CADE

CADE

THE STRIKING STEELE SAGA

DAWNLYN HOLMAN

Cade

Contact Info: www.dawnlynholman.com

Cover Design by: GetCovers

Editor: Sugar Free Editing

ISBN: 978-0-9835371-7-5

ALSO BY DAWNLYN HOLMAN

The Striking Steele Saga

Jackson (Book 1)

The Against the Odds Series

Take A Chance on Me

Never Give Up on Me

Count on Me

Collection of Short Stories

All That Glitters is Not Gold

Teenage Memoirs Duet

A Walk in the Park

A Closer Look

CHAPTER 1

Cade

I could already taste the open road and feel the ocean breeze on my face, the vision of our beachside escape almost in plain view, like a promise we'd waited too long to keep.

Megan called from the bathroom, her voice just barely reaching me over the whirr of the blender. I turned it off, wiped my hands on a dish towel, and made my way down the hall. The door was cracked open, and I could see her standing at the sink, her blonde hair damp and tousled as she brushed out the last tangles.

"What?" I asked, leaning against the doorframe.

She caught my eye in the mirror, her reflection bright, even in the dim bathroom light. "I asked if there was anything else you needed. Since this is the last trip to the store before we pack up the car, I figured you might have thought of a few extra things."

I paused, thinking about it. The house felt quiet, almost expectant, like it was listening in on our plans. "Actually, yeah. I thought it might be nice to strike up the fire pit one night. Roast some hot dogs, have some snacks . . ."

"Or s'mores," Megan cut in, her eyes twinkling at the thought. Her sweet tooth had been more insistent these last few weeks, and I wouldn't deny her a thing. "I think the baby would really love that," she added with that mischievous smile that always made me cave.

"Really?" I chuckled, stepping further into the bathroom and feeling the cool tile under my bare feet. I braced my arm against the doorframe, pretending to be skeptical. "And how could we forget s'mores?"

"It wouldn't be right." She secured her hair with one of those sparkly ties she loved.

"Exactly. So, if one of your stops includes the grocery store, think you could grab hot dogs and the s'mores stuff? I'll handle getting the heavier things loaded into the truck."

Megan turned, her smile growing, the sparkle in her eyes matching the hair tie. "You know, I think I can manage that. Anything for my husband and our soon-to-be little camper."

I felt something inside me ease, a knot of tension I hadn't realized was there. This trip would be good for us. A chance to leave behind the day-to-day grind and remember what it felt like to just . . . be. I reached out, tucking a stray lock of hair behind her ear. "Then let's make this trip something we'll never forget."

Megan smiled, and her hand touched mine. "It will be; I can feel it. I'll head out now so I'm back in time to help you pack up the last of our things so we can relax for the evening."

I followed Megan from the bathroom to the front door as she went to grab her shoes. "I like that. I'm thinking if we leave at four a.m., we'll be able to bypass the traffic and make good time." I'd gone over the route a dozen times with my brother Spencer, and I felt like I had this whole thing mapped out perfectly.

She nodded, slipping on the white sandals that matched her black-and-white striped T-shirt. "I think that sounds good. I know how much you hate driving in heavy traffic, so I'm all for anything that keeps you as relaxed as possible." She smiled up at me, her eyes full of that steady, reassuring calm I'd come to depend on.

I grabbed her purse and keys from the silver horseshoe-shaped hooks by the front door and held them out to her. They were one of Megan's many "lucky" finds at the antique shop downtown. She said it reminded her of my family's ranch.

"I think that's everything, but if I do think of something, I'll let you know."

"Thank ya, honey." Her sweet Texan drawl bounced through the room. She took both items from me, then stepped closer, pushing up on her tiptoes to bridge the gap between us. It was a gesture so familiar, so hers, it made me smile every time. She hooked her arms around my neck, drawing me in. "I'll see you when I get back."

"I love you," I murmured, leaning in.

"Not as much as I love you," she replied, as always, before pressing her lips to mine. It was our routine, one I'd grown to expect and cherish—a small piece of home in every kiss, a touch that never grew old, that I'd always crave.

"Drive safe," I whispered against her lips, feeling her smile beneath mine. "I'll be here when you get back."

"I'll be back before you have the chance to miss me," she teased, kissing me once more before turning toward the door. The screen door creaked as it swung open, then slammed shut behind her with a familiar clap.

I stood in the open doorway, watching as she climbed into her small SUV. The engine roared to life moments later, and I couldn't help but call out softly, "Too late," as if she could hear me. I waited until she drove down our paved driveway and out of sight before turning back inside.

Our house felt quiet in her absence. The hardwood floors creaked under my bare feet as I walked inside from the porch.

3

Sunlight streamed through the lace curtains Megan had sewn herself, casting soft, dappled patterns on the walls. I cut through our cozy living room to turn off the television. We spent a lot of time in this particular interior room. Family photos covered the walls: pictures of my folks; me with my brothers; Megan's parents and her three siblings; candid shots of us at the lake; Megan in her wedding dress, her smile so big I swear I could still feel it in the room.

Stepping past the pictures, I turned off the TV and returned to the kitchen, the heart of our home, with its old-fashioned stove and the white porcelain sink where we'd wash dishes together. I filled a cup with my Green Machine smoothie and leaned against the counter, drinking a few sips as the faint trace of lavender from the flowers Megan kept on the windowsill filled my nasal passages. I had a bunch of things I planned to do, but this nice little break felt good.

It was funny how a few small sips could lead to finishing the smoothie, searching social media, and engaging in a few friendly rounds of gameplay on Words with Friends with Jackson and Alden. When I finally noticed the clock, I knew I had lost too much time.

Break time is over.

I left the kitchen, passing by two of our three bedrooms. The first was a makeshift office, and the second would soon be our nursery. At the end of the hallway was our room—simple but comfortable, with a quilt Megan's grandmother had made folded neatly at the foot of the bed. Her side of the dresser was always a little cluttered. Jewelry and hair ties littered the base of a small mirror. Except for my old pocketknife and a few coins, my side was bare.

Right where I left it, a large suitcase sat near the door. We had started with the clothes, so that's what I'd load into the truck first. I grabbed the suitcase and headed back out to the front porch, only stopping to slip on my flip-flops.

Ah, our porch was probably one of my favorite things about our house. It wrapped around the front, just wide enough for a few chairs, where we'd sit and watch the sun dip behind the mesquite trees. I could see the yard, open and sprawling, where we'd shared more quiet moments than I could count. Our own private oasis amid all the chaos of work and planning for a future that seemed to change every day.

I walked over to my truck parked in the driveway. The red paint gleamed under the sun. Megan and I had decided to take the truck on the trip, planning to stretch out in the bed one night and fall asleep under a blanket of stars. I hefted the suitcase into the back, securing it beside my road toolbox. There was still more to do, but I'd promised Meg I'd handle it so she wouldn't have to worry.

As I turned back toward the house, I pulled out my phone and scrolled to my momma's number. I hit call, and she answered on the second ring, her voice warm and strong, the way it always was. "Hey there, Cade. How's it going?"

"Hey, Momma. Just wanted to check in on you while I'm packing up." I stepped back inside and made my way to our bedroom. "Megan's out running errands, and I'm getting things ready on this end."

"Well, aren't you just the good husband?" she teased. "You know I raised you right."

"You raised seven of us!" I chuckled. "How are you doing today?"

"I'm pretty good. I can't complain, especially when my sons call just to check on me." I could hear the smile in her voice. "Just finished baking some of those peach pies you like so much. Figured I'd bring a couple over before y'all head out tomorrow."

"That sounds perfect, Momma. I know Meg will love that," I replied, feeling a pang of nostalgia for those pies that always seemed to make everything better. "We're planning to leave at four in the morning."

"Oh, that's earlier than I thought. I'll bring them by this evening."

"It will be great to see you, but if you can't make it, we'll come by as soon as we get back."

"I'll be there, don't worry." There was no telling Elizabeth Steele to sit idle. Once she had her mind made up, that was it. "Well, I'll let you get back to packing. I hope you two have a wonderful trip," she continued. "You both deserve a little time away. And be safe, all right?"

"We will. Thanks. Love you."

"I love you too, Cade. I'll see you soon."

"Take care, Momma." I ended the call and stood there for a moment, looking around our bedroom. It felt like everything was in its place, and yet, the anticipation of leaving it all behind for a little while made me feel light, almost giddy.

With a deep breath, I went back to packing, knowing that in just a few hours, we'd be on our way to a long-awaited adventure.

CHAPTER 2

Megan

I gripped the steering wheel tighter than usual, feeling a flutter of excitement mixed with nerves in my chest. It had been two whole years since Cade and I'd had a real getaway. This trip felt like a dream come true, a chance to reset and just be together. And in the back of my mind, I knew it might be the last time we had a trip like this, just the two of us.

I couldn't help but smile, imagining our next adventure with a tiny third passenger in tow. A family of three. A baby. I pictured myself on a beach with a stroller, Cade cradling our little one against his chest. I wondered what our baby would look like. Maybe they'd have his eyes, that deep Steele brown that seemed to hold all the calm in the world. Maybe they'd have my blonde hair. The thought warmed me, made me feel a little giddy.

I brought myself back to the present and glanced at the bags half-filled with groceries and odds and ends in the passenger seat. I mentally ticked through the haul: sunscreen, snacks, extra chargers, and even the travel-size hand sanitizer Cade always forgot about. A small smile tugged at my lips. At least I hadn't forgotten the cooler bags this time.

"Small victories," I murmured to myself, shaking my head.

I tapped my fingers on the steering wheel, feeling the excitement in my chest bubble up again. Cade and I had talked so much about our future: this baby, the dreams we were building. It was overwhelming but in the best possible way. This trip was our chance to soak in these final moments, just the two of us, before everything changed. A good change, the best kind, but still . . . different.

The light ahead turned red, and I eased my foot onto the brake. The bags from Kilmer's, our town's local have-it-all store, were proof that I'd managed to grab everything we needed for the trip. It felt good to have one less thing lingering on my list. Now it was just home, finish packing, and then we were off.

I cracked the window to let in the warm summer air, then took a deep breath. The breeze felt nice on my skin. A few birds chirped in the distance, and a couple of kids on bikes zipped past the crosswalk. It was a peaceful day. Perfect for a drive, even to somewhere as mundane as Kilmer's.

I smiled, imagining Cade's face when he saw all the snacks I'd packed. He'd tease me for over packing, calling me his "snack queen," but he secretly loved it. A warmth blossomed in my chest just thinking about it. Thinking about us.

Thinking about—

A deafening crash filled my ears, and my body lurched forward. Pain exploded in my neck and shoulders; my chest slammed into the seatbelt with a force that knocked the air from my lungs. Metal crunched, and glass shattered—an orchestra of chaos that drowned out everything else.

"Oh God!" I gasped, trying to brace myself. My head whipped back against the headrest, and I was thrust forward again. My SUV was pushed through the intersection, skidding out of control. The world outside the window blurred.

Greens. Yellows. Reds. Spinning and spinning.

The steering wheel jerked violently under my hands. I heard

a scream, my scream, mingling with the screech of tires on pavement.

There was another jolt, sharper this time, and I slammed into the median. The impact was sudden, jarring, and then the airbag burst from the steering wheel, hitting me square in the face. At the same time, my arms protectively guarded my stomach on impact. My ears rang as the airbag inflated, pushing me back and filling the space with the harsh, acrid smell of burning chemicals and plastic.

"Help!" I tried to yell, but the sound came out more like a whimper. The taste of blood filled my mouth.

My head felt heavy. Everything was . . . muffled. The music, the chaos—it was all fading. I blinked rapidly, trying to clear my vision, but the edges were dimming, darkening. My heart pounded in my chest, but even that felt distant, like it was happening to someone else.

Voices filtered through the haze, but they were far away. Were they shouting? I couldn't tell.

I tried to reach for my phone. Where was my phone? Wasn't it right there, in the cup holder? My fingers fumbled, but they were sluggish and uncoordinated. "Cade . . ." I whispered, though I knew he wasn't there. I just needed to feel close to him, needed to feel . . . something.

Sirens. Faint but growing louder. Closer.

A strange sense of calm washed over me. Maybe it was shock. Maybe it was just . . . relief. I didn't know. I closed my eyes; they were too heavy to keep open. The sirens were louder now. So close. I let them become my lullaby, lulling me into the darkness spreading through my mind, wrapping me in its cool, quiet embrace.

Just before I slipped away, I thought of Cade. His smile. His laugh. I tried to hold on to it.

Then, nothing but sirens.

CHAPTER 3

After I finished loading the last of the suitcases into the truck, I tossed my own small duffle on top. It held the basics: a couple of pairs of jeans, clean shirts, and boots. That was enough for me.

I could already hear Megan's voice in my head, half-laughing, half-scolding as she zipped up her third bag. "*Cade, you can't tell me that's all you're bringing,*" she'd say, with her hands on her hips and that look of mock exasperation on her face.

"*Sure can,*" I'd always counter, "*I don't need much.*" Truth was, I'd let her pack half the house if it made her feel settled. She liked to be prepared. I just liked seeing her smile.

I had just zipped up the duffle bag when my phone rang. I glanced at the screen, expecting it to be Megan calling to let me know she was on her way and she'd need help bringing in everything.

But it wasn't Megan. It was an unknown number.

My eyebrows furrowed as I answered. "Hello?"

A woman's voice, calm but professional, came through. "Is this Cade Steele?"

"Yeah, this is Cade. Who's this?"

"This is Nurse Thompson from St. Mary's Hospital," she said. "Your wife, Megan, has been in an accident. She's here at the hospital now. You need to come right away."

My breath caught in my throat. "An accident? What happened? Is she . . . Is she okay?" My voice shook, and a knot began forming in my stomach.

"She's being cared for by our trauma team right now," the nurse said, her tone steady, but I could sense the urgency behind it. "I can't give you all the details over the phone. It's important that you come as soon as you can."

"I-I'm on my way," I managed to say, already grabbing my truck keys and heading for the door.

I hung up. My hands trembled as I pulled up the family group chat. I needed to let everyone know: my parents, my brothers, Megan's family.

> Emergency! Megan's been in an accident. Heading to St. Mary's Hospital now. Please meet me there if you can!

I hit send and raced out the door, my mind spinning. The drive to the hospital felt like the longest of my life. I could hardly breathe or think straight. I just kept whispering, "Please, let her be okay. Let her and the baby be okay."

I imagined what it felt like for Jackson when he lost Hannah. I couldn't lose Megan, too.

I can't.

Images of Megan flashed through my mind. Her smile, her laughter, the way she always touched her belly with a small, secret smile on her lips. My hands gripped the steering wheel tighter, knuckles white.

I hit a red light and nearly pounded the dashboard in frustration. I knew it wasn't rational, but every second I sat there was another second she might need me, another second I was failing her.

When I finally pulled into the hospital parking lot, I barely remembered to turn off the engine before jumping out of the truck. I rushed inside, my eyes scanning for the information desk.

"Nurse! Excuse me! I'm Cade Steele. My wife, Megan, was brought in after an accident. Where is she?"

The nurse checked the tablet in her hand. "She's in the back, Mr. Steele, with our doctors. They're taking good care of her. I'll let them know you're here."

I nodded, my heart pounding in my chest. I paced the waiting area, nerves stretched thin, until the flood of family started coming through the doors. My parents were first. Momma pulled me into a hug that said more than words could. Then my brothers appeared, their faces tight with the same worry I carried in my chest.

Megan's parents and siblings weren't far behind; her momma was already red-eyed. I gave them what little I knew, though it wasn't much.

After what felt like an eternity, a doctor came out, still in his scrubs. "Mr. Steele?"

I stepped forward. "That's me. How's Megan? Is she . . . is she okay?"

The doctor nodded. "She's stable, Mr. Steele. Her injuries could have been much worse. We've managed to stabilize her condition, and the baby appears to be unharmed. But . . ."

"But?" I prompted, feeling like I was on the edge of a cliff.

He sighed. "Megan's in a coma. It's hard to say when she'll wake up. We're monitoring her closely, but there's no way to know for sure. It could be hours, days . . . or longer."

A wave of relief and fear crashed over me. I gripped the back of a chair to steady myself, and my father's firm hand landed on my back for comfort. "But she's . . . she's alive. And the baby's okay?" I asked, needing to hear it again.

"Yes, Mr. Steele," the doctor confirmed. "Your wife is alive, and the baby is still with us. We'll continue to monitor both of them closely."

I exhaled, feeling some of the tension release from my chest, but the fear was still there, gnawing at me. *A coma. Megan is in a coma.* I turned to look at our families. I saw their worried faces, their silent prayers.

"She's strong," I said, more to myself than anyone else. "Megan's strong. She'll pull through this. She has to."

I felt Momma's hand on my shoulder, a gentle squeeze of reassurance. My brothers stood beside me, silent but present, their strength grounding me. And Megan's family, holding each other, eyes filled with the same hope and fear I felt.

I nodded to the doctor. "Can I see her?"

He nodded. "Yes, of course. Just be prepared for what you might see. She's resting now, and we're doing everything we can."

I swallowed hard, steeling myself for what I was about to see. "Okay," I whispered. "Okay. I just need to see her."

I followed the doctor down the sterile, brightly lit hallway. My hands trembled beside me with every step. I didn't know what I'd find when I walked into that room, but I knew one thing for sure; I wouldn't leave Megan's side. Not until she woke up. Not ever.

I walked into the room, and the first thing that hit me was the sterile scent of the place, sharp and clean, almost too clean. The blinds were partially drawn, letting in thin slivers of light that cut across the room in lines, turning everything into a stark contrast of shadows and brightness. The walls were a soft, pale blue, probably meant to be soothing, but it only made the room feel cold and empty.

There she was, in the middle of it all, lying on a hospital bed that seemed too big for her small frame. My heart twisted painfully at the sight of her. Megan, my Meg, usually so full of life and color, looked so still. Her hair, which she'd worn pulled back in a hair tie that morning, was now spread out against the white pillow, a few strands tangled. A line of dried blood stood out against her pale skin, right beside a small cut on her forehead, just below her hairline. Her cheeks were colorless, and a dark bruise had formed along her jaw.

I moved closer, and my eyes took in the wires and tubes connected to her. The steady beep of the heart monitor filled the room—a rhythmic, mechanical reassurance that she was still here with me. A canula perched below her nose, and an IV line ran down to her arm, delivering fluids. Her hands, usually busy with work, rested on the sheets, unmoving, with one wrapped tight in a white cast.

I took a deep breath, fighting the wave of panic rising in my chest. My hands trembled as I reached out, brushing a stray lock of hair away from her face. Her skin felt cold to the touch. I wanted to hold her and pull her close, but I was terrified of hurting her.

"Hey, Meg," I whispered, my voice breaking. "I'm here. I'm right here."

I sat in the chair next to her bed as the weight of everything pressed down on me. I stared at her face, looking for any sign of movement, any twitch of an eyelid, a flicker of her fingers, anything to show she was still in there, fighting her way back to me.

God, she looks so fragile, I thought. My heart pounded in my chest. *So damn fragile.* I'd never seen her like that, so . . . vulnerable. Megan was always the strong one, the one who kept us grounded when things got tough. She had a fire in her, a strength I'd always admired. Seeing her like this, still and silent, felt like someone had ripped the ground out from under me.

I swallowed hard, my eyes stinging with tears I refused to let fall. "You have to wake up, baby," I whispered, leaning closer, my forehead almost touching hers. "I need you to wake up. We've got a lot to do, remember? We've got a trip to take, a baby on the way. Our whole future, Megan. It's waiting for us."

I took her hand in mine, squeezing gently, feeling the coolness of her skin against my palm. *Please, God, please. Let her come back to me. Don't take her away. Don't take our baby away.*

Minutes passed, or maybe hours. I wasn't sure. Time felt strange in this place. It felt like it had stretched out and slowed down. Each second was a painful reminder of the uncertainty that hung over us. The muffled voices of doctors and nurses filtered through the walls. The hum of machinery, footsteps moving quickly past. But in here, it was just us. Just me, Megan, and the quiet fight for her to come back.

I felt a hand on my shoulder. I looked up to see my father, his face etched with worry, his eyes filled with the same fear and hope I felt. He didn't say anything. He didn't need to. He just gave me a nod, his grip firm, steady. It helped just to have him there with me.

I turned back to Megan, my fingers entwined with hers. "I'm not going anywhere," I whispered again. "Not until you open those beautiful eyes of yours and tell me I'm being dramatic." I tried to smile, but it felt weak, uncertain. "I love you, Megan. We all do. We need you . . . I need you."

I leaned back in the chair, never letting go of her hand, my thumb brushing over her knuckles in a slow, repetitive motion. I waited, watching, hoping. Praying that somewhere in the silence, she could hear me. That she knew I was there. And that no matter how long it took, I'd be right there, waiting for her to come back to me.

CHAPTER 4

*M*y head drooped and caused me to jerk awake. I blinked a few times, disoriented, the sharp, antiseptic smell of the hospital filling my lungs as I sat up. The dim lighting hadn't changed, casting soft shadows across the floor, and the steady hum of machines filled the quiet. I glanced over at Megan, still lying there, still as silent as she had been for the past three days.

I'd say it was peaceful, but the truth was, I just wished I knew if she was still in there. I hadn't left her side since they brought her in. I couldn't. I'd barely slept, not more than a few minutes at a time, and I hadn't changed clothes or even left the room. There was no way I could walk out of there while she lay in that bed.

Can she hear me? Does she know I'm here?

I reached for her hand again, like I'd done a hundred times since that first day. Her skin felt a little warmer now, not as cold as before, but she was still so pale. I leaned forward, resting my head against the edge of her bed, my fingers brushing over hers. My eyelids grew heavy again, the exhaustion finally starting to pull me under. *Just a few minutes*, I thought. *Just a little rest . . .*

A slight movement pulled me back from the depths. It was small, barely a shift, but it wasn't my imagination. My head shot up, my heart racing in my chest. I looked at her hand, then up at her face. Her eyelids fluttered, and her chest rose and fell a little faster.

"Megan?" I whispered, barely able to contain the hope bubbling up inside me. I leaned closer, searching her face for any sign. "Megan, can you hear me?"

For what felt like forever, there was nothing. Just the faint hum of the machines and the soft beep of the heart monitor. And then, slowly, her eyes began to open, just a crack at first, then wider, blinking against the harsh fluorescent light.

I could barely breathe. "Oh my God, Megan . . . you're awake," I said, my voice catching in my throat. I reached out, brushing her hair away from her face, my fingers trembling. "Baby, I'm here. I'm right here."

She blinked again, her gaze moving sluggishly, like she was trying to take in the room but couldn't focus. I glanced at the nurse who had just walked in to check her vitals, hoping she'd seen it too. She had. Her face lit with quiet urgency as she set down her clipboard and moved to Megan's bedside.

"You're okay, sweetheart." The nurse leaned over to examine her. "Welcome back. Just take it slow."

Megan's eyelids fluttered again, her lashes trembling like she was struggling to stay awake. Her breathing quickened, and I saw her chest rise and fall more sharply. Then, she coughed— deep, ragged, like her lungs were trying to catch up. The sound hit me like a jolt of electricity, and my heart leaped into my throat.

"She's coughing!" I exclaimed, looking at the nurse, desperate for her to do something. "She's—She's trying to—"

"It's okay," the nurse interrupted. She adjusted the bed so Megan was propped slightly higher, her movements steady and practiced, but my own hands trembled uncontrollably as I sat there, helpless. Megan coughed again, her face twisting in discomfort, her breathing uneven and strained, like her body was learning how to work again after too long in the dark. "Sometimes when patients wake up, they're startled. They breathe in quickly and swallow saliva or something, and they just need a few minutes."

"Hang on, Megan," I whispered, my voice breaking. "You're okay. Just breathe, baby. Just breathe."

The nurse checked her vitals, murmuring soothing words under her breath. Megan's eyes flickered toward me, confused, disoriented, and then darted to the nurse, as if she was trying to make sense of what was happening. Her lips parted slightly, but no sound came out, just a small, strained whimper that tore me apart.

"All right," the nurse said, keeping her focus on Megan. "You're doing just fine. Deep breaths if you can. There you go."

I leaned forward, my hands gripping the edge of the bed until my knuckles went white. Megan's coughing slowed, turning into shallow, uneven breaths. The nurse gave a small nod of approval and stepped back to check the monitor.

"That's it," she said. "Good job, Megan. Just keep breathing slow and steady."

Megan's eyes opened again, watery now, and she took a shaky breath. She scanned the entire room before her gaze finally landed on me, and for one brief, glorious moment, I thought I felt it—the relief I'd prayed for since I got the call.

But then . . . something changed. Her expression shifted. Her brow furrowed in confusion. She looked at me. No, she *stared* at me, and it wasn't the look I knew, the one that always made me feel like the luckiest man alive. This was different. Distant.

"Who . . . who are you?" Her voice, raspy and broken, finally came out. The words may have been barely above a whisper, but they hit me like a punch to the gut.

I froze. For a moment, I couldn't process what she'd just

said. I couldn't move. I couldn't think. "Megan, it's me," I said softly, my voice cracking. "It's Cade. Your husband. I've been here the whole time. I—" My words faltered as her confusion deepened.

As she shook her head slightly, her gaze slipped away from mine. "I don't . . . I don't know you." Her voice was hoarse and fragile, but it carried a weight that crushed me.

No. No, this can't be happening. My mind raced, trying to understand, to make sense of what was happening. "Megan, you —" I swallowed hard. "We're married. We've been together for six years." I stopped myself. I almost said that we were having a baby, but she seemed so disoriented, that might have made things worse.

Her eyes widened, and she looked down at her stomach, then back at me. There was fear in her gaze now, fear and confusion. "I . . . I don't remember," she whispered, her voice trembling.

I felt my world tilt, like the ground beneath me was slipping away. I'd spent the last three days praying for her to wake up, begging for it. And now she was awake, but it was like she wasn't really there. Like the Megan I knew, the woman I loved, was lost somewhere I couldn't reach.

"I'm your husband, Megan." My voice cracked, barely able to hold back the panic rising in my chest. I squeezed her hand gently, desperate for her to remember, desperate for her to see me. "We've been through everything together. We've built a life together. Please, just . . . just try to remember."

She pulled her hand away, and the motion felt like a knife to my chest. "I'm sorry," she whispered, tears filling her eyes. "I don't know who you are."

I stumbled back, dropping into the chair next to her bed. My mind spun as my heart broke into a million pieces. This wasn't right. This wasn't how it was supposed to go. She was supposed to wake up, and then we were supposed to hug, cry, and celebrate that she was okay. We were supposed to be okay.

But instead, she looked at me like I was a stranger. Like I meant nothing to her.

I sat there, staring at her, trying to hold on to something that would make this make sense. But all I could feel was the hollow ache in my chest and the cold, unyielding truth settling in.

She didn't know me.

She didn't remember *us*.

And I didn't know what to do.

CHAPTER 5

Megan

I blinked up at the man sitting beside me. His face was a strange mix of desperation and heartbreak. I didn't know him. Nothing felt familiar. Nothing made sense.

Who is he?

And why did he look at me like that, like I was the most important person in the world to him? I wanted to say something, anything, but my raw throat ached from disuse. Whenever I tried to speak, it felt like the words barely made it out.

He reached for my hand again; his fingers brushed against mine. I flinched, not from fear, exactly, but from something I couldn't quite name. Unease? Uncertainty? I pulled back my hand, and the movement sent a sharp ache through my arm and into my shoulder. I winced, trying to shift, but even that sent little jolts of pain radiating through my body.

"Hey, it's okay," he said softly, his voice breaking, like he was holding back tears. "I'm not going to hurt you. Megan, I just want to help."

Megan. Was that my name? It sounded right, but it didn't feel right, not coming from him. My head felt heavy and thick with fog. I glanced around the room, the sight bringing more questions than answers. How long had I been there? What happened?

The man—*Cade, he called himself Cade*—leaned closer, his face lined with worry. "You've been through a lot," he said. "You don't have to remember everything right now. But I'm here. I'll help you through this."

I looked away, focusing on the pale walls, the IV in my arm, the blanket draped over me. His words sounded sincere, kind even, but they didn't reach me. They floated somewhere above the haze clouding my brain, untouched.

"Mr. Steele?" The nurse's voice broke through the thick silence. I turned my head slightly, wincing again as the movement sent another pang of discomfort shooting through me. She stood near the door, watching us. "I think it might be best to give her some time. She's disoriented, and we don't want to overwhelm her."

"I can't leave her," he blurted, his voice tight, almost panicked. "She just woke up, I need to—"

"Mr. Steele. It's important that we give her space to process. Let me get the doctor, and we can talk about how to move forward. Please."

For a moment, he didn't move. His hands gripped the edge of the bed, his knuckles white, and he looked at me with a pleading expression that made my stomach twist. He didn't want to leave. That much was clear. But finally, with a heavy sigh, he stood up, his movements slow, reluctant.

"I'll be right outside," he said, his eyes never leaving mine. "I'm not going anywhere, Megan. I promise."

I didn't respond. I didn't know what to say. The nurse gently ushered him toward the door, her voice soft as she reassured him. Then they were gone, and the room was suddenly too quiet, too still.

I stared at the closed door for a long moment, my heart

pounding in my chest. He said he was my husband. Was that true? I didn't remember.

My gaze drifted around the room, taking in every detail. The machines, the wires, the monitors. I didn't recognize any of it. They beeped and blinked rhythmically, tethering me to a reality that felt foreign and unsettling. The steady hum of medical equipment filled the quiet that pressed in around me.

But it wasn't just the hospital machinery that filled the room. As my eyes adjusted and moved beyond the stark white sheets and sterile walls, I noticed color, bright and overwhelming.

Balloons floated in clusters near the window, tied to chairs and tables. They bobbed gently, shifting every time someone passed the door or the air conditioning kicked on. Some were shaped like stars, others round and metallic, with bold, cheerful words: Get Well Soon!, Thinking of You!, and We Love You! The reds, yellows, blues, and purples were too loud for the strange stillness of my mind.

On every available surface, flowers bloomed in various sizes and shapes. Bouquets spilled out of vases and mason jars. Lilies. Carnations. Sunflowers with wide, golden faces. Roses ranging from delicate pink to deep burgundy. Some were still vibrant and fresh, while others drooped slightly, their petals curling at the edges. The scent was thick, cloyingly sweet, and it mixed with the sterile antiseptic smell until I couldn't tell if I wanted to breathe deeper or throw up.

And then there were the cards.

So many cards. Tucked into flower arrangements. Propped on trays and windowsills. Balanced on the arm of the nearby recliner. Some were handmade, clearly by children, with stickers and drawings and misspelled names. Others were elegant, printed in gold foil or handwritten in neat cursive. I could barely make out the words from where I lay, but I caught enough. *You're so strong. Come back to us. We're praying for you. We miss you.*

Miss me?

A few cards had photographs attached to them, pictures of smiling faces I didn't recognize. Friends, maybe. Family. People who seemed to know me, to care about me. In one photo, I stood between two women, all of us laughing, arms linked. I stared at my face, but it didn't stir anything inside. Not a flicker of memory. It was like looking at a stranger who just happened to share my skin.

I let out a shaky breath. All of this . . . love, this care, this attention. It was meant for someone I didn't remember being. Someone everyone else seemed to know, but who I couldn't find inside myself.

I was surrounded by a life I didn't recognize. A room bursting with reminders that I was cared for, prayed over, hoped for . . . but I didn't know any of them. Not their names. Not their handwriting. Not their faces. Not even my own.

Tears pricked the corners of my eyes as I slowly turned my head, taking it all in again. The joy of the colors, the scent of the flowers, the kindness in the messages—all of that should have comforted me.

But instead, it only made me feel more alone.

My cast arm ached, my legs felt heavy, and my head throbbed with a dull, relentless pain. But worse than the physical discomfort was the emptiness in my mind. The blank spaces where memories should have been.

The nurse said I needed time, but time for what? To figure out who I was? To piece together the fragments of a life I couldn't remember?

I closed my eyes, willing the answers to come, willing anything to break through the fog. But all I felt was the cold, sterile air of the room, and the overwhelming fear that I was completely, utterly lost.

CHAPTER 6

Megan

The soft knock at the door pulled my attention away from the window, where the balloons bobbed lazily in the corner. The sunlight filtered through them, casting strange, colorful shadows on the wall. For a moment, I felt like I was in a dream, watching someone else's life play out from a distance.

The door creaked open, and a man in a white coat stepped in. He was tall, somewhere in his mid-forties, with salt-and-pepper hair that curled slightly at the ends. He had a calm, capable air about him. His dark eyes were kind, though they scanned me carefully, the way someone might look at a puzzle missing too many pieces.

"Good morning, Megan," he said, checking something on the chart in his hands before setting it down on the counter. "I'm Dr. Nathan Bellamy. I've been overseeing your care since you were brought in."

I just stared, unsure of what to say. My throat still felt raw and tight, and I wasn't exactly in the mood to fumble through another conversation where I was expected to know things I didn't. Still, I nodded faintly, acknowledging him.

Dr. Bellamy walked to my bedside and offered a warm but professional smile. "It's good to see you awake. You've had quite the ordeal."

I glanced away from his eyes and looked down at my hands. Bruised. Scraped. They didn't feel like mine, either.

"I'm just going to take a look at you," he said, his voice gentle. "We'll go slow."

I gave the smallest of nods.

He moved methodically, checking my pulse, my blood pressure, lifting my eyelids and shining a small flashlight into my eyes. His hands were steady, and I could tell he'd done this a thousand times before. But everything he did, every tap of the reflex hammer, every question, felt strangely disconnected from me, like I was watching it happen to someone else's body.

He sat on a rolling stool and asked me simple things at first. "Do you know your full name?"

My lips parted slightly. I hesitated, embarrassed. "Megan . . . I think. That's what everyone's been calling me."

He nodded, made a note. "Do you know where you are?"

"A hospital."

"Do you know why you're here?"

I paused. "No."

He didn't react, just kept writing. "Can you tell me today's date?"

I frowned, looking toward the window, as if the world outside might help jog something loose. But the only thing that came was a heavy emptiness. "I don't know."

"And what's the last thing you remember?"

I shook my head slowly, frustration prickling in the back of my throat. "I . . . don't. I remember waking up. Today. That's all."

Dr. Bellamy put the clipboard down and walked the stool closer to my bedside. He folded his hands in his lap and looked at me with the kind of patience I wasn't sure I deserved.

"Megan," he said. "I believe you're experiencing something

called retrograde amnesia. It's a type of memory loss where you're unable to recall events that occurred before the injury, or sometimes days, weeks, even years leading up to it."

I stared at him, trying to process the words even though they felt like they were coming from underwater.

"It's usually caused by trauma to the brain," he continued. "You were in a car accident. Pretty serious. From the scans, there's some swelling and a fractured wrist, but no bleeding. That's a good sign. Physically, you're healing remarkably well."

"But I don't remember anything," I said, my voice barely audible. "Not my name. Not the people in the pictures. Not even the crash."

"I know." He nodded. "That can be incredibly disorienting. Sometimes the memories return gradually, pieces at a time. In other cases, they don't come back at all. Everyone's brain is different. What's important is that we give you space and support, and we'll monitor you closely in the coming days."

"So, what do I do now?"

"You focus on healing," he said. "You take your time. There's no pressure to force anything."

I looked down at the blanket covering me. My body ached, my head throbbed with a slow, pulsing pain, and my chest felt empty. Like someone had scooped out everything that made up *me* and left nothing behind.

Dr. Bellamy stood up, smoothing the front of his coat. "I'm going to step out and update the team. I'll be back shortly to check on you again. If anything changes, or if you remember something, no matter how small, please let your nurse know."

I nodded again. That was all I seemed capable of doing lately.

He gave me one last reassuring look, then exited the room, the door clicking softly behind him.

I was alone again.

The balloons caught my eye once more, floating like distant

memories out of reach. I turned my head to the side and glimpsed a framed photograph propped beside a vase of lilies. It was me again, or who I was supposed to be, smiling wide with that man, *Cade*, his arm around my waist like he belonged there.

I stared at the photo until my eyes stung.

If I had once loved him, I didn't remember it. If I'd built a life with him, shared secrets and laughs and kisses, I didn't remember any of that, either. All I had was a hollow space where something used to be.

Was I supposed to pretend? Try to step back into someone else's life? Or wait there until something came back?

I hated the not knowing.

And more than anything, I hated *that everyone else knew*, and I didn't.

I curled slightly on my side, careful not to disturb the IV or the sore muscles beneath the thin gown. The puffs from the air conditioner caused the balloons to dance where they sat, and I closed my eyes against it all.

But even in the darkness, I still felt lost.

CHAPTER 7

Cade

I'd worn a hole in the floor with the pacing.

The rubber soles of my flip-flops slapped softly against the polished hospital tiles as I passed the same row of faded artwork and informational posters for what had to be the fiftieth time. I could've counted every tile with my eyes closed.

The white linoleum floors gleamed under the fluorescent lights, and the quiet hum of machines behind closed doors followed me like a shadow. Nurses passed by every so often, giving me that familiar, soft smile. The one meant for the family members holding on by a thread.

I kept glancing at her room, at the door I'd been asked to step out of. Every second away from Megan felt like a lifetime. My body ached from the lack of sleep and the tension of waiting, but I didn't care. I'd sleep when she was at home, safe and sound.

The second I saw Dr. Bellamy approaching, I stopped in my tracks, heart thudding. His white coat flared slightly as he walked, clipboard in hand. His expression was neutral, but I knew better. Doctors didn't put on that face unless they were bracing you for something.

"Mr. Steele, do you have a moment?"

My throat tightened. "Yeah, of course."

He gestured toward a small waiting area just off the hallway. It was empty, the TV in the corner playing silently, a stack of magazines untouched on the table between two plastic chairs.

I followed him in, but I didn't sit. I couldn't.

Dr. Bellamy didn't rush. He settled into one of the chairs and looked up at me with that same even expression. "I know this is a lot to take in," he began. "I wanted to walk you through what we've found, now that Megan's awake."

"How is she?" I asked, my voice raw. "Really?"

"She's stable. Physically, she's doing well, all things considered. A few cracked ribs, bruises, a concussion, and her fractured wrist. Nothing life-threatening. She's a strong woman." He paused.

"Doc . . ." I ran a hand through my unwashed hair. "Talk to me straight. What's going on with her memory? She didn't recognize me. She looked at me like I was a stranger."

Dr. Bellamy took a breath and folded his arms. "We're seeing signs of retrograde amnesia. It's likely trauma-induced, caused by the impact and the brain's protective response to the concussion. She's alert and coherent, but she can't access memories from before the accident."

"How far back? Like, does she remember her childhood? Her job? Us?"

He shook his head. "It's hard to say with certainty. Memory can be unpredictable after trauma like this. Some patients regain fragments. Others, everything. And unfortunately, some never fully recover what was lost."

"Okay . . . okay." I swallowed hard, trying to wrap my head around it. "So, what now? What do we do? Is there some kind of treatment? Therapy?"

"There's no magic solution. Time is the most important

factor. Sometimes, memories return slowly. They can be triggered by familiar environments, people, smells, and voices."

I stared at the floor, heart hammering. "So . . . I just keep showing up. And hoping."

"Exactly," he said. "She'll remain here for a few more days. We want to monitor her brain activity, ensure there's no further swelling, and evaluate any physical limitations. She may need physical therapy, especially once she starts moving around more. But emotionally and mentally, what she needs most is familiarity and patience."

I nodded slowly, feeling the weight settle on my shoulders. I'd do whatever it took. I didn't care how long it took. I wasn't going anywhere.

Dr. Bellamy paused, watching my face. "Was there something else on your mind?"

I rubbed the back of my neck. "Yeah. There's something I haven't brought up yet. How do I talk about the baby?"

His brow lifted slightly, his expression softening. "Ah. Yes, that does add an extra dimension."

"She doesn't even remember me. How are we supposed to tell her she's pregnant? I don't want to overwhelm her or make things worse."

"That's a delicate situation," he admitted, "and you're right to be cautious. We usually recommend easing patients into new or unfamiliar information. Too much too fast can lead to emotional distress, especially in cases like hers."

"You think we should wait?"

"We give it time. You know her better than anyone, Mr. Steele. When you feel the moment is right, when she begins to feel safe and grounded again, you'll know. Until then, the priority is her recovery. Let her adjust to her surroundings, her condition, and the people in her life. Let trust rebuild. Then the truth can follow."

I let out a shaky breath and nodded, the weight of his words pressing against my chest. "Okay. Thank you. For everything."

Dr. Bellamy stood and offered me a firm, steady look. "You're doing everything right, Mr. Steele. I'll be back in to check on things later this evening."

"Thank you," I murmured, watching him leave the room, his footsteps fading down the hallway.

When he left, I slumped into the nearest chair. I reached for my phone and scrolled to Megan's mother's number—Sherry. My thumb hesitated over the call button.

And then I hit it.

She answered immediately. "Cade?"

"Hey, Sherry." My voice broke slightly.

"Oh, honey," she said. "Is she . . . did something happen? What's going on?"

"She's awake," I said softly. "Finally. She came to a little while ago."

"Oh, thank God. How is she? What did she say?"

I hesitated, trying to find the right words. "She doesn't remember anything. Not me. Probably not y'all. The doctor called it retrograde amnesia. Her brain's protecting itself after the trauma, but she's scared. Confused."

Sherry repeated what I said to whoever was in the room with her. Within a moment, Megan's daddy's voice came into the background. "Put it on speaker," Matthew said. Then, louder, "I'm glad to hear she's awake, but I didn't expect that to be what happened when she woke. Sorry you had to be there alone. That must've been hard."

"It was," I admitted. "I'm trying to keep it together, but it's difficult when she looks at me like I'm nothing to her. But I'm not going anywhere. I'll stay right here and wait as long as it takes."

Sherry's voice softened. "We want to come. We're already

dressed, and we'll be there in a few minutes. I want her to see familiar faces. I want you to have support, too."

Tears threatened, but I blinked them away. "Thank you. That means more than you know."

Matthew chimed in. "Tell her we're on our way. We'll bring more photos, maybe some things from home. Just . . . hang in there, Cade. You're not alone in this."

"I appreciate it. Really."

We talked for a few more minutes—about the hospital, the doctors, and the prognosis—before ending the call.

I stood and stretched, my back popping from the chair's stiffness. Then I turned and walked back down the hallway, feet slapping softly against the floor. My heart thudded in my chest as I reached her door.

I eased it open, peeking in. Megan lay there, awake again, propped slightly higher than before. Her eyes were open, watching the soft light filtering through the blinds.

"Hey," I said, clearing my throat gently. "Um, your parents are on their way. They'll be here soon."

Her gaze flicked toward me, unreadable. Distant.

I stepped inside, unsure of how much space to give her. "Thought you might want to see some familiar faces."

She didn't respond. Instead, she turned her head toward the window again.

I wasn't sure if I should sit or speak or just disappear for a while, so I stayed silent.

But I wasn't going anywhere.

Not then. Not ever.

And I couldn't shake the feeling . . . that something was about to change.

CHAPTER 8

Megan

a dust mote drifted lazily through the sunlight slicing across the hospital room. It danced like it didn't have a care in the world while I sat there, weighed down by a fog of confusion and uncertainty so thick I could barely breathe through it.

The past few days had passed in a blur of faces coming and going, voices speaking gently, like I might shatter if they weren't careful. My body was healing slowly, but my mind remained a mess of fragmented thoughts and blank spaces. Memories that should've been mine, that should've belonged to the life I lived, remained stubbornly out of reach.

I knew my name. Or what they told me it was, at least. I knew what year it was, who the president was, and that peanut butter went better with chocolate than jelly. But I didn't know why the man with the warm brown eyes and tired face looked at me like I was his whole world. Or why hearing his voice made something deep inside me ache.

Cade.

He said we were married. That we'd been together for years. That we had plans, a life, a future. But it was all stories to me, tales told by a stranger. Sweet, gentle, patient . . . but still a stranger.

A soft knock at the door pulled me from my thoughts. I glanced up as it creaked open.

"Hey, sweet girl," a warm voice said.

It was Sherry, my mom. I knew her in flashes of sensation more than pictures. The smell of her perfume, the cadence of her voice. She'd been there every day since I woke up, fussing over my blankets, stroking my hair, trying not to cry when I didn't call her "Mom" without hesitation.

Behind her trailed Matthew, tall and stoic. Within his kind eyes, I could see my own, another person I hesitated to call by their title. Dad.

And then came my siblings, Lindsey, Rebecca, and Jacob, each of them bringing their own swirl of emotions into the room.

Cade was already sitting in the corner chair, looking like he hadn't slept again. His hair was a little longer than I imagined he liked, curling at the ends. I felt this more than I knew it. He rose from what had become his chair next to my bed when my family walked in, nodding politely.

"Morning," he murmured, eyes flicking briefly to mine.

"Morning," I replied, unsure of whether to smile or not. I hadn't long been up and wasn't even sure if it was morning anyway.

Jacob made a beeline to my bed and tossed himself down in the chair beside it. "You look better. Not like a zombie anymore."

I managed a soft laugh. "Thanks. I think?"

Lindsey rolled her eyes. "Ignore him. He's an idiot. How are you feeling?"

"Okay, I guess." I glanced down at my hands folded over the blanket. "Still confused. Still . . . floating."

They all nodded sympathetically, but then Sherry, a woman I

was probably close to, cleared her throat and clasped her hands. She looked as familiar to me as a stranger on the street. How could I see her as anything more?

"We, uh, we've been talking," she began, glancing around at everyone in the room. "Since they're releasing you in a day or two, we want to make sure you have the best setup possible for your recovery."

My chest tightened. "Setup?"

"Well," she said, "we think it would be best if you came to stay with us for a while. Just until you're back on your feet. You'd have your own room, lots of help, and constant care."

I opened my mouth to reply, but Cade spoke first.

"Actually, Megan and I live a few minutes from here. Her stuff's already there. And it's her home. She should come home with me."

The temperature in the room dropped like a rock.

Sherry's smile faded. "Cade, I'm not trying to overstep here, but she doesn't even remember you. How can we expect her to live with someone she sees as a stranger?"

"I'm not a stranger," Cade said, his jaw tight. "I'm her husband."

"But right now, to her, that's just a word," Lindsey chimed in, arms crossed. "It's going to take time. Maybe being around her family, her real family, is what she needs."

"I *am* her family," Cade shot back. "What she needs is familiarity. Her room, her house that we've made a home, her routine."

I shifted slightly under the covers, my pulse quickening as their voices edged higher. All these decisions were being made like I wasn't even in the room. Like I was some fragile thing about to break if someone looked at me wrong.

Matthew stepped forward, his voice calm but firm. "I don't think this needs to be a fight. We all want what's best for her. Maybe we should ask Megan what she wants."

All eyes turned to me. I felt the weight of it, the pressure of choosing when I didn't even know what I was choosing between. One path was built on memories I didn't have. The other was filled with people I recognized only because I was told I should.

Panic swelled in my chest. What *did* I want?

"I don't know," I whispered. "I don't know what's right."

Silence.

"I don't remember any of you the way I want to," I continued. "Some of you feel familiar. Some of you . . . don't. I don't know what I'm supposed to do or where I'm supposed to go. I don't want to hurt anyone. I just want to feel normal again."

Sherry's face crumpled, and she stepped toward me, taking my hand. "Sweetheart, we love you. No matter what. We'll support whatever you decide." That must have been hard for her to say since she clearly wanted me with her.

"I want to remember," I said softly. "I want to know what my life used to feel like. But everything's just out of reach."

Cade took a careful step closer. "Let me help you remember. No pressure. No expectations. Just . . . let me try."

Sherry started to speak again, but Matthew laid a hand on her arm. "Let her decide."

I looked around the room, at the faces I was supposed to know by heart. And still, I felt like I was playing a role in someone else's story.

Cade's eyes lit with hope, the kind that made my chest ache with guilt.

But I wasn't saying it for him. I was saying it because I needed to see it for myself. The place everyone kept insisting was mine. The place where all the pieces of my life were supposedly waiting to click back into place.

I looked over at Cade. "What's it like? Our house."

He straightened a little. "It's small. Cozy. White siding, navy shutters. You painted the kitchen yellow because you said it felt like sunshine, even on cloudy days. There's a swing on the porch. You picked it out at a flea market and made me promise I'd hang it up that same weekend."

I looked down at my hands in my lap, trying to imagine what that might look like. Trying to picture a version of me who felt at home somewhere. A person who felt safe with a man that I couldn't even recognize. My mind searched for something that connected, but the images were all foggy. Words with no pictures. Feelings with no source.

Another question came to mind, so I cleared my throat and asked. "Is there a spare room?"

He hesitated, and I looked up to meet his unknowing expression. One that I wished I understood.

CHAPTER 9

"Is there a spare room?"

The question hit harder than I expected.

I wished I could've answered right away. When we first moved in, yeah, there was a spare room. A blank canvas. But that space had started becoming something else entirely.

The beginnings of a nursery.

It wasn't finished yet, but it didn't need to be. The paint samples on the wall, the open crib box in the corner, the folded onesies still in their packaging—it was enough to say what that room was meant to be.

How was I supposed to tell her she had a future in a house she didn't even remember?

She wasn't ready for that, not yet. She needed peace, not pressure.

So, I nodded. "Yeah, there's a spare room."

That small lie twisted in my chest. Not because I regretted it, but because I knew why I'd said it. Because she needed somewhere that felt hers again. Somewhere that didn't come with expectations or questions she wasn't ready to ask.

"I just have to clean it out a little," I added quickly. "I'll handle that."

Megan gave a faint nod. "Then that's what I'll do." Her voice was calm but thoughtful. She glanced around the room, her eyes resting on each face. "I'll go home. To the home that I prepared."

Her words made my throat tighten. She didn't remember building that life with me, but some part of her still claimed it. That had to mean something.

Right?

Sherry stepped closer to the bed and folded her arms. Her eyes flicked toward me, uncertain, wary. "Are . . . are you sure, Megan?"

I got it. I really did. She was a mom, and this was her daughter. Of course she was protective. But ever since the accident, there'd been a tension building between us. In this silent tug-of-war, each of us believed we knew what Megan needed. And maybe we were both right. Or maybe neither of us was.

Still, the way she looked at me now, like I was something to guard Megan *from*, cut deeper than I cared to admit.

Megan didn't flinch under the attention. Her shoulders squared, subtle but sure. "It's what seems best," she said, her voice quiet but clear. "I want to know who I am . . . and I can't think of a better place to do that."

Across the room, Rebecca's brows pinched together, her arms still bound tightly across her chest. Matthew gave a slow, almost imperceptible nod. It wasn't approval exactly, but maybe an acknowledgment that Megan was claiming something for herself. Her choice.

Sherry, though . . . She didn't speak right away. Her lips pressed into a thin line, and she looked like she wanted to say a dozen different things at once. But then she simply exhaled, brushing Megan's hair behind her ear.

"Okay," she relented. "Okay, sweetheart. If that's what you want."

For a moment, silence settled over the room. Not heavy. Not angry. Just . . . uncertain.

I stayed quiet, letting Megan sit with her decision. Allowing her the control she deserved. But inside, my mind was already moving, calculating what needed to be done. I'd have to run home that night. Pack away the tiny shoes by the closet door. Take down the mobile from the ceiling hook. Fold the ultrasound photo we'd stuck to the fridge, the one with her name in typed font at the top.

It was going to wreck me.

But I'd do it.

Because right then, what she needed wasn't a husband reminding her of a life she didn't remember.

What she needed was space.

Even if it meant I had to pretend parts of our life hadn't happened yet.

Even if I had to grieve in silence, alone.

Because I loved her.

And love, real love, wasn't always loud.

Sometimes it was quiet. Patient. Waiting just outside the door until she was ready to come home to you. And right then, that was the emotional homecoming that I was waiting for.

THE HOUSE WAS quiet when I pulled into the driveway. Too quiet.

I hadn't been there in days, not since the accident. Even though I'd driven this same paved path a thousand times before, everything felt foreign. I turned off the engine and sat in the silence for a beat, staring at the front door. Megan's door. Our door.

As I approached, the sharp tang of cut grass and motor oil curled into my lungs with every breath. The porch creaked beneath my weight. I turned the knob and stepped inside.

The familiar scent of pine cleaner and the soft citrus of Megan's favorite candle still lingered. Those scents stopped me cold for a second. A part of me had expected the house to feel hollow, abandoned, like I'd been gone for weeks, but it didn't. It felt lived in.

"Cade?" Jackson's voice called from down the hall.

"Jackson?" I kicked the door shut behind me, surprised to hear his voice.

Jackson, my older brother, appeared around the corner, his gray T-shirt spotted with sweat, a rag slung over his shoulder. Dust streaked his jeans. "We've just been tidying up. Figured the place could use a reset before you brought her home."

Spencer, our younger brother, followed close behind, holding a spray bottle and a roll of paper towels. "Didn't think it was right for her to walk into a mess," he added, glancing around like he was still mentally taking inventory. "We hit the kitchen, living room, and got most of the laundry caught up."

I nodded slowly, grateful, even though I felt like there was a world of pressure pressed against me. "Thanks, guys. That means more than you know."

Jackson leaned against the doorframe. "How's she doing?"

I rubbed the back of my neck. "Better, I guess. Still confused, still asking questions. But she's stable. Might even be released tomorrow."

Spencer gave a low whistle. "That soon?"

"Yeah." I exhaled and looked down the hall toward the back of the house. "But there's one thing I gotta do before that happens."

My throat tightened. I walked past them into the spare room

—no, the nursery. The walls still bore the faint robin's-egg-blue paint we'd started to test, and Megan's handwriting sprawled across a sticky note taped near the closet: *Do we like this color??* She'd drawn a smiley face next to the words.

I swallowed hard and nodded. "She asked if we had a spare room. I told her yes."

Jackson used the rag to dust off his jeans. "You didn't tell her?"

"How could I?" I sighed, dragging a hand through my hair. "She doesn't remember me, Jackson. What's she gonna do with news about a baby?"

He didn't answer right away. Instead, he gave me a slow nod and started unpacking a drawer, careful with everything he touched. As a father, I was sure he understood how hard this was.

Spencer exhaled. "So, what's the plan?"

"She's coming home," I repeated. It felt good to say. "She wants to figure out who she is. Said this house might help her."

Jackson glanced at me. "And do you think it will?"

I looked around the room again. The crib still waited in the box, unassembled. A rocking chair huddled in the corner, half-covered with a sheet. A folded stack of baby blankets stood on the dresser.

"I don't know," I admitted, "but it's the only shot I've got."

We worked in silence for a while, boxing up memories we hadn't had the chance to make. Spencer asked a few quiet questions. He wanted to know how she'd been eating and whether she could walk around yet. I answered them as best I could, the way you do when the facts are clear but the future isn't.

Eventually, Jackson placed the last blanket in a tote and dusted off his hands. "We'll leave the frame and furniture for now," he said. "We'll just remove the stuff that might make her ask questions you're not ready to answer."

"Yeah," I said. "Thanks. For being here."

Spencer clapped me on the shoulder. "We're always here. You know that."

Just as he said it, a gust of wind rattled the windows. The sun had nearly disappeared behind the trees, casting the hallway in a dull gray.

Jackson grabbed his keys. "You need anything else before we go?"

I shook my head. "Nah. I just need to figure out how to keep going."

Spencer paused near the front door. "You don't gotta figure it all out tonight. Just keep showing up, Cade."

They left with a few boxes and an unspoken promise to return. I stood alone in the middle of the room, surrounded by packed-away hopes and quiet walls.

As I turned to shut the door, something caught my eye. Something was tucked behind the dresser, nearly hidden under the edge of the rug. I kneeled and pulled it free.

Within my hand rested a small, framed photo of Megan and me. It had fallen, probably during the commotion of the last few days. The two of us were sitting on the back porch, her head on my shoulder, a messy milkshake between us.

She was laughing. And I was looking at her like she was my whole world.

I stared at the photo for a long time, my thumb brushing over the glass. The next day, she'd walk into that house and not remember that moment. Or the porch. Or me.

And the worst part?

I'd have to stand there, pretending it didn't break me.

CHAPTER 10

Megan

I'd spent days staring at the same pale walls, listening to the same beeping machines, seeing the same careful faces watching me like I might shatter if someone blinked too hard. Maybe I would. I hadn't decided yet.

I sat in the wheelchair while a nurse helped with the discharge papers. A new pair of sneakers covered my feet, and a bag of folded clothes rested across my lap. Clothes I didn't recognize, but everyone insisted they were mine. Even that detail was unsettling. How do you forget your own wardrobe?

"Ready?" Cade asked as he stood beside me.

Ready? That was a stretch. I gave a small nod anyway, trying to hide how my stomach had been turning circles since I woke up that morning. That man, my husband, waited patiently, reaching to take the bag off my lap, then stepping back to let the nurse roll me down the hallway.

I glanced at him out of the corner of my eye as we moved. He was tall and broad shouldered, with suntanned skin and a full, dark beard that matched his black hair. He looked like he belonged in the pages of a country-life magazine. I'd studied his face enough over the last few days, but I felt a slow panic rising inside. I'd be alone with him, in a house that was supposedly mine.

When we reached a big red pickup truck, he opened the passenger door and helped me inside. His warm hand brushed against mine in a firm, familiar way that made my heart thump harder, even as my mind screamed that he was a stranger. The door closed with a dull thud, and then it was just the two of us.

I buckled the seatbelt, fingers fumbling slightly.

He climbed into the driver's seat and started the truck. The low rumble of the engine vibrated through the floorboard and into my bones. He adjusted the mirror and glanced over at me. "You okay?"

No. "Yeah."

We pulled out of the parking lot. The road rolled out in front of us, the landscape slowly changing from medical buildings to trees and wide-open skies. I shifted in my seat, noticing the scent that clung to the cab—clean soap, worn leather, something warm and woodsy. It was his. That was Cade. My . . . *husband.* Even thinking those words sounded odd to me.

My gaze drifted to him as he drove. One hand draped over the steering wheel, while the other rested on the console between us. His profile was calm but alert, his jaw tense. He was close, just a few inches away. Close enough that I could see the way his eyes creased when he blinked. It was weird, knowing this was supposed to feel like home.

I wanted to ask him so many questions. What did he do for a living? What did he do for fun? How did we meet? What was our first date like? What were his favorite foods? Did he snore? And if so, did I tease him about it?

I should have known the answers, but I didn't, and I couldn't bring myself to ask any of those questions. So, I settled for something safer.

"Is it far?"

"About fifteen minutes," he replied. "We're just outside of town. We got a place with land, so it's quiet out there."

"Did I want that?" I asked before I could stop myself.

He glanced at me. "You did. At first, you were nervous about being so far from where you were raised, but it grew on you. You said you liked the peace. That it helped you think."

I nodded like I believed him. Maybe I did. I didn't know anymore.

The drive continued in silence after that. I stared out the window at the passing trees, mailboxes, barns with peeling paint, long driveways that disappeared into green pastures. When the truck turned off the main road, my breath caught. A nicely paved driveway wound beneath a canopy of tall trees. The branches tangled overhead, casting dancing shadows across the truck's hood.

Then I saw it.

The house.

The one-story Craftsman was beautiful, with wide porches and freshly mulched flower beds out front. The porch swing Cade mentioned at the hospital swayed gently in the wind. A wind chime tinkled at the edge of the eaves. Everything looked so lived in. So loved.

Cade parked the truck and got out, circling to open my door. "Take your time," he said, holding out his hand.

I hesitated, then placed my palm in his. His fingers curled around mine. My feet hit the driveway, and I just stood there for a minute, staring up at the house that was supposed to be mine.

"How long have we lived here?" I asked.

"Almost two years."

I looked around. "It looks like a magazine cover."

He smiled faintly. "You picked the color of the shutters. Said they reminded you of the ocean."

I let him lead me up the front steps, my sneakers brushing

the welcome mat that read *Home, Sweet Home*. The door opened with a soft click, and warm air brushed against my face.

I stepped inside and froze.

Everything felt familiar . . . and foreign. The walls were a soft cream, the floors a warm wood, with a braided rug near the door. A coat rack held a few jackets, one of which I assumed was mine. The scent of vanilla and cedar clung to the air, delicate and comforting.

Photos lined the hallway. Dozens of them.

I drifted toward the wall, fingers twitching. There we were. Over and over again. Cade's arm around my waist. My smile too bright, too real to be faked. Us in front of a mountain. Us at a bonfire. Us laughing in a kitchen I barely recognized.

"Those are from our anniversary trip last year," Cade said behind me. "You loved that mountain cabin. Kept talking about how peaceful it was."

I stared at the photo. "I look . . . happy."

"You were."

I moved down the line, to an image of us dancing in the living room, blurry with motion. Another image showcased the two of us painting a room together, with a splash of blue paint on my nose. I paused before a picture where I wore a white dress and held a bouquet. My wedding dress.

My throat tightened. "This was our wedding?"

"Yeah," he said, stepping closer. "Best day of my life."

I stared at the picture in its frame, at the way I leaned into him. My hand rested on his chest. My eyes sparkled.

"I don't remember it," I whispered. "Not even a second."

He didn't say anything, but I didn't need him to. The silence said enough.

I moved away from the wall and into the living room. A soft sofa with throw pillows in warm tones, a coffee table with a candle, and a stack of books—it looked like a museum exhibit.

Cade stood nearby, watching me. Not pushing, not hovering. Just watching.

I turned to him. "Do I work? What do I do?"

Cade glanced at me, then looked back at the wall of photos. "You used to work as a secretary at a small doctor's office in town. Real sweet place, good people. But it closed last year. Some folks got transferred. Others were downsized."

I absorbed the words slowly, watching as he made his way toward me.

He continued. "You didn't look for anything else right away. I told you to take your time to figure out what you really wanted. So right now, you've been looking into classes. Thinking about going back to school, getting a degree."

There was something soft and familiar in his voice, like the words came from a place of shared dreams. But then his words started to slow, his mouth opening slightly, like he was about to say something else. Instead, he just stopped.

I waited for a beat, maybe two, and when he didn't continue, I turned my gaze out the window.

He must've been about to bring up some memory, something important, something I didn't remember. My chest tightened a little at the thought. This man clearly knew so much about me, and I couldn't even remember where I used to keep the coffee mugs.

I cleared my throat and pressed forward, needing something else to hold on to. "Okay. So, what do you do?"

"I have two jobs, technically," Cade said, glancing over at me. "I work as a firefighter. Started out volunteering when I was a teenager, and now I'm on the payroll. I'm only part-time, though, because the other half of my time is spent helping my parents on their ranch."

He gestured toward a banner hanging in the living room that read Striking Steele Ranch, the bold yellow lettering stitched against a faded navy background. The worn edges spoke of years of use, but the strip of fabric was clearly cared for, based on the way he spoke about it with quiet pride and unspoken history.

"A firefighter?" I echoed, trying to picture him in that role. And honestly? It wasn't hard.

Everything about him, from his broad shoulders to the steady, grounded way he spoke, made sense in that context. His presence felt dependable. Safe. I didn't know much right then, but I could already tell that Cade Steele was the kind of man who ran toward the fire, not away from it.

"And a ranch," I added, glancing back at him. "You spend your time running into burning buildings *and* chasing cattle?"

The corner of his mouth twitched into something close to a smile. "More or less, yeah."

I shook my head, half amused, half in awe. "That sounds exhausting."

"Some days, it is. But I love it. Both jobs, in different ways."

"And we live here . . . just the two of us?" I asked as I roamed the room a little more.

"Yeah. Well, we've had friends visit. Then, of course, some of my brothers like to come over to crash every so often if they need a break from life." A small chuckle escaped his lips. It was the first time I'd heard him laugh. I guess this situation hadn't left a lot of room for humor.

My eyes flicked back to the hallway. "And the room at the end of the hall. Is that the bedroom?"

He hesitated. "Yeah, the primary and the guest room, which I've been cleaning up for you."

I nodded. "Good. I don't want to be a burden on you."

"You're not," he said immediately. "Megan, you're my wife."

I swallowed hard and looked around again. This place was filled with memories, our memories. But none of them lived in my head. Only in these frames, these walls. In this man beside me, who clearly loved me in a way that I didn't understand at that moment.

I rubbed my arm, suddenly cold. "I think I need to lie down."

"Of course. I'll show you the guest room." He led me down the hallway, past a door I guessed was our bedroom. He didn't pause there. He just kept walking. "That's the bathroom." He gestured to his left as he continued.

When he opened the guest room door, I took in the small bed against the wall, which had been freshly made, and the air faintly scented with lavender. The room was simple and calming. Nothing overwhelming.

"This okay?" he asked.

"It's fine."

He nodded, then lingered a moment longer. "I'll be in the room across the hall if you need anything."

I nodded. "Thanks."

He stepped back, hand on the doorknob, then stopped. "For what it's worth, I'm glad you're home."

I didn't know what to say to that, so I just offered a small smile.

When the door clicked shut, I sat down on the edge of the bed. My fingers toyed with the hem of the comforter. The silence stretched around me, heavy and strange.

I was home.

But it didn't feel like mine.

And for the first time since waking up in that hospital bed, I was starting to wonder if I'd ever feel like I belonged in this life again.

CHAPTER 11

Cade

The house was quiet. Too quiet.

I stood at the stove, a wooden spoon in one hand. My other hand gripped the handle of the skillet as something sizzled beneath it. The aroma of garlic, rosemary, and pan-seared chicken filled the air. I'd added roasted potatoes and green beans to the mix too, hoping the comfort of a familiar meal might help. It was my rustic chicken skillet bake—Megan's favorite. Or, at least, it used to be.

Behind me, the soft tick of the wall clock sounded louder than usual. Every second, the knot in my stomach felt larger.

She was down the hallway, napping. At least, that's what I assumed when the door closed after I'd shown her the guest room. She'd crawled into bed without much to say. She hadn't asked where *our* bedroom was. Maybe she didn't want to know.

Maybe I didn't want to open the door to a conversation she wasn't ready for.

I stirred the chicken absently, barely noticing the slight char to one of the edges until the scent shifted. "Dammit," I muttered, flipping the piece before it scorched. The rest still looked fine, but the burned corner felt like a metaphor I didn't want to touch.

That's when my phone buzzed on the counter.

I reached for it, swiping at the screen—a calendar alert, bright and bold.

Prenatal Appointment – Dr. Langston @ 3:15 PM Tomorrow

My chest tightened as I stared at the reminder. My thumb hovered over the alert for a second too long before I finally dismissed it. The date, the time, the name—all of it felt like a flashing neon sign above my head.

She doesn't know.

She didn't remember *me*, let alone the life we'd been planning. The little life growing inside her. And now I had less than twenty-four hours to figure out how to break the biggest news of her life . . . again.

"I can't keep this from her much longer," I said under my breath. The words stuck in my throat like splinters. "God, how the hell am I supposed to do this?"

"What are you supposed to do?"

My head jerked toward the voice, eyes landing on Megan standing at the kitchen threshold. Her hair was tousled from sleep, her eyes a little heavy, but she was awake and watching me like she'd caught me doing something I wasn't supposed to.

I swallowed hard. "Dinner," I said, quickly forcing a smile. "I was just talking to myself about . . . whether or not I should add some more garlic."

Her brow rose. "Sounds serious."

I let out a soft laugh, trying to keep the mood light. "Only if you're a garlic enthusiast. You, uh, can grab a drink if you want. It'll be ready in a few."

She gave a small nod and inched toward the fridge, her movements cautious, unsure, like someone walking through someone else's house. And maybe that was exactly how it felt to her.

I turned back to the stove, trying to act normal, like I hadn't just been ambushed by reality. The smell of the food was warm, familiar, but my chest still felt cold.

BEFORE WE SAT down at the table, I lit a candle in the center. Stupid, maybe, but it felt right. Megan sat across from me, her hands folded neatly in her lap. She barely touched her plate at first.

"I used to do this every Thursday," I said, cutting into the silence. "Dinner like this. You'd always roll your eyes at the candle, but you'd leave it lit anyway."

She didn't look up from her plate.

"You said it made the green beans taste more sophisticated," I added with a small smile.

That earned the slightest tug at her lips. "That does sound like something I'd say."

Encouraged, I continued. "And that time I tried to make homemade spaghetti? You pretended it wasn't a disaster, but I caught you sneaking frozen meatballs from the microwave twenty minutes later."

She let out a quiet laugh, but it faded too fast. Too hollow.

I glanced at her, at the way she kept pushing food around her plate. Not eating. Not really listening anymore, even if she tried to seem interested. Her eyes were glassy, distant, like she was in a room with me but had already started drifting somewhere else.

"I'm not trying to overwhelm you. Just thought maybe . . . a few stories might help."

"I appreciate it." Her fork went down with a quiet *clink*. "But it's a little hard to laugh at memories that don't feel like mine."

The smile dropped from my face. I leaned back slightly, heart pinching. "Right. Yeah. Of course."

She rubbed her temples and let out a shaky breath. "I'm trying, Cade. I really am. But it's like trying to connect puzzle pieces that aren't in the box."

I nodded slowly, but the silence that settled between us turned heavy, suffocating. Still, I pressed forward, like maybe if I just found the *right* memory, it'd break through.

"Remember that time we went camping out by Silver Ridge? That storm rolled in and flooded the tent, and we ended up sleeping in the truck with wet socks and a space heater that nearly caught fire." I let out a weak chuckle. "You swore off camping forever that night. Said next time we go, it better have walls and a working bathroom."

Nothing.

She blinked slowly, her lips parting, but no recognition flickered across her face.

"And then there was your birthday last year," I tried again, searching her eyes, desperate to see even a flicker of something familiar. "You didn't want a party, just a quiet night in. I made that chocolate chip skillet cookie you like. I burned the edges, of course, but you ate around it and said it was perfect anyway."

Her fingers trembled slightly as she reached for her glass of water, but she didn't take a sip. Just held it there, white knuckled.

I swallowed. "You wore those ridiculous fuzzy socks with the lemons on them. Said they were your 'birthday armor.'"

She stood up so fast that her chair scraped against the floor.

"I . . . I need a minute," she said, voice tight, almost strangled.

"Megan—"

She held up a hand. "I know you're trying. I know all of this means something to you, and I feel like the worst kind of person for not being able to meet you halfway, but Cade . . . it's too much. These aren't memories. They're stories. They're all about me, but none of them feel *like* me."

Her voice cracked at the end, and she turned away before I could respond. The hallway stretched behind her like an escape route, her silhouette swallowed by the soft light as she walked away. Not storming. Just retreating.

Again.

The sound of her door clicking shut echoed louder than it should have.

I sat there at the table, the meal going cold in front of me, the shadows stretching long as the candlelight flickered against the walls. Her plate sat mostly full. Mine, untouched.

It felt like I'd just read her a bedtime story from a book she didn't like. One where she was supposed to be the main character, but the plot was unfamiliar, the voice foreign, and the happy ending a blur she couldn't quite believe in.

And now I'd driven her further away.

I leaned forward, pressing my elbows on the table, hands in my hair.

She was slipping through my fingers.

And tomorrow . . .

Tomorrow, I had to hand her another story, one that could shatter everything.

Because this one involved *both* of us.

And someone we hadn't even met yet.

CHAPTER 12

Megan

I closed the door behind me and pressed my back to it. My hand remained on the knob, like letting go would somehow undo everything that had just happened.

The dim, soft light from the hallway spilled through the cracked door until I closed it and turned the lock. I wasn't afraid of him. But right then, I needed the kind of space that a simple door couldn't really give.

I crossed the room and let my fingers trail along the edge of the dresser as I moved past it. The top was bare except for a folded towel and a small dish of lavender-scented soap. It smelled like something I might've liked once. Like something a version of me had picked out with care.

I sat on the edge of the bed and stared at the floor, my legs swinging slightly above the wood like I was a child again, too small to touch the ground. My chest felt too tight. Like my ribs were shrinking, and everything inside me was being crushed inward.

Cade's voice still echoed in my mind. The stories. The laughter. The way his eyes softened when he looked at me as if he were holding something fragile in his hands.

Me.

But I didn't feel fragile. I felt broken.

I was a stranger with a photo album full of memories that didn't belong to her. I lived in a house with my name on the mail, but I had no sense of ownership. I was married and had a husband whose smile stirred something deep in me, but it wasn't enough.

My stomach twisted sharply, and I doubled over a little, pressing my hand to the ache as a wave of nausea rolled through me. I squeezed my eyes shut.

Breathe. Just breathe.

It had to be the stress. All the stories. The smells. The pressure. Everything built up until it cracked like a dam inside me. I hadn't eaten much. Maybe that was it. Maybe it was just being back there, surrounded by a life I supposedly built but couldn't remember laying a single brick of.

A sob broke from me without warning, the sound quiet, sharp, and raw. It surprised me. I hadn't even felt it coming.

I crawled further onto the bed and curled onto my side, pulling the blanket over my shoulders even though the room wasn't cold. My face burrowed into the pillow that smelled faintly of linen and lemon and maybe something else. Something I couldn't name but that made my chest ache.

I wanted to be her, the version of me that smiled in the pictures on the wall. The woman who knew how to laugh with her husband over burned spaghetti and fuzzy socks. The woman who didn't flinch when her husband reached for her hand. The woman who could remember.

But I wasn't.

Not at that moment.

And maybe not ever again.

Hot tears slid down my cheeks and soaked into the pillowcase. I didn't wipe them away. I didn't try to stop them.

I just lay there, holding on to the ache in my chest, whispering the only thing I could manage. "I wish this were easier."

And in the silence that followed, not even the walls could comfort me.

CHAPTER 13

Cade

I sat at the table long after Megan disappeared down the hallway, the silence pressing in on me like a second skin. The candle had burned low. A thin curl of smoke trailed toward the ceiling when the flame finally flickered out. Her plate still sat there, barely touched. Mine too. The green beans had gone cold, the chicken dry, but the ache in my chest? Still fresh.

I rubbed a hand over my face and leaned back in the chair, letting my eyes tip toward the ceiling. They burned, not from tears, exactly, just . . . everything. I was trying to hold a life together with hands that couldn't grip tightly enough.

I pulled my phone from my pocket, thumb hovering over the screen for a second before I opened the group chat titled *Steele Boys + Momma & Pop*. That chat was where the real stuff went down. Jokes were thrown around like footballs, but the serious stuff never got left hanging.

I typed slowly, deliberately.

> First day home. Not great. I'm trying to take it slow, but tomorrow we have a prenatal appointment, and I'm not sure what to do. Why can't this be easier?

I stared at the message before hitting send. It was quiet for maybe thirty seconds before the buzzing started.

POP

> One day at a time, son. She's scared. You're scared. That doesn't mean you're failing. You're there. That counts for a lot more than you think.

JACKSON

> Just keep showing up, Cade. Don't try to fix it all at once. Just be the guy she fell in love with, even if she doesn't remember him yet.

SPENCER

> You're doing everything right, man. None of us has the rulebook for this. But she came home to you. That means something.

GRAHAM

> This sucks, no way around it. But you're stronger than this mess. And she's in there somewhere. Just keep holding the light.

I read them all twice, then hit "like" on each one before typing one final text.

> Thanks, everyone. I know there's not one answer for this, but it helps to have your support. Love you all.

My thumb hovered for a moment after sending the text. Then I set the phone on the table. The screen dimmed as the messages faded from view.

I tried to eat a few more bites. Going to bed hungry wasn't an option, just like we used to promise never to go to bed angry.

That was our thing, one of those little vows we made to each other outside of the big ones. It had always helped before. Now, everything felt like a half-remembered rule in a life Megan didn't recognize.

When I'd had enough, I stood and gathered the plates, scraping the leftovers into a Tupperware container. Megan's fork rested on the plate's rim, like she'd abandoned more than just her dinner. I rinsed everything in the sink, letting the hot water run over my hands for longer than necessary.

I packed the rest of the food away and wiped down the counters. The house felt heavy with the kind of stillness that settles into old bones and quiet spaces. I needed to move. Fresh air had always done me good, ever since I was a kid. Whether it was a hard day on the ranch, a rough shift at the station, or at that moment, while trying to piece together a life that looked the same on the outside but felt completely foreign.

I grabbed my jacket from the hook by the door and stepped outside, letting the screen door ease shut behind me with a soft *click*. The crisp night air brushed against my skin, just cool enough to remind me that summer was ending. Stars blinked overhead, scattered like someone had tossed a handful of glitter across the sky.

I walked slowly, the heels of my boots sinking in the grass, the quiet hum of crickets filling the spaces that words couldn't reach.

And somewhere between the porch and the fence line, I let out a sigh from deep in my soul.

I just needed a minute. Just a little space to think before the next day came crashing in.

THE NEXT MORNING, I found myself standing outside the guest room, my hand paused mid-air, just inches from the door. I hadn't slept much, if at all. My thoughts had circled endlessly, rehearsing lines I knew wouldn't come out right. I imagined her reaction one hundred different ways. None of them had felt good. None of them felt fair.

The morning air filtered through the windows. A low hum vibrated the fridge in the kitchen, and the ticking clock in the hallway provided accompaniment. The world felt too normal for what I was about to do.

I finally knocked. Just lightly. Barely louder than a whisper. "Megan?"

There was a long pause. Then, the soft rustle of blankets, the creak of floorboards, and the metallic click of the door unlocking. It cracked open a moment later.

She locked the door? What is she afraid of? I shook off the thoughts.

She stood in front of me, still wearing the oversized sleep shirt that used to be mine, though I didn't mention it. Her hair was pulled into a loose knot on top of her head, and her eyes were puffy with sleep, but alert. Guarded.

"Hey," I said gently. "Sorry to wake you."

She blinked once, twice. "It's okay."

"I just wanted to make sure you had enough time to get ready," I said, rubbing the back of my neck. "I was gonna make some eggs, toast . . . coffee, if you want it."

A small furrow formed between her brows. "Ready for what?"

I shifted my weight from one foot to the other, feeling a tight knot twist behind my ribs. "We have an appointment this afternoon. It's at 3:15. I . . . we scheduled it a while ago. Before the accident."

She pushed the door open a little wider, clearly trying to piece things together. "What kind of appointment?"

I hesitated, swallowing hard. "It's a doctor's appointment."

Her eyes narrowed. "For me?"

"Yeah," I said, voice dropping a notch. I forced myself to hold her gaze. "It's a prenatal checkup."

The silence that followed felt loud. Deafening.

Her expression didn't shift at first. She just stared at me like I'd spoken in a foreign language. Then, slowly, too slowly, her lips parted. "Wait . . . what?"

I nodded. "You're pregnant, Megan."

The breath left her body in one sharp exhale as the news punched the wind out of her. Her hand tightened on the edge of the doorframe, knuckles white.

"I didn't want to keep it from you," I blurted. "I just . . . didn't know how to tell you. And the appointment's today, so I knew I had to say something."

Still nothing. Her face had gone pale, her eyes wide and wet around the edges.

"We're . . . we were excited," I added, softer now. "When we found out, we kept it to ourselves for a few weeks, just to enjoy the moment. We'd just told everyone shortly before everything happened."

Her mouth opened, then closed again, as she struggled to find a foothold in a landslide of information. She wanted to match my words with something that made sense to her. But there was nothing.

CHAPTER 14

Megan

I blinked. Once. Twice. Like maybe if I opened my eyes wide enough, Cade's words would rearrange themselves into something else.

Pregnant.

He said I was pregnant.

I stared at him, the sound of blood rushing in my ears louder than anything else in the room. My lips parted, but no sound came.

Pregnant?

I didn't even remember kissing him or sharing a bed with him. How could I be carrying his child?

It wasn't just the kiss. It was everything. I didn't remember falling in love. I didn't remember the first time he made me laugh or the first fight that made me cry. I didn't remember saying yes to a future with him, trusting him with my heart, with my body, with a baby.

Everything in me twisted into a knot. The panic was quiet but rising fast, like water filling up a room, inch by inch, and I stood in the center, pretending not to drown.

"Megan? Are you okay? Again, I'm so sorry to spring this on

you. The doctors at the hospital said to let things happen gradually, but with this, I couldn't wait. It didn't seem right."

I swallowed, my throat dry. "I still think someone should've told me sooner than this. I mean . . . how far . . . How pregnant am I?"

He exhaled, rubbing the back of his neck. "Fourteen weeks. Just crossed into your second trimester. It's why we planned the trip. We knew the next one would be with a baby, so we figured this might be the last real getaway for a while."

Fourteen weeks. That was three and a half months. And I didn't remember a single day of it.

The thoughts in my head were autumn leaves caught in a windstorm, swirling around. I grasped at memories I didn't have, trying to anchor myself to feelings I didn't feel.

How did I react when I found out? Did I cry? Laugh? Did I wrap the test in a ribbon and surprise him after dinner? Or did I panic and sit on the bathroom floor with a hand over my mouth?

I didn't know. And not knowing felt like grief.

"I—" I tried to form a sentence, but the words stuck in my throat. I wasn't sure what to say that would be appropriate for the situation. For my life. For this version of me I couldn't seem to reach.

All I knew was I couldn't ruin it. Whatever this was, whatever we were, I couldn't undo it just because I felt like a stranger in my own skin.

"I'll need to get ready," I finally said, voice thin and brittle. "May I shower?"

Cade nodded quickly. "Of course. The bathroom's right there." He pointed down the hall. "All your stuff's still in the cabinet. The lower shelf inside the shower is yours. Shampoo, conditioner, body wash, same brand you've always used."

He stepped back from the doorway, giving me space. I nodded and walked past him without meeting his eyes.

"Oh," he said behind me, his voice a little louder now, like he was trying to steer us away from the emotional wall that had settled between us. "Water pressure's a little weird in there. The pipes are old. Spencer's been helping me work on a few things around the house, but the bathroom's one of the last things on the list. The shower knob can be a little touchy, so turn it real slow." He ran his fingers through his slightly disheveled black hair, then gave a half-smile. "Actually, let me just go turn it on for you. It's easier that way. Otherwise, it'll either be freezing or burn your skin off."

I stepped aside and nodded, grateful for the pause in the conversation. Grateful that he was filling the air with something practical and safe that I didn't have to overthink.

He disappeared into the bathroom, and a second later, I heard the familiar creak of pipes, followed by the rush of water splashing against tile. "Just give it a minute," he called from inside. "It takes a bit to get warm. Once it does, though, it'll stay hot."

The sound of running water filled the hallway, a strange comfort in the quietness of everything else.

He came back out a moment later, brushing his hand against the side of his jeans. "You're good to go. Towels are under the sink. Let me know if you need anything else."

There was something gentle about his voice, a kind of practiced softness that told me he was used to caring for me. I just wished I could remember what it felt like to be cared for by him.

I nodded again, fingers tightening around the edge of the doorframe. "Thanks," I said, then stepped inside and shut the door behind me, the latch clicking into place with finality.

Just me now. Me and the sound of the water and a thousand thoughts I don't know what to do with.

I placed my hand against the door.

I locked it.

Not because I didn't trust him, but because I needed a second to breathe. True time alone with my thoughts.

The room was small and neat, with soft gray walls and a navy-blue rug beneath my bare feet. A hand towel hung too perfectly, like someone had been tidying up in hopes I'd feel at home. Decorative wall clings lined the tops of the walls, almost like a border. Had I hung those?

Steam already fogged the edges of the mirror as I peeled the oversized T-shirt off and tossed it into the small wicker hamper beside the sink. I hesitated in front of the mirror, heart hammering, then stepped forward.

My reflection stared back at me. The same blonde hair piled messily on my head, same face, same pale skin.

But different, too. Softer.

I turned to the side and placed my hand over my lower stomach.

It wasn't a bump. Not really. Just a subtle swell, like I'd eaten a big lunch or had one too many late-night snacks. It was something that I hadn't noticed until that day. It was real. Something was growing inside me. A life.

My hand ghosted over my skin, fingers pressing lightly, tracing the invisible curve of what I couldn't remember building.

Who was I when I found out? Hopeful? Scared? Excited?

Did I cry in Cade's arms? Did we pick out names over ice cream? Did we sit on the floor of this very room, dreaming about what kind of parents we'd be?

The ache came fast and sharp. A deep, hollow hurt that bloomed behind my ribs.

"I don't know who I am," I whispered to the mirror. "I don't know who you are. I don't know how to be her."

The reflection didn't answer. It just stared back with glassy eyes, shoulders trembling, a stranger in my skin.

I stepped into the shower. The warm spray cascaded over

my body like a curtain, trying to blur out the chaos in my mind. The scent of lavender and citrus rose with the steam and wrapped around me in a cloak that used to mean comfort.

I tilted my face into the stream, letting the water hit me full on, letting it wash over the panic, the uncertainty, the heartbreak of not knowing what I was supposed to be feeling.

But then, just beneath it all, there was something else.

A flicker.

A quiet pull, soft but insistent, like a thread wound too tightly around my chest. I pressed my hand against my stomach and felt the warmth of my own skin under my fingers.

Inside me, a life was growing. A tiny heartbeat I hadn't heard. A future I hadn't planned. A child I didn't remember creating or choosing . . . but already somehow couldn't imagine leaving behind.

"I don't remember you," I whispered into the steam. "But I will."

I didn't know how, or how long it would take. But I meant it.

I owed that to the person I used to be.

And to the little someone waiting on the other side of all this confusion, someone who hadn't asked for any of this but deserved everything.

"I'll find my way back," I said. "For you."

Not for Cade.

Not even for myself.

For the one person I hadn't met yet but already loved more than I could understand and could probably ever describe.

CHAPTER 15

Cade

*A*fter a while, she crept out of the guest room, almost like she was afraid her presence might disrupt the morning's stillness. Her damp, straight hair was pulled into a loose ponytail, and she wore one of her favorite blouses, though she probably didn't realize it—blue with tiny floral stitching around the neckline. A pair of jeans hugged her hips and thighs just right. I had moved a lot of her clothes over to the *guest* room closet when I cleaned it out so that she had easy access to everything.

I was leaning against the kitchen counter, coffee growing cold in my hands, but the moment I saw her, I straightened.

"You look beautiful," I said, offering her a small smile.

She glanced down at her clothes, then looked back up and nodded. "Thanks."

And there it was, just the hint of a blush brushing her cheeks. It nearly made my heart stall. Even with the distance, Megan still had this way of knocking the wind out of me.

"I'm ready whenever you are," she said, adjusting the strap on her purse.

I nodded and set down my mug before grabbing my keys

from the hook near the door. "Okay. Let's get you and our little one to the doc."

She followed me through the house, her footsteps quiet on the hardwood floor. I held the front door open and waited for her to step through. Outside, the sun had barely burned through the haze, and the gravel crunched under our feet as we made our way toward the truck.

"Watch your step," I murmured, guiding her around a spot where the rain had pooled earlier in the week.

When we reached the truck, I jogged ahead a bit and pulled the door open for her.

"Running ahead to get the door?" she said, a hint of question in her voice.

I looked up at her with a grin. "I was raised to be a respectable gentleman. Especially for you."

She blinked at that. Then she climbed in without another word, settling into the seat and seeking comfort in a place she didn't recognize. I shut the door and circled to the driver's side.

The silence between us hung low as I started the truck and eased it out of the driveway. I stole a glance at her. Her hands rested in her lap, her left slightly elevated, as it was still in a cast, and her eyes on the horizon.

"Your momma called this morning." I cleared my throat to break the quiet. "Just checking in. She's gonna be the one taking you to your physical therapy appointments for the next few weeks."

Megan turned her head slightly. "Why?"

"Because . . ." I hesitated, fingers tightening on the steering wheel. "Since your car was totaled, we only have one car right now, and I'm heading back to work this week. Between the fire station and the ranch, I've got some long shifts coming up. I didn't want you stuck without a ride."

She looked out the window again. "Oh."

A beat of silence passed.

"I can take the bus or something," she offered, though her voice lacked conviction. "She doesn't have to go out of her way."

I shook my head. "No way. It's not safe, Meg. Not right now. Besides, she thought it would be a great way for you two to reconnect. Spending time with someone you've known longer than me might even help your memory."

She didn't reply to that, but I saw her fingers tighten just a little on her jeans.

"I know it's weird," I said, trying to tread carefully. "Having to rely on people like this. I just don't want you to feel like you're doing this alone."

She turned to me slowly, eyes narrowing. "But I am doing it alone. Or at least . . . it feels that way. No one else is going through what I am."

The words hit harder than she probably meant them to. I gritted my teeth and kept my eyes on the road. "You're not the only one going through this, Megan. We all are. And I'm trying to make it easier. I don't know how else to help."

She sighed and leaned her head against the seat. "I didn't mean to sound ungrateful. It's just . . . a lot."

"I know. Believe me, I know."

The road stretched on. A line of trees flanked the two-lane blacktop. In the spring, those boughs were full and plentiful. Wind whispered through the cracked window, and the occasional thump of the tires rolling over seams in the pavement provided a backbeat.

"This appointment today," she said after a few minutes, "what exactly do they do?"

I glanced over. "They'll check on the baby, listen to the heartbeat, and maybe get a look with the ultrasound. You'll probably answer a bunch of questions. And they'll make sure you're okay, physically."

"And mentally?" she asked, a hint of sarcasm playing at the edge of her voice.

I smiled, but it faded fast. "Dr. Langston knows about the memory loss. I gave her a heads-up on a call this morning. She's been our doctor since the start, and she's solid. Kind. Smart. I figure it's better she knows."

She nodded. "Right. That makes sense."

Another stretch of silence.

"I packed your water bottle," I said, trying to lighten the mood again. "And some of those crackers you like are in the glove box, just in case."

She looked at me out of the corner of her eye. "Thanks."

Her voice was small, and something in it twisted inside me. I missed her. I missed the ease between us, the way we used to talk without thinking, without weighing every word. Whenever we rode in the truck, she would slide closer, even though she didn't have to, just to be near me. Now every sentence felt like stepping through a minefield. Careful. Deliberate.

And we were always one word away from blowing it all up.

We reached the clinic ten minutes early. I pulled into a shaded spot near the front entrance and turned off the engine. Megan unbuckled her seatbelt but didn't reach for the door. I watched her, waiting.

She turned to me finally. "So . . . what do we say if someone asks me something I should know?"

"I'll step in. You don't have to pretend. Just be honest. You're recovering, and anyone who matters will understand."

She nodded once and then opened the door. I met her at the front of the truck and walked beside her up the path to the clinic.

As we passed through the automatic doors and entered the waiting room, I couldn't help but glance down at her. She walked in with a strength, like she knew where she was going. For a moment, she was the old Megan, my Meg. But there was a quick, unsure glance from her, and I remembered.

And I couldn't stop the thought that flickered through my

mind about what it would be like, months from then, if she still didn't remember.

Could we build something new? Would she ever feel like mine again?

I pushed aside the thoughts and forced a smile for the receptionist as we stepped up to the front desk, but inside, I was a mess of worry, hope, and the quiet, gnawing fear that maybe we'd never quite find our way back.

CHAPTER 16

My eyes scanned the framed photos of smiling babies and proud parents that lined the pastel blue walls in the waiting room at Dr. Langston's office. Even though my nerves were coiled tight, the room had a calming effect. Megan sat beside me after we checked in, her arms resting on the armrests that separated us. She wasn't saying much, but every now and then, her gaze lingered a little longer on a photo.

It felt like hope. A flicker, but I'd take it.

"You okay?" I asked, leaning in just enough for my words to stay between us.

She nodded once. "Just . . . watching."

She didn't elaborate, and I didn't press her. I was learning quickly that silence wasn't always a bad thing with Megan. Not then, at least. Sometimes she just needed space to breathe. And honestly, so did I.

"Megan Steele?"

We rose together when the nurse called her name. Instinct guided my hand to the small of her back as we followed the woman down the hallway. Megan didn't flinch. She didn't lean into me, either, but she didn't pull away.

Progress.

The bright exam room was the kind of clean that made you trust the place instantly. A patterned curtain hung half-closed near the exam table, and a fetal Doppler sat ready on the counter beside a container of gel. Everything was sterile, quiet, waiting.

Dr. Langston walked in moments later, clipboard in hand, glasses perched on the bridge of her nose. She was in her mid-fifties, with a calming presence that reminded me a little of my momma—grounded, thoughtful, and steady.

"Good afternoon," she said, smiling at Megan first, then at me. "Megan, I'm Dr. Langston. I understand we've had a bit of a rocky start."

I sat down beside Megan as she gave the doctor a hesitant nod. "That's . . . one way to put it."

Dr. Langston's face softened as she lowered herself onto the rolling stool. "Cade mentioned what happened in his message. I'm so sorry for what you're going through. I can't imagine how hard this must be."

Megan didn't respond, but her shoulders eased just a little. I figured that was as close to comfortable as she'd allow right then.

"I know everything might feel unfamiliar," she continued, "but medically speaking, your pregnancy has been progressing well so far. Today's visit is just a standard checkup to make sure the baby's growing the way we want and that you're staying healthy, too."

She spoke to Megan like she was still the same woman from before, not a fragile shadow trying to remember how to fit into her own life. I was grateful for that.

"Let's go ahead and get your vitals first," the nurse said, stepping in again. Megan stood and followed her instructions as the doctor checked her vitals, which were all routine. She didn't say much through it, but she didn't look scared, either. Just focused. Observing. Taking it in.

After that, Dr. Langston invited her to lie back on the table. The crinkling paper beneath her seemed unnaturally loud, but Megan moved smoothly, positioning herself with care. "This might be a little cold," the doctor warned before applying the gel to her stomach.

Megan flinched, then let out a surprised little laugh under her breath. "You weren't kidding."

And just like that, the tension in the room shifted. That one smile. I breathed it in like it was oxygen.

Dr. Langston pressed the Doppler probe against her abdomen and moved it in slow, practiced circles. For a moment, the only sounds were static and soft thuds.

Then the baby's heartbeat filled the room, strong and rhythmic. The same sound we'd heard once before together, only now it was like hearing it for the first time all over again.

Megan's lips parted as she turned toward the monitor. Even though it wasn't showing anything visual, her eyes widened. She didn't say anything, but she didn't have to.

She was listening.

Feeling.

Connecting.

"That's your baby," Dr. Langston said with a warm smile. "A healthy heart rate, just over 150 beats per minute. Perfect for fourteen weeks."

Megan swallowed hard, and I watched as she blinked, brushing her thumb absently against the curve of her belly. "It's real," she whispered.

My heart clenched.

"Yeah," I said, barely above a breath. "It's real."

Dr. Langston continued with the rest of the checkup, talking us through measurements and the baby's development. "Baby is roughly the size of a peach right now. Around three and a half inches long. In the next couple of weeks, you'll probably start to feel fluttering. Almost like bubbles, at first. It'll be subtle, but once you recognize it, it's hard to miss."

Megan glanced at me, then down at her stomach. "Do you remember when we found out?"

I nodded. "I remember everything."

Her eyes flickered with something unreadable, perhaps longing or regret. I couldn't tell. But she didn't ask me to explain, and I didn't offer. Not yet.

When the appointment finished and she was upright again, wiping away the excess gel, she looked lighter. Like hearing that heartbeat had settled the storm, if only for a moment.

The ride back home was quiet at first. Peaceful.

Until . . .

"So . . . my mom's taking me to PT?" she asked, glancing at me from the passenger seat.

"Yeah." I eased onto the road. "I talked to her earlier. She's got a flexible schedule this week. Said she'd be happy to help."

"Because you'll be working?" she said, almost as if she were testing her memory.

I nodded, keeping my eyes on the road. "Firehouse shifts start back up in two days. And between that and helping my folks on the ranch . . ." I exhaled. "There's just a lot to juggle. I want to make sure you don't miss anything important."

She was quiet for a beat. "That makes sense."

But there was something in her tone; it wasn't dismissive, but it wasn't warm, either. Almost like she was trying to say she understood, even if the whole situation still felt unfair.

"I know it's not ideal," I said, "but until we can figure out a better setup, this is what we've got."

She nodded. "It's fine. Really."

I didn't press. I didn't want to argue. But I also didn't want to keep pretending like everything was easy when it wasn't. Not for either of us.

Back at the house, she climbed down from the truck before I could come around and open the door. That used to be one of her favorite things, when I'd do it without thinking. Now she just walked ahead of me, arms folded, head slightly down.

I watched her pause at the porch steps. Her hand rested briefly on the railing before she looked back.

"Thanks for taking me," she said softly. "For . . . everything."

The air between us shifted again.

"You don't have to thank me, Meg. This is still your life, even if it doesn't feel like it right now."

She gave a tight nod, then stepped inside.

And as I stood there, keys still in my hand, the wind stirring the trees around me, I couldn't help but wonder how long until this version of her stopped being temporary?

And would she ever really come back?

CHAPTER 17

Megan

$\mathcal{A}$ few days later, I found myself alone in the house for the first time. Cade had left for work early that morning. I wasn't sure he'd had a chance to eat breakfast, as I hadn't heard him clanging around in the kitchen, but he'd taken the time to leave a note beside my phone. The note let me know the battery was fully charged and anyone I wanted to call could be found in the contacts.

He didn't need to do that, but that was just how he was.

The house felt so different without him in it, though. Quieter. Lonelier. Wider somehow, like the walls were pushing outward, and I was just this tiny thing floating inside them.

Granted, it was nice to move around freely without him constantly worrying if I was okay. I could explore at my own pace without feeling guilty for making him hover. But even as I wandered from room to room, a strange ache settled in my stomach, heavy and persistent.

It didn't make any sense. I barely knew Cade. My mind didn't remember him.

But that didn't seem to stop my heart from missing him when he was gone.

How was that even possible? How could you miss something you didn't even remember having?

I ended up in the living room again, like a moth to a flame, drawn toward the same bronze-colored frame sitting proudly on the coffee table.

Our wedding party.

I kneeled in front of it, brushing my fingertips lightly against the cool metal edge. Six men stood beside Cade, and six women beside me, smiles bright and eyes full of excitement. The date etched at the bottom in sweeping cursive read: *October 24th.*

Our wedding day.

I stared at the photo until the faces blurred together. There was Kaleigh, Cade's niece, clutching her basket of rose petals, and Hayden, my nephew, his bow tie slightly crooked. My sister had called yesterday, and I'd heard Hayden's voice through the speaker. That loud, silly, familiar sound had twisted something deep inside my chest.

I didn't know this life.

It still felt like trying to step into someone else's shoes. Someone braver, happier, someone who *belonged.*

I wanted to ask Cade about it. About everything. How we met. What that day was like. What promises we made under the sky on a day I no longer remembered. But fear stopped me. I worried I would hurt him, or he would hurt me. I worried that no matter how hard I tried, I might never get it all back.

A sharp knock at the door broke through the fog of my thoughts, making me jump. My heart leaped into my throat before logic caught up and I remembered my ride.

I wiped my hands down the front of my leggings and glanced at the clock on the wall. *10:58 a.m.* Exactly when Cade said my mom would come by. She'd volunteered to take me to PT when the time came, but I wasn't sure why she'd planned to stop by on that particular day.

I tucked a few loose strands of hair behind my ears, gave myself a shaky nod, and moved toward the door.

When I opened the door, my mom stood there, smiling in that overly bright way that always seemed a little forced those days. Her reddish-brown hair was pulled into a simple ponytail, and her blue eyes—my blue eyes—searched my face with a quiet sort of tenderness. She wore jeans, sneakers, and a soft teal sweater that made her look younger. I hadn't seen her since being released from the hospital; she seemed more relaxed than she did then.

"Hi, sweetie," she said, pulling me into a quick hug before I could react.

I let her, wrapping my arms loosely around her as her perfume hit me. The scent was so familiar it made my throat ache.

"Hey, Mom," I said, stepping back. "Thanks for coming."

"Of course! You didn't think I'd leave you stuck in this house all day, did you?"

Her smile widened as she nudged past me into the living room, her gaze flicking around like she was taking mental inventory.

I closed the door and followed her, heart thudding strangely in my chest.

"You ready for our girls' day?" she asked brightly. "Thought we could drive around a little. Maybe see some familiar places. Jog that memory of yours."

I hesitated, biting my lip, unsure if driving around town would feel more like pressing on a bruise than healing anything.

But I nodded anyway.

"Sure," I said. "Sounds good."

Mom beamed like I'd given the perfect answer. "Great! Grab your purse, and let's go." She reached for my hand but stopped herself halfway, lowering her arm awkwardly. For a moment, she seemed to forget that she was a stranger to me, but my hesitation was a sharp reminder.

"You look beautiful, honey," she said. Cautious optimism filled her eyes. "That color looks really good on you."

I glanced down at my simple blue top and dark jeans, cheeks flushing with sudden warmth. I hadn't thought much about what I'd worn. I'd just grabbed something clean and easy. As she studied me, however, I couldn't think about anything else.

"Thanks," I mumbled, tugging at the hem.

She smiled wider, her eyes misty but still shining. "You're welcome."

I stepped onto the porch and pulled the door shut behind me after grabbing my purse. The cool breeze kissed my cheeks, and for the first time all morning, a tiny thread of comfort weaved through my nerves.

Mom led the way to a silver SUV parked neatly by the curb. She opened the passenger door for me like it was second nature, and I slipped inside, tugging my seatbelt across my chest.

As she rounded the front of the car, I swallowed the lump in my throat.

It was strange.

I didn't remember her from before the hospital.

Not the way I should have.

But somehow, sitting in her car with the faint scent of the air freshener hanging between us, I felt something I hadn't expected to feel.

Safe.

Anchored.

Almost . . . home.

Maybe memories weren't the only way to find my way back to the people who loved me. Maybe sometimes, I just needed to start where I was and let my heart do the remembering.

The drive started out nice. She pointed out shops we used to visit together. The coffee shop where I'd supposedly spent hours on the weekend with friends. The little bookstore tucked away behind Main Street that hosted weekly author signings.

"Remember when you dragged me to that midnight release party for that fantasy series you loved?" she said, laughing as she turned down a side road. "You insisted we dress up. You made me wear a cloak, Megan!"

I smiled faintly. The image was blurry in my mind, more like a feeling than a memory, but it was something.

"I wish I remembered it better," I admitted, voice soft.

Her hand tightened slightly on the steering wheel. "You will," she said, a little too quickly. "It just takes time."

The longer we drove, the more places she pointed out, rapid-fire, like she was afraid I might slip further away if she stopped. And with each new landmark, a pressure started building in my chest.

We pulled up outside a two-story white house with blue shutters. A swing set sagged slightly in the backyard.

"Your dad and I bought this house right before you were born," Mom said, her voice thick with nostalgia. "You learned to ride your bike on that sidewalk. You used to race the neighbor's boys down to the mailbox. I loved watching you and your siblings play tag in the yard."

I stared at the house, willing something, *anything*, to stir in my mind. Nothing came. Just an empty hollowness, yawning wider by the second.

Tears pricked the backs of my eyes, hot and furious.

"I don't remember," I whispered.

Mom reached across the console and squeezed my hand. "It's okay, sweetie. We'll just keep trying."

We sat there a few more minutes, the silence between us growing heavier.

Finally, she shifted the car back into drive. But her good mood was cracking around the edges, and mine was splintering right along with it.

She started the car again and took us down unfamiliar streets. Along the way, she peppered me with too many "You remember this place, don't you?" comments, and by the time we reached the diner, the inevitable happened.

She pulled into the parking lot, claiming we used to have Saturday breakfasts here, just the two of us, then parked the car with a little too much force.

"You're pushing," I said quietly as I stared out the windshield.

"What?" Her voice was sharp, defensive.

"You're pushing me to remember things I'm not ready to," I said, turning to face her. "I'm trying, but it's not like flipping a switch, Mom." It was the first time I'd said "Mom" out loud. It didn't feel wrong, yet it grabbed my attention.

"I know that!" she snapped. Her seatbelt unbuckled with a harsh *click*. "But you *could* try harder. You just sit there like . . . like you don't even want to remember!"

I flinched. The words landed like a slap, even though I could see the regret on her face the second they left her mouth.

"That's not fair," I said, my voice shaking. "You think I don't want to remember? You think I *like* feeling like a stranger in my own life?"

Mom pressed her fingers to her temples and squeezed her eyes shut. "I didn't mean it like that," she said, voice tight. "I just —" She blew out a breath. "I just miss my daughter."

The anger drained out of me, leaving only sadness behind.

"I miss her too," I whispered.

We sat there in the stifling silence, both of us too stubborn or too scared to say anything else.

Finally, Mom reached for the door handle.

"Come on," she said, her voice rough but gentler now. "Let's get some lunch. We'll call it a win just for getting out of the house."

I hesitated.

Part of me wanted to tell her no, to crawl back into bed, to hide from the mounds of everything I couldn't remember. But another part—the part that still hoped, still fought for scraps of familiarity? That part pushed me out of the car and into the afternoon sunlight.

The bell above the diner door jingled as we stepped inside, the smell of frying bacon and fresh coffee wrapping around me like an old quilt. It was a small place, with vinyl booths lining the windows and a bar with chrome stools beneath the counter. Two older men sat hunched over their coffee cups, chatting quietly.

A waitress with a pink apron and a messy bun caught my mom's eye and gave a warm wave. "Pick wherever you want, hon!" she called out.

Mom smiled at her and led us to a booth by the window. I slid into the seat opposite her, the leather squeaking under my jeans. For a few minutes, we busied ourselves with the menus, though I wasn't really reading. The words blurred together.

"You used to get the chocolate chip pancakes here," Mom said after a while, peeking at me over the top of her menu. "You wouldn't even look at the rest of the menu. You'd just bounce in and order them right away."

Something about the way she said that made something shift inside me. Chocolate chip pancakes—the words evoked a flash of melted chocolate, sticky fingers, and powdered sugar dusting a plate.

It wasn't clear, but it was there. A feeling.

I looked up, surprised to find my throat tight.

"I . . . think I remember that," I said slowly, blinking hard.

Mom's eyes widened as her hand flew to her mouth. "You do?" she whispered, as if the moment might vanish if she spoke too loudly.

"Not everything," I said quickly, not wanting to give her false hope. "Just, I don't know. The feeling of it. Chocolate chips. Sitting in a booth like this."

Her eyes shone with sudden tears, but her smile was real this time, soft and trembling. "That's something, sweetie." She reached across the table to squeeze my hand. "That's a start."

I squeezed her hand back, feeling the tiniest flicker of something unfamiliar but welcome in my chest.

It wasn't everything. Maybe it wasn't even close.

But it was *something.*

When the waitress came over, pad in hand, Mom looked at me with a smile still tugging at the corners of her mouth.

"Ready to order?" the waitress asked.

I glanced down at the menu again, but the choice was already made.

"I'll have the chocolate chip pancakes." And for the first time in days, I felt a flicker of peace.

Maybe memories didn't come all at once.

Maybe they were just waiting, tucked into the small, ordinary corners of my life. Waiting for me to find them again.

One tiny victory at a time.

BY THE TIME Mom dropped me off at home, long shadows stretched across the driveway. The house looked different—not physically, but lighter somehow. Maybe it was just me.

Mom hesitated at the curb, looking like she wanted to say more, possibly to apologize again, but I gave her a small, tired smile. We'd already said what needed saying. We needed space to breathe.

I waved as she pulled away, then turned toward the porch once she was out of view. Inside the house, I slipped off my shoes and wandered into the living room, letting my fingers trail lightly over the back of the sofa, the edge of the coffee table, the wedding photo in the bronze frame.

October 24th.

The date stared back at me, looping elegantly and permanently across the glass.

With my eyes, I traced the outline of Cade's face in the picture. It left a strange ache deep inside my chest. A longing for something I couldn't remember but desperately wanted to feel again.

Sighing, I lowered myself to the sofa, always careful of my arm, which was still in a cast. Parts of my body were also still a little sore from the accident. I was about to grab the blanket folded neatly over the back of the sofa when my phone buzzed against the end table, the screen lighting up.

Cade.

My heart thudded stupidly loud in the quiet room.

I picked it up, my thumb hesitating over the screen before swiping to open the text.

CADE

Hey, hope everything went okay today. Thinking about you. Let me know if you need anything, okay? 🩶

The tiny heart emoji at the end made my throat tighten.

It was...different.

I think I remembered something today.

Before I could set my phone down, the bubbles popped up on the screen.

CADE

You did? What happened?

I smiled, curling my legs up under me, and typed back.

> My mom took me to a diner we used to go to a lot. I remembered the chocolate chip pancakes. Not a big deal, but I thought you'd like to know.

The reply came almost instantly.

CADE

> That's a big deal! It's amazing, baby. I'm so proud of you.

My heart twisted at the word *baby*. I didn't know if he even realized he'd typed it. It sounded so natural, so easy, like breathing.

I hesitated, then asked the question that had been gnawing at me all day.

> Are you coming home tonight?

It took a little longer this time, and I tried not to read into it, but the bubbles appeared again.

CADE

> I wish I were. Still at the station. Long shift. I'll be home tomorrow morning, promise.

I swallowed around the sudden lump in my throat. *Tomorrow morning. Okay.*

> Be safe. I'll see you then.

CADE

> Always. And Megan?

My heart jumped a little as I waited for the next message to come through.

CADE

You're doing great. One step at a time. I love you.

I stared at the words until they blurred together. I didn't know if I was supposed to say it back. I didn't know if I could. But I pressed my fingertips lightly against the screen, wishing he could somehow feel it across the distance.

After a moment, I sent a simple reply.

Thank you. Have a good shift.

I set the phone beside me on the sofa and leaned my head back, staring up at the ceiling. There was so much I didn't know. So much still missing.

But that day, just for a few minutes, I'd felt something real. And that was enough.

CHAPTER 18

$\mathcal{T}$he firehouse had a rhythm all its own, a heartbeat you could almost feel in the walls—steady, humming, waiting. I leaned back in the worn recliner in the dayroom, thumb brushing over the screen of my phone as Megan's reply came through.

MEGAN

Thank you. Have a good shift.

A small, relieved breath escaped my chest.

It was simple. Just a few words, but they meant more than I could explain.

She's trying.

She was trying to meet me halfway across the canyon her memory loss had dug between us. And damn it, I'd walk the rest of the way if I had to.

A grin pulled at my mouth, and I pressed to like her message. Right as I did, the bell shrieked through the station. The sound slammed through the air like a gunshot. Instant and electrifying. No matter how many times I heard it, the alarm always punched the breath out of me for a second.

Fire run.

I bolted upright. Around me, the room exploded into motion. Boots thudded against the floor. Gear bags hit the tiles. Voices shouted across the bays.

"House fire! Residential structure!" Captain Morales barked, slapping the run sheet into my hand as I ran past him. "Two-story. Possibly occupied."

Adrenaline hit my bloodstream like a shot of ice water and fire all at once.

There wasn't time to think. Only to move.

I hauled open the locker door and grabbed my bunker pants. I yanked them over my uniform in one practiced motion. The jacket went on next, thick, heavy, scarred from a dozen other fires. The helmet swung by my side as I sprinted toward the engine.

The massive firehouse bay echoed with the roar of engines kicking to life.

Sunlight slashed through the open doors, lighting up the rigs like something out of a movie. Polished chrome, gleaming red paint, and ladders glinted in the light.

I swung into the rig, helmet slamming onto my head, gloves stuffed into my jacket pocket. Fitz was already in the driver's seat. His mouth pinched into a grim line as he white-knuckled the steering wheel.

"Let's move!" Captain barked from the passenger side, radio already crackling with updates.

The engine roared onto the street. Sirens screamed, and the tires spit water as we tore down the bay apron and into traffic. Inside the cab, we sat in the heavy, bracing silence that only comes before you throw yourself into the fire.

Literally.

I braced my boots against the floorboard, feeling the heaviness of the gear pressing into my shoulders, feeling the old familiar tension winding up inside me like a spring.

I thought about Megan.

About the tiny, brave message she'd sent me.

About the baby we hadn't even named yet.

And I made myself a promise, a silent promise that I always made before every call.

I'm coming back. No matter what. I'm coming back to them.

The truck veered left, siren howling as we blew through an intersection. Cars scattered to the sides to make room for us to get through. Up ahead, a thick plume of black smoke punched into the sky, curling and shifting with the breeze. The flames were already licking out of the second-story windows.

"Man," Fitz muttered under his breath. "That's been burning for a while."

"Looks like the kitchen and maybe the back bedrooms," I said, studying the structure as we pulled up.

"Neighbors said they thought someone was inside," the captain grumbled over his shoulder. "Primary search first. Get your masks on. Go fast."

No need to tell us twice.

I cinched my Air-Pak straps. The weight settled across my back like an old, stubborn friend. Next, I snapped my gloves on and pulled the face piece tight. In that moment, the world narrowed to a few simple things: Air. Fire. Search. Save.

We hit the ground running.

I followed my crew to the front door, thermal camera in hand. The door was already half gone, charred black at the edges. I kicked it open the rest of the way, and heat slammed into me like a living thing. The world inside the house was a wall of smoke, thick and choking, swallowing up everything in sight.

I dropped low and crawled forward. The camera flickered and pulsed in my hand, showing faint outlines of furniture, doorways. Not the heat signatures I was looking for, though. No people.

"Cade, right side! Fitz, left!" Captain's voice crackled over the radio.

"Copy!" I bellowed back, pushing deeper into the blackness.

Every instinct screamed at me to hurry. That fire above us wasn't going to wait for us to clear the lower floor. It was hungry, greedy, and fast.

I swept my empty hand in front of me, feeling along the baseboards, checking the sofa, the floor beside it.

Nothing.

My heart hammered against my ribs as I moved into the hallway, the floor groaning ominously beneath me. Ahead, the kitchen glowed orange. A terrifying, beautiful light show of flames chewed through cabinets and countertops.

"Clear here!" Fitz shouted from the living room.

"Primary clear downstairs!" I echoed into my radio. "Advancing to the second floor!"

We moved as a team, fast and sure, navigating the smoke-blind world with practiced ease. Upstairs, the air was even hotter. Flames ate the far wall. Paint blistered and peeled like melting skin. The heat was so intense that it made your brain want to shut down, but you couldn't let it.

You kept moving. You kept searching.

Finally, finally, we reached the bedrooms.

Clear.

Clear.

Clear.

"No victims!" I shouted, relief punching through the haze in my brain.

The captain confirmed, and within minutes, the hose teams hit the main body of the fire, knocking it down with the low roar of high-pressure water.

When it was over, we stood in the ruined shell of someone's home, breathing hard, dripping sweat and soot and adrenaline. I peeled off my helmet. Blinking through the grime, I caught Fitz's eye.

We bumped fists, silent but solid. Another one in the books. Another fire we walked away from.

Outside, I slumped against the engine for a second, dragging in a lungful of fresh, sweet air. In the quiet that followed, the hum of engines idling, the distant chatter of radios, I pulled my phone out again.

No new messages. Just that last one from Megan, still sitting there like a lifeline in my inbox.

I smiled to myself as I scrubbed a hand through my hair, grabbed a bottle of water from the rig, and got ready to load up for the next call.

Because this was the life.

This was the *other* promise I'd made long before memory loss or babies or anything else. To be the one who runs in when everyone else is running out. The most important lesson I learned as a firefighter was never to leave a partner behind. Who knew I would need to use that in my daily life? But that was what I'd pull from. Megan was my life partner, and I'd never leave her behind.

CHAPTER 19

Cade

The house was dark and still when I finally pulled into the driveway. The early morning sky was still caught somewhere between night and day, in that soft, misty blue hour before the sun even thought about waking up.

I killed the engine and sat there for a moment, scrubbing my hand over my face.

It had been one hell of a shift.

Two structure fires, one medical call that went sideways, and a whole lot of paperwork. I was running on fumes and the promise of seeing her.

I climbed out of the truck, made my way up the porch steps, and unlocked the front door quietly. The house smelled like home—a mix of fresh laundry, vanilla candles, and something sweeter underneath I couldn't place. I dropped my bag just inside the door, kicked off my boots, and padded down the hallway toward the guest room. Toward her.

When I nudged the door open, the soft creak gave me away, and I froze. She was curled up under the covers, one hand tucked beneath her cheek, the faint rise and fall of her breath the only movement in the room.

God, she looked so peaceful, so heartbreakingly beautiful, that it almost hurt to look at her.

I started to back away, ready to let her sleep, but the door betrayed me again with another soft groan. Megan stirred, blinking sleepily until her gaze found mine across the room. She appeared disoriented at first, the way she always seemed since the accident, but then her face softened into something like relief.

"Cade?" Her voice was husky with sleep.

"Hey." I stepped inside and eased the door shut behind me. "Sorry. Didn't mean to wake you."

"It's okay," she whispered, sitting up a little and pushing her hair from her face. "You're home."

I crossed the room and crouched beside the bed, resting my arms on the mattress so I could look at her properly. "Yeah. Long night," I admitted, offering a tired smile.

She studied me for a second, like she was trying to read between the lines of my face. "Was it . . . bad?"

I shrugged. "Could've been worse. We got everyone out safe. That's what matters."

"You're exhausted," she said, softer now, like she hated seeing it.

"Little bit," I admitted with a chuckle. "Nothing a few hours of sleep won't fix."

She smiled faintly, then glanced down at her hands twisting the edge of the blanket. "I'm glad you're okay."

Something in my chest tightened at the quiet sincerity in her voice. Even if she didn't remember everything, parts of her heart still knew how to care. We sat there for a second in the comfortable stillness, and then Megan shifted, drawing her legs up a little closer.

"I was thinking about something."

"Yeah?"

She hesitated, like she wasn't sure if it was safe to ask. "How did you propose?"

I blinked. Of all the things she could've asked, I hadn't expected that, especially at this moment.

A slow smile pulled at my lips as I remembered.

"It was fall," I started, voice low and rough with memory. "Your favorite time of year. We went back to that sunflower field we used to sneak off to when we first started dating."

Her mouth tugged into a soft half-smile, like maybe the place sounded familiar.

"I had Jackson help me set it up earlier that day. We strung some lights through the trees around the edge of the field. You couldn't even see it from the road, just this little hidden world once you got close." I laughed under my breath, remembering how nervous I'd been. "I packed a picnic, your favorite drinks, those brownies you love that I always mess up somehow. I thought about hiding the ring in the brownies, but Jackson said you'd probably swallow it, and then we'd be spending the night at the ER."

She gave a soft little giggle at that, and it knocked the wind out of me. God, how I'd missed that sound. It was real, and that was most important.

"So . . . what did you do?" she asked, leaning in like she didn't want to miss a word.

"I waited until the sun started to set. You were walking ahead of me, picking flowers or something, and I called your name. When you turned around . . ." I smiled wider, feeling the emotion all over again. "I was already down on one knee. You cried. A lot. Pretty sure I barely got the words out."

"And I said yes?" she whispered, like she needed to hear it.

I nodded, reaching out instinctively to tuck a loose strand of hair behind her ear. She didn't pull away. "You said yes before I even finished asking. Practically tackled me into the dirt."

A soft laugh broke free between us, and something warm and aching moved through my chest. For a few seconds, it was just us. No amnesia. No fear. Just the lingering truth of who we were.

But then I saw it, the flicker of frustration behind her eyes, and I knew the moment was about to shift.

"I wish I could remember it," she murmured, her voice cracking at the edges. "It sounds like something I'd want to remember."

I exhaled slowly and rested my forehead against the edge of the bed. "I know. I wish you could too. But you will. And if not, we'll make new memories."

She bit her lip, struggling with something inside herself. "What if I'm not the same person you proposed to?"

I met her gaze. "Then I'll fall in love with you all over again."

Her eyes shone with unshed tears, but she blinked them away. We stayed like that for a while, just breathing each other in. Finally, she broke the silence.

"You should go sleep," she said. "You look dead on your feet."

I pushed my hair away from my face. "You kicking me out of your room, Mrs. Steele?"

A blush rose on her cheeks, and she ducked her head. "I'm just worried about you."

I pushed to my feet, stretching my back with a quiet groan. "Fair enough, but if you need anything, anything at all, you just yell, all right?"

She nodded, still watching me like she wasn't quite ready to let me go.

I hesitated at the door. "Megan?"

"Yeah?"

"I love you," I said, simple and sure.

Her fingers tightened in the blanket, and she offered a small, trembling smile.

"Thank you," she whispered.

It wasn't *I love you, too.* Not yet. And that was okay because that was something.

And for the moment, that was enough.

CHAPTER 20

*W*hen I finally woke up, the sun was high in the sky, pouring soft golden light through the bedroom window. I lay there, letting the warmth seep into my bones, trying to shake off the heavy exhaustion still clinging to me.

The house was quiet, but not in the lonely way it had been when I left for my shift. There was a hum to it now, the distant clink of dishes, a faint hint of music playing low from the kitchen.

She's here.

I smiled to myself, swung my legs over the side of the bed, and stretched until my shoulders popped. That day, I had decided, was going to be about her. About us. No pressure. No expectations. Just being together.

When I stepped into the hallway, the smell of coffee hit me first, rich and familiar. I found Megan standing at the counter, wearing one of those soft sweaters that always looked like they belonged on her. She'd pulled her hair into a ponytail.

She turned when she heard me, offering a shy, sleepy sort of smile. "Morning."

"Morning," I echoed, voice still rough from sleep. "You made coffee?"

She nodded and handed a mug to me. Our fingers brushed, the sensation light, fleeting, but it was enough to send a jolt of awareness through me. I caught the faintest pink rising to her cheeks.

"I figured you'd need it. Doing things like this with one arm isn't easy, but I managed."

"I'm sure it isn't. You did great, though." I took a grateful sip. "Thanks, baby."

She flinched, almost imperceptibly, at the endearment. The reaction twisted something sharp in my chest. It used to be second nature, the little names. Now every word felt like walking a tightrope, balancing between what we had and what we were trying to rebuild. I leaned back against the counter and studied her over the rim of my mug.

"You busy today?" I asked.

She shook her head. "No. Just wandering around the house, I guess."

I set the mug down with a decisive thud. "Then let's get out of here."

Her eyes widened slightly. "Where?"

"Anywhere you want. It's a beautiful day. Feels like a crime to waste it."

She hesitated, worrying her bottom lip between her teeth. "I don't know if—"

"No pressure," I said, holding up my hands. "Just . . . a drive. Some sunshine. Maybe lunch if you're up for it."

A slow smile tugged at her mouth, uncertain but real. "Okay, I'd like that."

THE OLD TRUCK rumbled down the back roads. A cool breeze filtered through the cracked windows as we passed patches of trees already flaming with hints of orange and red. The fields had turned gold.

Megan sat beside me, her hair dancing around her face with the wind. Every now and then, I caught her watching the scenery, a small, thoughtful smile playing on her lips.

It felt good. Easy, almost, even with the undercurrent of everything we weren't saying.

I stole a glance at her, my chest tightening. "Anything look familiar?"

She was quiet for a moment, then pointed out the window. "That old red barn . . . I think we drove past it before. On the way to that festival?"

I grinned, heart flipping a little. "Yeah. The Fall Harvest Festival out by Miller's Creek. You wore those boots you loved. The ones you refused to throw out, even after they got wrecked in the rain."

She laughed, really laughed, and the sound filled the cab like sunshine.

"I remember them!" she said brightly. "Brown leather. Scuffed to hell."

"You said they had character," I teased. "Wouldn't let me buy you new ones."

She beamed, and I drank in the sight of her.

A piece of her. Coming back to me.

We drove a bit further and ended up at a little diner just outside town, the kind with checkered floors and chipped mugs and a jukebox in the corner that hadn't worked right since I was a kid. Afternoon light spilled across the table as we slid into a booth by the window.

Megan studied the menu like it was a puzzle, then looked up at me with a mischievous glint in her eye. "Did I always get the same thing?"

I laughed. "Yeah. Grilled cheese and tomato soup. Every time."

"Predictable?"

"Consistent," I corrected, flashing her a wink.

She rolled her eyes but smiled, and damn if it didn't feel like the easiest thing in the world to fall for her all over again.

When the waitress took our order and left, Megan propped her chin on her hand, studying me across the table. "Tell me more."

"More?"

"About us," she clarified. "Before."

I leaned back, folding my arms loosely. "You want the highlight reel or the embarrassing moments?"

"Both," she said, grinning.

I chuckled and scratched the back of my neck as I thought. "All right. Let's see. First date: total disaster. I was so nervous, I spilled soda all over you at the movies."

She gasped, laughing. "No!"

"Yep. Thought for sure you'd never talk to me again. But you just laughed and made some joke about me 'breaking the ice.'"

She shook her head, amused. "Sounds like something I'd say."

"You kissed me first."

Her eyebrows shot up. "I did?"

"Bold move. Totally threw me off my game."

She looked both pleased and a little embarrassed by that. "What else?" she asked.

I glanced out the window as memories crowded in. "You loved stargazing. We used to drive out to the ridge behind the ranch, lie on the hood of the truck, and just . . . watch. You knew all the constellations by heart."

A flicker of something crossed her face. Longing, maybe. Or sadness.

"I wish I remembered that," she murmured.

"You will," I said, willing it to be true. "Or we'll do it again. Start new."

She smiled at that and reached across the table.

For a breathless second, I thought she was going to take my hand. But she just brushed her fingers lightly against the saltshaker instead, pulling back like she wasn't sure she was allowed that closeness yet. It almost broke me. But I smiled anyway, because she was trying. And so was I.

After we finished our meal, we spent the rest of the afternoon wandering. We went past the old library and the park where we'd spent lazy Sunday afternoons, then through the little antique shop she used to drag me into even though I had no clue what half the stuff was.

Everywhere we went, Megan asked questions. Every answer felt like weaving another thread between us. And even though there were moments when the shadows crept back in, when she'd look lost or uncertain, she never pulled away completely.

She was letting me in.

Piece by piece.

By the time we made it home, the sun was low on the horizon, bathing everything in gold. I parked the truck and cut the engine, but neither of us moved to get out right away.

Megan turned toward me, her face serious in the fading light. "Thank you."

"For what?"

"For today. For being patient with me."

I reached out, brushing my knuckles gently across her cheek. She leaned into the touch, so subtle it might've been imagined, but I felt it, all the same.

"I'm not going anywhere, Meg."

She closed her eyes for a second, like she was trying to hold on to the moment. When she opened them again, something had shifted—a softness, a quiet kind of hope.

"Maybe we could . . . go stargazing again soon," she said.

My heart almost burst.

"Yeah," I said, voice thick with emotion. "I'd like that."

And for the first time in what felt like forever, I knew we were finding our way back.

One small, steady step at a time.

CHAPTER 21

Megan

*T*he days and weeks blurred together after that night. Not in a bad way, but in the way life seems to have when you're waiting on a memory. Cade's shifts got longer. Between the fire station and the ranch, he was running himself ragged. I tried not to complain. He was doing all he could; he was who he was.

On that particular morning—one that was a bit less blurry than the others—I sat at the kitchen table and flipped through the daily newspaper. Reading the newspaper didn't seem like something I would normally do. Absentminded flipping felt more natural, so I assumed Cade was the one who wanted the daily paper. Maybe there was something specific he looked for. A certain section that piqued his interest.

My cell phone rang, vibrating against the wooden table and yanking me from my thoughts. I glanced at the screen.

Dr. Bellamy.

I smiled a little as I answered. "Hello?"

"Megan? Hi, it's Dr. Bellamy. Just checking in to see how you're doing. And how's your wrist?"

I flexed my left hand instinctively, wincing at the stiffness, but I felt no pain. The cast still covered most of my forearm, but I could already feel the difference compared to the first days after the accident.

"I think I'm doing okay. It's much better."

"Good. Based on your last X-ray, it looks like we're on track. If everything continues healing properly, we should be able to remove the cast in another week or two."

Relief flooded through me, fast and unexpected. "Really?"

"Really," he said warmly. "We'll set up a final check, but I'm confident."

We hung up after a few more instructions, but the second I set my phone down, my mind started racing. Getting the cast off didn't just mean freedom from the clunky, itchy thing that made showers a nightmare and folding laundry a two-hour project. It meant independence. Freedom in a bigger way.

A knot twisted low in my gut.

Cade had been great, and I assumed that was how he'd been the whole time I'd known him. For some reason unbeknownst to me, I could feel it. My heart insisted this was a fact, even when my mind faltered.

But being stuck at home while he was gone for 24-hour shifts? Dependent on rides from his mom or my family for every appointment or errand? It gnawed at me.

I wasn't broken, and I didn't want to be treated like I was. I bit my lip and stared at my phone's dark screen. Was it crazy? Was it selfish? Maybe, but I had to ask. I opened my messages and started typing before I could talk myself out of it.

> Hey. Dr. Bellamy called. I might get my cast off soon. I was thinking... I want to start looking for a car. I don't want to be stuck here when you're gone. I need to be able to do things on my own.

I stared at the words, my heart hammering.

Then I hit send.

The three dots appeared almost immediately. Cade was still on shift, but he must have had a minute to check his phone. His reply was slower than usual, though.

> CADE
>
> That's great news about your wrist.

> CADE
>
> We can talk about the car thing when I get home.

Short. Tight.

Not angry . . . but not exactly thrilled, either.

I leaned back in my chair, chewing the inside of my cheek. I could already feel the tension creeping in around the edges.

I knew Cade would worry. I knew he'd want to protect me, to keep me close until I was one hundred percent. But part of me, the part waking up again after returning home from the hospital, didn't want to be protected anymore.

I was told I could've died, but I fought for life. I wanted to live.

I wandered into the living room, running my fingers over the worn spine of a photo album I found on the bottom shelf. When I opened it, there we were, a younger Megan and Cade smiling in dozens of pictures. Camping trips. Fishing at a lake. Riding in the bed of an old pickup with the stars above us.

A girl who laughed easily, who didn't second-guess herself, who trusted the world a little more. I didn't know if I could be her again, but maybe I could start trying. And it started with regaining my independence.

I WAS STILL SITTING on the edge of the sofa, the photo album open in my lap, when I heard the rattle of keys in the front door. The familiar sound of Cade's boots stepping into the foyer stirred something in my chest—relief and nerves tangled up in a tight knot.

"Hey," he called out, voice low and tired but still warm.

"In here," I answered.

He came into view a second later, brushing dust from his jeans and yawning into his sleeve. His flannel was half untucked, the sleeves rolled just past his elbows, revealing strong, sun-bronzed forearms dusted with a bit of dirt. As he walked further into the room, he absently began unfastening the top few buttons of his shirt, probably out of habit. With each unfastened button, he revealed a glimpse of his tanned, broad chest, sculpted from years of honest, physical work. The edge of a scar traced one side of his ribcage, and I wondered what story that mark carried.

Something fluttered low in my stomach. I didn't remember everything about our life together, but in that moment, watching him move across the room with a smooth and slow stride, I could recognize that I'd once made a very, very good choice in my choosing him.

He paused when he saw me with the album, his eyes falling on the pages like they were ghosts.

"You found the old one." He stepped closer.

"Yeah," I murmured. "I didn't mean to go looking. I just . . . wanted to feel something familiar."

He nodded slowly, then walked around the coffee table and crouched beside me. "And did you?"

I looked down at the photo of us laughing in a canoe, water glistening around us. "A little. Just pieces."

Cade didn't say anything at first. He just studied my face like he was trying to read between the lines of what I wasn't saying. "So, you wanted to talk?"

"Well . . ." I shifted in my seat. "First, I probably shouldn't have started this by text; that wasn't right."

"It's fine. I would've given more of a response, but I wasn't sure what to say. I need more context. Why do you feel like you need a car?"

"Didn't I have one before?" That came out a little snippier than I meant, so I tried again. "I might not remember what my life was before the accident, but I've learned a lot. I had a car, which means I was an independent person who didn't wait for people to drive me around all the time."

"But—"

I held up my finger. "I also remember you telling me that I was starting to consider taking classes. You'll do what you can, Cade, but you won't be able to take me every time. It's not fair. To either of us."

"But this isn't a permanent situation. At some point, you'll—"

I closed the album and exhaled. "I'll get my memory back? I would love that, but we don't know that. I'm doing all I can, but it's like waiting for a light to magically turn on, and I can't make it work like that."

"I'm trying to stay as positive as I can." He moved to sit beside me, his weight dipping the sofa cushion. "Megan, you're doing incredible. Seriously. I don't say it enough. But this, driving alone, getting out there . . . it's not nothing. It's huge. And I get why you want to do it."

"But?"

"But it scares me too. Because it's not just about the car or getting lost. It's about something happening and you not knowing how to reach out. Or you being too proud to ask."

I swallowed hard. He wasn't wrong.

"I'm not trying to prove anything to you," I whispered. "I'm trying to prove it to myself."

His eyes softened. "I know. And that's what makes this so hard."

"Cade, I don't want to feel like I'm just sitting in the house, waiting for the next memory to show up. I need something that's mine. Even if it's just buying milk or walking around a park. And I understand that I don't have my memories of a year ago or five years ago, but I remember yesterday. I remember the day before. I remember every day since I woke up from the accident, and to me, that's something."

He was quiet for a long time, rubbing his hand along his jaw like he always did when he was thinking. That was one of the quirks I'd noticed about him. I found myself studying his mannerisms, intrigued by them, by him.

Finally, he said, "You're right to want to have your own life. I get that. I do." He looked down at his fingers for a moment, his strong hands that seemed so warm and comforting. "You really want to buy a car?"

"I do." I nodded. "Not to go joyriding. Just something small. Practical. Cheap, even. So I can start making decisions for myself again."

Cade leaned back, head resting against the cushion as he let out a long breath. "You'd promise to be careful?"

"I would."

"No long trips?"

"No long trips."

"Only short errands until the cast is off and . . . until more of your memory returns?"

"Yes. I swear."

He turned to look at me, that same cautious smile playing at the corner of his mouth. "You'd let me install one of those GPS apps so I can see where the car is if you ever get turned around?"

I laughed softly, feeling the tension ease in my chest. "Yes, if it'll give you peace of mind."

"It will," he said. "I won't pretend this is easy. I want to hold on tight because I'm scared of losing you again. But I also don't want to be the one holding you back."

"Then let's figure this out together."

He reached over, touched my hand, and before I could react, he laced his fingers with mine. "We'll go look at cars tomorrow." Then he brought my hand to his lips and kissed it gently.

A grin broke across my face. I was happy about the car, but something about that gentle kiss caused me to smile, too. I didn't remember falling in love with him, but I could see why I had. "Really?"

"Really," he said. "You've earned it. And maybe this is a step toward everything coming back."

I leaned into him, resting my head on his shoulder, and for the first time in a long time, I felt like I wasn't just floating through someone else's life. I was beginning to rebuild my own. Bit by bit.

And I had Cade right beside me.

CHAPTER 22

Megan

*T*he dealership was bigger than I expected. Row after row of shiny vehicles lined the lot like soldiers at attention, each one silently promising adventure, freedom, or just a reliable way to get to physical therapy without needing someone else to take me.

I wasn't sure which promise I needed more.

Cade parked the truck and cut the engine before turning to me. "You okay?"

I nodded, eyes still scanning the lot. "Yeah. Just . . . feels weird to be shopping for a car when I don't even remember what kind I used to like."

He smiled, his hand brushing mine for a second before pulling away. "You liked cars that had good gas mileage, weren't flashy, and had heated seats. You always said your butt deserved luxury."

I let out a small laugh with him. "That sounds like something I might say."

The truth was, I didn't know if it did. But it felt good to laugh with him, to see that familiar twinkle in his eyes, even if my brain hadn't fully caught up with my heart.

We walked through the rows together. Cade kept his hands in his pockets most of the time, giving me space to browse, to explore. I appreciated that more than I could say.

A blue SUV caught my eye. Not too big, not too small. I reached for the handle, hesitated, then glanced back at him. "Is it weird I'm nervous about test driving?"

Cade shook his head. "Not at all. But I'll be right there. We'll go slow." He walked around the car. "It's funny you're drawn to this one, though."

"Why?"

"It looks very similar to the car you had before. It's a different make, but the color and size are similar. Great minds think alike?" He flashed a smile.

"I think that works more if it's different people, but it is interesting. I think even more so now, I need to at least test drive this one."

The salesperson appeared then, smiling, polite, a little too peppy, but I appreciated the way Cade kept the conversation directed back to me. He didn't take over. He didn't treat me like I was fragile. He let me try.

The test drive wasn't perfect. My wrist ached a little on the turns, and there was a moment at a four-way stop where I panicked and forgot who had the right-of-way. But Cade's voice was calm beside me, grounding. "You're doing fine," he said. "Breathe, Meg. You've got this."

By the time we pulled back into the lot, my palms were sweating, and I wasn't sure whether I wanted to cry from pride or scream from nerves. Maybe both.

"I think I like it," I admitted as we stepped out of the car.

He nodded, shielding his eyes from the sun. "Then let's talk numbers."

While Cade worked with the salesperson, I sat on a bench by the showroom window, watching a dad lift his daughter into the back of a minivan. I wondered what it would feel like to do that with our baby. I wondered what kind of mom I would be. I rested my hand on my stomach and imagined how it would feel to carry the baby as he or she grew inside of me, and what it would feel like to hold a person who's never seen me as different to them.

Cade returned a few minutes later, with two water bottles and a hopeful smile. "They're running numbers. Want to come look at the financing stuff?"

I rose to my feet, nodding, but as I followed him into the office, that strange feeling twisted in my chest again.

The deal took longer than expected. Paperwork, signatures, small talk with the manager. By the time we finally walked out with the keys in hand, I was exhausted but oddly exhilarated.

"Want to drive it home?" Cade asked, holding out the keys. We had taken a rideshare to the dealership so we could ride back together.

My first instinct was to shake my head. But then I reached for the keys. "Yeah," I said. "Yeah, I do."

The drive was quiet but not uncomfortable. I cracked the windows slightly and enjoyed the cool air against my face. Cade adjusted the radio but kept the volume low. Every so often, he glanced over at me, and I could feel the unspoken pride in his expression.

"I know this doesn't change everything," I said after a long stretch of silence, "but it feels like something. A step."

"It is something," he agreed. "It's a big something."

We were only a few blocks from home when the car jolted with a sharp *thump-thump-thump*. My stomach dropped as I eased us onto the shoulder.

"Flat," Cade said while unbuckling his seatbelt.

We both climbed out, and sure enough, the back tire sagged low. Cade moved toward the trunk, but I touched his arm. "Wait —let me try."

He gave me a skeptical look. "You want me to walk you through it?"

"Yes," I said, squaring my shoulders. "Just . . . tell me the first step."

Cade pulled out the jack and spare, then set them down. "Okay. First thing, loosen the lug nuts before you lift it. Otherwise, the tire spins."

I nodded, crouched, and put the wrench to the first bolt. Something clicked inside me. My hands knew the rhythm, the order, the little details that shouldn't have been familiar but somehow were. I loosened one, then the next, moving with a strange, sure confidence.

"All right, Megan, slow down—" Cade started, but I was already positioning the jack, sliding it into place without asking.

When I glanced up, he wasn't frowning or teasing. He was watching me like he'd just witnessed a miracle.

I set the last nut in the hubcap and leaned back, breathless. "I did it."

"You did." He nodded as he spoke.

"But . . . how did I know how to do that?"

His eyes softened, the corners crinkling with quiet pride. He crouched next to me, brushing his fingers lightly across mine. "Because I taught you. See? You've still got us in you."

Something warm spread through me, sweeter than the relief of a fixed tire. It was a piece of us slipping into place.

By the time the spare was tightened and the tools put away, I slid back behind the wheel, hands trembling just a little. I pulled into the driveway with a small sigh of relief and parked. I didn't even care if it was crooked. I'd done it.

CHAPTER 23

The morning breeze pushed through the open kitchen window, giving me the slight cooldown I needed. Megan sat across from me, her hair still damp from the shower, her hands wrapped around a steaming mug of coffee. She looked more rested than she had in days, and something in me eased at the sight of it.

"I should get going. Jackson will be ready to disown me if I'm late," I joked.

Megan laughed a little. She had a good relationship with Jackson and my brothers. She just didn't remember it. We'd been so busy getting her familiar with her family, we hadn't had time to get to mine yet, but we would.

"I think I might go out for a little drive later."

"Is there something you need? I could stop on the way home."

She shrugged. "Nothing in particular. I just wanted to pick up a few things."

"Okay. Well, you be careful out there."

"I will. I won't go far."

I'd hesitated, but this was the whole reason we'd gotten a car for her. Even with her agreement to stay close to home, the thought of her driving on her own still worried me.

I stood and carried my empty plate to the sink, where I rinsed it off. The familiar clatter of dishes was a small comfort, but the weight of the coming day pressed at the edges of my mind. Work at the ranch wouldn't slow down just because my heart was sitting here at this table, sipping coffee across from me.

I glanced over my shoulder at her. I couldn't help it. She took a few sips of her coffee and stole casual glances around the room. Every so often, she tousled her hair with her fingers, looking more beautiful than any memory I could ever try to hang on to.

On impulse, I dried my hands and turned to lean against the counter. "Hey." I caught her eye. "What would you say to me taking you out Friday night?"

Her spoon clinked softly against her mug as she paused. A flicker of surprise crossed her face, then a slow, shy smile bloomed. "You're asking me on a date?" she teased, laughter hiding something softer beneath it.

I smiled too, feeling the ease between us settle like a second skin. "Yeah, I want to take you somewhere nice. Just you and me."

For a second, she just looked at me, like she wasn't sure if I was serious. Then her head tilted a little, and her voice came, quiet and curious. "Do we still . . . date?"

With my hand still holding the dish towel, I froze as my heart caught somewhere in my chest. The way she said it, half shy, half unsure, made something ache deep inside me. I turned around and crossed the kitchen until I was leaning against the counter just a few feet from her. Close enough to see the small flicker of vulnerability in her eyes. Close enough to feel it settle between us like a living thing.

I could have said something simple. I could have laughed it

off. But this—*we*—would never be something simple. I dropped my gaze for a second, gathering myself, then looked back at her.

"Yeah, baby," I said, my voice rougher than I meant it to be. I stepped closer, closing the last of the space between us. "We date. We dream. We keep building us, no matter what. Losing a few memories doesn't change the way I love you. If I have to, I'll spend forever reminding you that you're my home."

Her eyes widened, shining with something soft and glassy. She dropped her gaze to her coffee cup, a faint flush blooming high on her cheeks. She traced the rim of the mug with her thumb and remained silent for a long heartbeat.

When she finally looked up at me, her smile was small but real—a delicate thing that had survived a storm.

"I'd like that," she whispered.

God, I *wanted* to kiss her. I wanted to take her face in my hands and tell her every piece of our story until she didn't have a single doubt left.

But this, this slow rebuilding, it mattered. It had to be on her terms. At her pace.

So instead, I just smiled, reached out, and brushed a loose strand of hair behind her ear. The brief touch was enough to leave my hand aching for more.

I cleared my throat and stepped back, knowing if I didn't then, I wouldn't. "You free Friday night?"

Megan gave a soft laugh, still playing with her coffee mug. "I think I can pencil you in."

"Good." I flashed her a grin. "Because I've got plans to remind you just how much fun you used to have with me."

"Used to?" she teased, arching a brow.

I chuckled and headed to the coat rack by the door. "Still do. Always will."

As I shrugged on my jacket, I caught her watching me, and it sent a bolt of something warm straight through my chest.

She walked me to the door, bare feet padding softly across

the hardwood. When I turned to say goodbye, she stood on tiptoe and pressed a quick kiss to my cheek, surprising us both.

"Be safe," she said, her voice barely above a whisper.

"Always. Enjoy your day, Meg."

I lingered there for a second longer than I should have, memorizing the way she looked in the morning light, bright-eyed, beautiful, and mine. I didn't need her to remember every chapter we'd written. I just needed her to trust that our story was still worth writing, one *new* memory at a time.

As I stepped outside, the door clicked shut behind me. I tucked my hands into my jacket pockets and smiled to myself.

Friday couldn't come soon enough.

CHAPTER 24

Megan

The house felt a little too quiet after Cade left for work.

I stood by the door for a long moment after it shut, one hand resting on the worn wooden frame. I could still smell the faint scent of his cologne in the air. Clean and woodsy, like fresh pine and something unmistakably him. It lingered in the empty spaces he left behind, stirring something restless inside me.

I padded back into the kitchen. The floorboards creaked gently under my bare feet. My half-empty coffee cup sat on the table, cooling fast, but I wasn't in any rush to sit down again. Not after the way Cade had looked at me that morning, like he was already counting the hours until Friday night.

The thought made my chest warm in a way I couldn't explain. We were going on a date. A real one. As if we could pick up all the broken, scattered pieces and start stitching something new from them. I ran a hand through my hair and wandered aimlessly through the living room, my fingers brushing the edge of the sofa, the shelves lined with little bits of our life. Photographs. Books. The blanket that smelled like him.

Pieces of my life, tiny flashes, tugged at the edges of my memory like soft whispers.

I found myself at the coffee table again, drawn to the same photo album I'd kept flipping through those previous few weeks. The one filled with our smiles, frozen in moments I couldn't place but desperately wanted to remember. Camping trips. Nights under the stars. Dancing barefoot somewhere that looked like heaven.

There, in those pictures, I caught glimpses of the girl I had been. The girl who had once known without a doubt that Cade Steele was her whole world.

I didn't know if I could ever get back to her. But maybe it was about becoming someone new, someone who could still choose him, every day, even if the past was blurry.

The thought left a hollow kind of ache in my chest, sweet and a little frightening.

I closed the album and straightened, glancing at the clock on the wall. It was late morning already, and I needed a breath of fresh air.

Without giving myself time to second-guess it, I grabbed my purse and the keys off the hook by the door. The car Cade and I had picked out was sitting in the driveway. The shine from the paint gleamed and made me happy. It was as if I was gaining my life back. However, I wasn't sure I deserved that yet.

I could do something simple. Go to the store. Pick up a few groceries. Nothing crazy, and I'll be helping out around here instead of relying solely on Cade.

Just a small step. A small win.

My heart thudded hard in my chest as I stepped outside. Crisp air brushed against my cheeks. I made my way to the car and slid behind the wheel, then adjusted the seat and mirrors the way Cade had reminded me.

For a second, my hands froze on the steering wheel. Fear

whispered doubts in the back of my mind. What if I got lost? What if I forgot where I was going?

But then I remembered the way Cade had looked at me—proud, hopeful, trusting—and I swallowed the fear. I could do this. I had to believe I could.

I turned the ignition, and the soft rumble of the engine grounded me. With a deep breath, I eased out of the driveway and pointed the car toward the long shadows over the road ahead.

I kept my hands steady on the wheel, focusing on each turn, each landmark Cade had pointed out on our drives together. There was the faded barn with the peeling white paint, the stretch of open fields where cows dotted the hills like black-and-white stones. I even passed the little gas station with the crooked sign, the one Cade joked looked like it would fall over if you sneezed too hard near it.

For a while, everything was okay. I could breathe. I could even hum a little to the radio when a familiar country song floated through the speakers.

But then, somewhere between trying to find the small grocery store Cade mentioned and convincing myself I remembered the way, I realized with a sick sort of certainty that I had no idea where I was.

The road ahead didn't look familiar anymore. Neither did the rows of shops blurring past my window. Panic tightened its grip around my chest, sharp and quick, but I forced myself to slow the car, pulling into the first place that looked safe.

A diner. The neon "open" sign flickered weakly in the window, and a handful of trucks were scattered across the cracked parking lot.

I killed the engine and sat there for a long moment with my hands clenched in my lap.

You're okay. You're okay. Just breathe.

I didn't want to call Cade. Not for that. Not when he was

trying so hard to believe I could handle things on my own. Squaring my shoulders, I got out of the car and pushed through the diner door, the bell above it chiming softly.

Inside, the warm air smelled like bacon and fresh biscuits. A few people sat in booths and at the counter—old men reading newspapers, a waitress refilling cups between multiple tables without being asked. I hovered awkwardly near the entrance, unsure of what to do. Maybe I could just sit for a minute. Clear my head. Figure out how to get home without looking completely helpless.

I was debating sliding into a corner booth when a voice caught my attention.

"Well, if this isn't a small world."

The voice was deep, teasing, and oddly friendly. I didn't know anyone there, but I turned sharply, just to see who he was talking to.

Two guys leaned against the counter, both wearing jeans and worn baseball caps, casual and easy, like they belonged there. The taller one flashed a wide grin and stepped closer, his hands lifted in mock surprise. Short, dark hair poked from beneath his hat.

"Megan?"

I stiffened instinctively. How did he know my name?

The other one looked slightly younger, with longer hair, sharper features, and a dimple in his cheek. He elbowed the first and whispered something I couldn't catch.

My eyes bounced back and forth between the two men, and I scrambled through my mind, searching for any anchor. Then it clicked. The wedding photo. The picture I stared at nearly every day. They were two of Cade's brothers. The family resemblance was clear and strong, but for the life of me, I couldn't remember their names. I hadn't asked Cade, though I knew I should have.

I must have looked panicked, because the taller one softened and held out a hand like I was a wild animal he didn't want to spook.

"Hey, it's okay," he said gently. "It's Spencer. And that's Alden." He patted his brother's back. "We're Cade's brothers."

Spencer. Alden.

I tried to fit the names to the faces, to the memories that refused to come cleanly.

"I . . ." My voice cracked a little, and I cleared my throat. "Sorry. I . . . recognized you from the pictures. I just . . . I got a little turned around."

Alden flashed a grin that was pure Steele charm. "You're not the first. This town's a maze if you don't know it. Or if . . ."

I assumed he meant if someone were in a situation like mine. The other version of myself knew this town very well.

Spencer nodded and pulled out his phone like he was already formulating a rescue plan. "You want me to call Cade? Or you wanna just sit for a minute and catch your breath?"

Pride prickled uncomfortably in my chest. I didn't want to be the reason Cade worried. Not again. "I'm okay," I said quickly, though my voice wobbled. "Really. I just . . . need a minute."

Spencer exchanged a glance with Alden. They held a silent conversation in a language brothers seemed to be fluent in before he motioned toward a booth by the window.

"Come on," he said. "Sit. You're family. You don't have to handle everything alone."

Family.

The word felt fragile and too big for me all at once. But some part of me, the part that remembered laughter and bonfires and warm, safe arms, ached toward it.

So, I nodded and let them guide me to the booth, letting myself sit down in the small, sun-dappled corner of the world that still felt a little like home.

Spencer slid into the booth seat across from me with an easy grin. Alden grabbed a few menus from the counter and plopped down beside him. The vinyl seats let out a soft squeak under our weight. For a moment, the normalcy of it all, the clink of coffee cups, the low murmur of conversation, the faint smell of frying bacon, almost tricked me into thinking this was any other Saturday morning.

But it wasn't. Not for me. I sat stiffly, unsure of where to put my hands, my mind racing, even as my body stayed frozen.

Spencer leaned back against the booth and flipped open a menu, scanning it like he had it memorized. "First time at Fran's?" he asked casually, trying to make conversation.

I nodded. "I think so." Then I caught myself. "At least . . . it's the first time that I remember."

Alden's smile dimmed a little, but he recovered quickly. "Best pancakes in town. Terrible coffee, though. Tastes like someone boiled shoe leather."

That earned a small, reluctant laugh from me, and Spencer's eyes softened like he was cataloguing every little victory.

The waitress came by with a pot of coffee balanced on one hip. Without asking, she poured three steaming cups.

"Cups of coffee on the house for you three."

I shook my head. "No, no, that's not necessary. I can pay. We were just talking through the menu."

"You're with the Steele boys, honey," she said kindly, patting my shoulder. "That makes you family around here. All the help Mr. and Mrs. Steele have given me over the years? Free cups of coffee aren't payment enough."

I nodded. *Family.* There was that word again, and it sat heavy and hopeful in my chest.

"Thanks," I murmured, wrapping my hands around the mug for warmth, even though I didn't plan to drink it.

As the three of us sat there quietly, I stole glances at them over the rim of my cup. Spencer looked so much like Cade. He wasn't as muscular, but he had the same broad shoulders and sharp jawline. There was a boyish mischief in his eyes that softened the resemblance.

Alden's face was more angular, but when he smiled, it held the same easy charm Cade had, the kind that could probably talk you into or out of just about anything. I hated how much I wanted to ask them everything to fill in all the aching gaps.

Finally, I cleared my throat. "So . . . um, how long have you guys lived around here?"

Spencer chuckled and folded his arms behind his head. "Born and raised."

"Yeah, and in the same house our whole lives. The Striking Steele Ranch," Alden added. "Though it wasn't much when Momma and Pop first moved there. I'm sure you've heard about all of that."

"No, I actually haven't." I shook my head. "I've been trying to fill in the gaps, and Cade's been doing his best to answer all my questions. We've started with details about me, then my family, but we haven't gotten all the way to his yet. Honestly, we haven't even finished mine."

"It's okay." Alden waved me off. "You can't expect to cram over twenty years' worth of memories into a few weeks."

"Talk about information overload," Spencer added with a grin. "If there's anything you want to know about the Steele family, just ask. I'd say we know a little something about them."

Before I could respond, the waitress returned to take our orders. The boys rattled theirs off quickly like regulars, but I'd been too wrapped up in conversation and hadn't looked at the menu yet, so I ordered a grilled chicken BLT and fries. I figured I couldn't go wrong with that.

I leaned forward, heart hammering a little with nerves once the waitress walked away. "I would love to know more."

"Ask anything you want," Spencer encouraged, nudging his coffee aside to make room for the glass of sweet tea he'd ordered.

"In our wedding photo, I noticed Cade and I had a pretty big wedding party. Was that because we couldn't decide who to ask?"

Alden laughed. "There was probably a little of that. But Cade said it would've been hard to get married without having all of us stand by his side."

Spencer nodded in agreement. "With your three siblings and his six brothers, it gave you a big group without even trying."

I blinked. "Wait, six brothers? I kept hearing about 'the brothers' and assumed there were just a few, but six?"

"Yup," Spencer said, amused. "There's Jackson—he's the oldest—then Cade. I'm next, then Alden here. After us, there's Graham, Braxton, and Dallas."

"Momma and Pop always wanted a big family," Alden added, "and they sure got it."

"Wow," I breathed, trying to picture it. A house full of seven boys, the noise, the chaos, the laughter. It was overwhelming . . . and kind of wonderful.

"And the ranch where Cade works sometimes . . . that's your family's home?"

They nodded.

"Has he always wanted to be a firefighter? And stay in Remington? I'm guessing having such a big family might have had something to do with that?"

"Yeah, Cade's always loved the ranch," Spencer said. "It's in his blood, just like helping people is. That's where the firefighting started. You should definitely ask him about that; it's a good story. He tells it better than any of us could."

He and Alden shared a quick, knowing look, one of those wordless conversations only brothers seemed able to have. I caught it but didn't press. It made me wonder what I *wasn't* asking.

"Thanks," I said. "I look forward to hearing it. We actually have a date planned." A warm flutter stirred in my stomach. "Maybe that'll be the perfect icebreaker."

Before long, our food arrived, and the conversation shifted to more casual topics, such as funny ranch stories and favorite hometown hangouts. I listened as much as I talked, soaking it up like rain after a drought. The boys were sweet. They made me feel like I belonged, even though there was a part of me that still wasn't sure if I did.

Eventually, I glanced at the clock on the wall and felt a jolt of panic at how much time had passed.

"I should probably get going," I said as I slid out of the booth and brushed crumbs from my jeans.

Spencer stood too, tossing a few bills onto the table for the coffee. "You want us to follow you? Make sure you get back okay?"

My pride prickled a little. I wanted to prove I could do it on my own, but I wasn't stupid, so I nodded. "Yeah. Thanks."

Alden shot me a wink. "Can't have Cade skinning us alive if we let his girl get lost again."

His girl.

The words echoed through me, warm and bittersweet, settling somewhere deep in my chest. I tucked that feeling close as we stepped out of the diner and onto the pavement.

The day hadn't gone the way I'd planned, but I was beginning to feel it was about more than getting lost. It was about finding my way back to the life I once loved.

I placed my hand on my stomach. Even if I didn't fully remember everything, the life inside of me was real. It was a physical representation of the relationship Cade and I had, and a representation of my wants and desires.

I just have to figure out what those are.

THE DRIVE back felt longer somehow. Maybe because every turn, every familiar road sign, carried just a sliver of doubt with it.

I tightened my hands on the steering wheel, heart beating faster with each decision I made. *You're doing fine,* I told myself. *You're learning.*

Spencer and Alden sat in the same truck, tailing me like loyal bodyguards. They did more than follow me home, however. They also escorted me to the grocery store to get the things I'd meant to get in the first place.

Alden rolled down his window and grinned as I pulled into the driveway. "See? Told ya you'd find your way."

I smiled back, grateful, but a gnawing unease threaded through my chest. If they hadn't been there, would I have made it back? I parked in front of the house and climbed out, watching as Spencer and Alden tipped their hats at me before pulling back down the long drive.

Just like that, I was alone again.

The house loomed, familiar and foreign. I hugged the grocery bag to my chest and went inside. The door creaked slightly as I shut it behind me, and I was unsure what to do next.

The logical thing would be to text Cade. Tell him I made it home. Tell him about running into Spencer and Alden. Tell him . . . I'd gotten lost. How close I'd come to panicking.

I slid my phone out of my pocket and stared at it.

His name was right there at the top of my messages, like it always was, or at least, recently.

My thumb hovered.

But what if he worries even more? What if he starts doubting that I can handle any of this?

The idea twisted painfully inside me. I wanted him to see the *good* parts. The strong parts. Not the girl who needed rescuing because she couldn't even make it to the grocery store and back without second-guessing herself.

I tossed the phone onto the sofa, frustration prickling the backs of my eyes.

I wouldn't bother him with it. *Not today.*

Instead, I unpacked the groceries and grounded myself in the simple rhythm of the actions, the crinkle of bags, the cool press of cans, the steady hum of the refrigerator. I told myself I wouldn't think about the fact that I'd nearly gotten lost in the middle of nowhere. About how the words *his girl* still echoed sweetly in my mind, even when the fear tried to drown them out.

I was going to be ready. For him. For our date. For whatever came next.

Even if part of me still felt completely, utterly off the map.

CHAPTER 25

I scrubbed my hands over my face as I sat on the porch Thursday night. I felt jittery, not necessarily because of nervousness, but because I wanted everything to be perfect.

The days leading up to Friday had crawled by slower than a cold molasses spill. I threw myself into work just to keep my mind on other things. No matter how sore my muscles got at work, no matter how dead on my feet I was when I finally stumbled into bed at night, one thought stayed sharp and alive in my chest: Friday. Her. Us.

I hadn't realized how much I missed this part—the planning, the nerves, the wanting. It felt like I was a teen again, trying to figure out how to impress the prettiest girl in the county, who somehow thought I hung the moon.

Only now, I wasn't starting from scratch. Now, I was fighting for something we already had, even if she didn't remember it all yet. This date was really important. It was a chance for us to be us and not two people existing in the same house who *used* to have something. We didn't used to have anything. We had everything, and I hadn't given up on that.

I didn't want her tired or overwhelmed. Didn't want to push too hard when she was still piecing herself back together. But she needed this just as much as I did. A night where it wasn't about her memory. Or the questions. Or the careful sidestepping around all the missing pieces. A night where it was just her and me. The way it was always meant to be.

I leaned back in the porch swing and stared up at the first stars winking into existence. My hands curled into fists at the thought of everything we had survived. Everything she was still surviving.

She had no idea how proud I was of her. How much she amazed me, every single day.

Something scuffled behind me, so I glanced over my shoulder. Megan stood just inside the doorway, arms folded across her chest. She wore an old sweatshirt that swallowed her small frame, and her hair was a little messy from her shower, falling in loose waves around her shoulders. She looked beautiful in a way that made my throat tighten.

"You okay?" she asked, stepping onto the porch.

"Yeah." I patted the swing. "Come sit?"

She padded over and sank down beside me, her bare leg brushing against my jeans and sending a jolt of heat through my already restless body.

I wrapped an arm around her shoulders, tugging her closer. She came willingly, resting her head against my chest, just like she had the other night.

"I'm excited for tomorrow," she said.

"Me too, Meg." More than she knew.

I let the silence settle between us, the kind of silence that didn't need filling. The cicadas sang somewhere out in the fields, the air thick with that end-of-summer sweetness.

I pressed a kiss into her hair and closed my eyes. *Tomorrow's the big night, and it can't come fast enough.*

"Cade?" Her voice broke the quiet between us, soft but carrying weight.

"Hmm?" I turned toward her.

"I have something to tell you. I'm not sure how you'll feel about it, but I hope you won't be upset."

"Upset?" My stomach tightened when she pulled back from my hold. I searched her face, trying to read the hesitation in her eyes. "You can tell me anything, but when you start with a warning like that, it doesn't make me think upset. It makes me think worried." I kept my voice even and waited for her to go on.

She drew in a breath. "The other day, while you were at work, I wanted to help out, so I told myself I'd go to the store. Everything went well . . ." Her voice trailed off, mouth parting like she couldn't quite make herself say the rest.

I gave her a small nod, urging her forward.

"It started out well," she corrected quietly.

My chest clenched. "Started? What happened?" I should've let her finish at her own pace, but my pulse was already ahead of me.

"I was happy that I noticed several of the places and things that you had pointed out to me when we were out together. It felt good to recognize things. But then, all of a sudden, nothing was familiar. It was like the world flipped. I didn't know where I was anymore, and it was . . . scary."

A spike of panic pushed through my ribs, but I tried to keep my tone steady. I slipped my arm around her shoulders again, pulling her closer. "I'm sure it was. Probably felt like trying something brand new. And in a way, it was. What happened after that?"

"I drove a little, hoping I'd find something I recognized, but my mind just blanked."

"Why didn't you call me?"

Her eyes widened. "I didn't want to bother you. You were at

work, Cade. You shouldn't have to look after me like I'm a child. That's not your responsibility."

I shook my head hard. "How many ways do I have to show you? You *are* my responsibility. You're my wife. I vowed to love and care for you. That means all of this, Megan. Every bit of it."

She let out a long breath and shook her head, but she didn't answer. The quiet was worse than if she'd yelled at me.

"Look, I didn't mean to come down on you," I said. "I just—"

"I know," she cut in. "I didn't mean to worry you. That's why I didn't want to tell you. But keeping it back felt wrong, like a secret I shouldn't keep."

"No. We don't keep things like that from each other." Regret stirred low in my gut. Was it a mistake to let her drive so soon? But I kept that thought buried. It wouldn't help now. "So, what happened? Did you ask for help?"

"Not really," she admitted. "I thought about it, but then I saw a neon *open* sign at Fran's Diner. I figured I could stop, ask directions, or just sit for a while to regroup. So I did."

Megan looked down at her fingers, tapping them together slightly. I watched her fidget and wondered what she thought through all of this.

"I'm glad you didn't stay out on the road," I said. "Going inside someplace is much safer."

Megan nodded, her fingers twisting in her lap before she finally looked at me. "It almost seemed meant to be that I ended up at Fran's."

My brows knit. "Meant to be?"

A small smile tugged at her mouth before she spoke. "Because when I walked in, Spencer and Alden noticed me. They approached me and started talking to me. I just felt safer with them. We had lunch together, and afterward, they helped me finish the shopping and even followed me home to make sure I got back okay."

I dragged a hand over my jaw, torn between relief and the

echo of panic still in my chest. Of course my brothers had stepped in. Of course they'd looked out for her. But damn, the thought of her lost, scared, driving around by herself before that —it knotted my gut tight.

She must've read it in my face, because her smile softened into something more cautious. "I wasn't alone, Cade. And I wasn't unsafe. It actually helped to talk with them in that diner. It reminded me that Remington isn't a foreign place. It's ours; it's mine."

I wanted to argue, to say she *was* unsafe. I wanted to insist she never try something like that without me again. But I bit back the words. Her eyes held a glimmer I hadn't seen in a while, a flicker of pride, of ownership in her own progress. I couldn't snuff that out, not when she needed it.

Instead, I took her hand, brushing my thumb across her knuckles. "I'm glad they were there. And I'm glad you told me."

She nodded, swallowing hard, as if my acceptance mattered more than she wanted to admit. Still, the worry clawed at me. The image of her behind the wheel, streets turning strange, and fear creeping in was enough to make me question whether I could trust her to try again. And maybe she knew it, because her voice came quieter, steadier, as if she were answering my thoughts.

"I'll get better at this, Cade. I know I will. I don't want to scare you, and I don't want to scare myself either. But I need you to believe I can do it . . . because I believe I can."

I let out a long breath and squeezed her hand. She was stubborn, brave in ways she didn't even realize, and God help me, I wanted to believe it too.

Her chin lifted, determination sparking in her eyes, fragile but fierce. "Next time, I won't get lost. I'll figure it out. I won't let this beat me."

CHAPTER 26

I slipped out the back door like a teenager breaking curfew, the screen door clicking shut behind me as I cut across the yard. The sun was just starting to dip low, casting long golden shadows across the porch and the dewy edges of the grass. Crickets had already started their nightly chorus, and the warm air buzzed faintly.

It was stupid, maybe, walking around the house just to knock on the front door. We lived together. We shared a home and a life I was still trying to help her remember. But that night wasn't just about routine. It was a date. A real one. And I wanted to *court* her the way she deserved.

So, I climbed the porch steps and knocked once, then stepped back, smoothing my hand down my light-blue, freshly pressed shirt. I'd even shrugged into the charcoal-gray button-up jacket Megan once told me brought out my eyes, though she didn't remember saying that now. Still, I hoped maybe something about it would stir a spark.

The door creaked open.

And there she was.

Megan.

She stood in the warm pool of light spilling from the hallway behind her, framed like something out of a daydream. Her hair was loose, curling gently around her face, and she'd chosen a soft cotton sundress in a pale shade of blue. The outfit was simple, yet so stunning on her it practically knocked the breath out of me.

She blinked up at me, a bit surprised. "Did you . . . knock?"

I rubbed the back of my neck, grinning sheepishly. "Figured if I was taking you on a real date, I ought to pick you up properly."

Her mouth curved into something soft and slow. Not quite a smile, more like the start of one, and it hit me square in the chest. "You're ridiculous," she said, but there was no heat behind it. Just something quiet and warm.

I held out my hand. "May I escort you, ma'am?"

That got the full smile.

She slipped her hand into mine, and for a second, we just stood there on the porch. Her fingers fit perfectly with mine, like they always had, and some part of her still *knew* me. Trusted me.

We walked hand in hand to the truck, the sky above us streaked in rose gold and fading indigo. I opened the passenger door for her and helped her in, stealing one last look as she settled into the seat. The light kissed her shoulders, and the curve of her mouth lingered even when she wasn't speaking.

Lord, she was beautiful.

I rounded the front and climbed in, stealing more glances as I started the engine. One hand rested loosely on the wheel, and the other rested close enough that if she wanted to reach for it, she could. She hummed some half-forgotten tune under her breath, and my chest ached with wanting.

I cleared my throat, but the words still came out thick. "You look beautiful."

She turned her head toward me, cheeks flushed, smile

radiant. "Thank you. You clean up pretty well yourself, Mr. Steele. Very handsome."

I chuckled low in my throat, savoring the easy back-and-forth that was starting to feel more natural between us again. But underneath it all, a current of nerves buzzed. "Thanks. It's nice to dress up every so often, especially when it matters."

And that night mattered.

WE TURNED off the main road, tires crunching over gravel. Ahead, the wide-open fields of the Striking Steele Ranch stretched out. The tall grass swayed like waves in the light evening breeze.

As we crested a small hill, she sucked in a breath. Spread out beneath a cluster of towering oak trees was the little world I'd made just for her. It was a lot easier to prepare ahead of time, considering my family owned the land.

A heavy quilt lay on the grass, surrounded by old mason jars filled with flickering candles, the soft light dancing in the early twilight. A basket sat nearby, filled with food, two glasses, and a chilled bottle of her favorite peach tea. A few strands of fairy lights dangled from the low branches, twinkling like fireflies.

"Oh, Cade," she breathed, her hand pressing against her heart.

I parked under the trees and rushed around to her side, opening the door like a man possessed by old-fashioned manners.

"Come on, baby," I said, offering her my hand again. "This night's all yours."

She slipped her hand into mine, her skin warm against my palm, and let me lead her down to the picnic. The scent of honeysuckle floated in the air. In the distance, the horses in the pasture snorted softly, and a low hum of peace wrapped around us.

I helped her settle on the blanket, my heart pounding in a rhythm that had nothing to do with physical labor and everything to do with her.

"I figured we'd keep it simple," I said, kneeling beside her and pulling out the food. "I didn't want you feeling like you had to act fancy or anything like that. Just us."

I unpacked sandwiches—turkey and cheddar on fresh-baked bread—a container of fresh strawberries, a couple of bags of kettle chips, and a slice of peach cobbler from the diner. Nothing flashy, but everything was picked with her in mind.

Megan laughed softly and scanned the expanse of land around us. "So, this is the infamous ranch, where you spend a lot of your time?" Megan looked over at me while picking up her drink and took a small sip. "This is perfect," she said, her voice catching a little at the end.

"It is. It's my second home. Or first, depending on how you look at it." I laughed. "Sorry, I probably should give you a tour one of these days."

"It's okay. I've seen *a lot* of pictures while you've been out working. It really is a beautiful piece of land. I can understand why you'd want to come here a lot. Even if you didn't have family here. What was it like growing up here? That's not something I can get from the pictures."

These were questions and things we didn't have to talk about, but the fact that she wanted to made this time together feel even more special. She was trying, really trying, to piece together the life we had, and that meant the world to me.

I leaned back a little, propping myself up on one arm as I looked out over the fields. The sun was low now, casting everything in amber light, catching the tops of the grass and making them glow.

"It wasn't always what it is now," I said. "When we were kids, it was just a modest house on a whole lotta land. No fancy barns or arenas, no welcome signs or event setups. Just chickens that wouldn't stay in their pen, a few cows that always seemed to find the one broken part of the fence, and a stubborn pony named Rascal that all of us boys tried and failed to train."

I glanced over at her, and the smile tugging at her mouth made me continue.

"We had one bathroom for nine people, and that meant a lot of elbow-throwing in the mornings with my brothers getting ready for school. Winters could be chilly, and summers were hotter than the devil's coffee. We didn't always have much, but it was home. It still *feels* like home."

Megan stayed quiet; she just listened. I wondered what she thought.

"What made it special wasn't the land, not really. It was Momma yelling at us to wipe our muddy boots, Pop teaching us how to fix a busted water line with duct tape and prayer, and Jackson hauling us all out of bed before sunrise like he was the foreman of a company we weren't paid to work for. We fought, sure. But we laughed a whole lot more. And every single one of us . . . We knew we were safe. We were loved."

I looked back at her then, and her eyes were locked on mine, wide and quiet and shining in the golden light.

"It's why I come here. Even when it's hard. Even when I don't know how to fix things. This land, this place, it pulls me back to the kind of man I want to be. The kind of man I *hope* I've been . . . for you."

She didn't speak at first. Just reached across the blanket and laid her hand over mine. It was the smallest touch, but it rooted me to the spot. And just for a moment, the air around us felt still, as if even the wind had paused to listen.

She looked down at our hands, her fingers brushing over mine like it was the most natural thing in the world. I could see her jaw tighten, the way she was holding something back. And then, her voice, soft but steady.

"You have been," she said. "The kind of man you hoped to be . . . I think you've been that. Even when I couldn't remember anything, when I didn't even know myself, you made me feel safe. You made me feel *known*."

Those words landed deep in my chest, sharp and tender all at once.

She turned her face toward the horizon, her profile catching the last wash of sunset like something out of a dream. I didn't say anything. I didn't want to break the moment.

"There's so much I don't know," she continued. "About this place. About you. About *us*. But hearing you talk about it like that, your family, your childhood, how much it shaped you . . . it makes me want to know more."

Then she looked back at me, and something in her eyes hit me right in the gut. That open, searching kind of gaze that felt like a door cracking open. Like maybe she was starting to find her way back.

"I want to remember," she said. "I want to remember all of it. But even if it doesn't come back the way we hoped, I want to know you again. All over again. From the ground up."

I couldn't move or speak, so I just took her in, this woman who had already stolen my heart once. And she was doing it all over again without even trying.

I reached for her then, letting my hand cradle her cheek as my thumb brushed her soft skin. She leaned into my touch on instinct.

"You will, but even if you didn't, I'd spend the rest of my life helping you fall in love with me again."

Her eyes glistened just a little in the fading light. In that moment, I knew, no matter how hard the road ahead might be, we were walking it together.

I pulled the basket closer and pulled out a few more items.

As we ate and talked, the conversation came easy, full of laughter and new memories that were beginning to feel like a bridge to our future. When the food was picked over and the sky had begun to darken, I leaned back on my elbows and looked up. Thousands of stars scattered across the velvet sky like someone had spilled a jar of sequins.

I tilted my head toward her. "Remember when we used to come out here to watch the stars?"

She shook her head slowly, regret clouding her features. "I wish I did."

I shifted until our shoulders brushed. "You will," I said softly. "I'll help you find all those memories again. Even if you can't, we can make new ones. Just as good."

She looked at me then, really looked, and something flickered in her eyes. Recognition, maybe. Or just the beginnings of hope.

"Lie back," I said, tugging gently at her hand.

She hesitated, then smiled and let me pull her down beside me. We lay there, side by side, staring up at the sky, the world around us falling away until it was just her breathing next to me and the universe stretching out above.

The evening sounds filled in the quiet between us: crickets tuning up, cattle shifting in the pasture, chickens clucking somewhere near the coop. It was peaceful

"Cade?" Her melodic voice broke the silence. "Can I ask you something?"

"Of course."

"You have a scar that I've seen a few times now. It looks like it might have been painful." She shifted beside me to get more comfortable. "Where did it come from?"

I sucked in a breath, surprised she'd noticed. Most people never asked. When they did, it was usually firefighters—guys who wanted the story, the adrenaline, the hero piece. But

Megan was looking at it like it meant something, like it was a mystery she wanted to gently unfold.

"There was a barn fire a couple of years ago. Some kids set off fireworks in an old place off Miller Road. The roof was already caving in by the time we got there."

Her eyes widened with concern, and even though she didn't remember loving me, she cared. I felt it.

"We thought everyone was out," I continued, eyes still on the sky. "Then one of the guys heard coughing inside. I went back in and found a kid of probably eight or nine hiding behind some equipment. The smoke was bad, and the beams were weak. I hoisted the boy over my shoulder to carry him, and part of the loft came down." I tapped my rib where the scar rested. "Board caught me as we were getting out. Had to shield him when we hit the ground. It took a good chunk out of me." A smile ghosted across my face. "But the kid made it."

For a moment, she didn't say anything. Megan just looked at me with this stunned, quiet awe that made my chest feel too tight.

"You saved him," she whispered.

"I did my job," I said, shrugging like it was nothing. It wasn't nothing; saving the kid was the right thing to do, and I'd do it over again if it happened tomorrow. "Anyone in my position would've done the same."

But she didn't look convinced. Her hand drifted closer, allowing her fingers to brush my scar with a gentleness that stole the air from my lungs.

"Maybe, but not everyone would have gone back in. You're a hero, Cade. Not just to that young boy, but to me too."

I swallowed hard as words climbed up my throat, desperate to be spoken. "You know, I fell in love with you under these stars."

She turned her head toward me, her hair brushing my cheek. "You did?"

"Yeah. Was probably too young and too stupid to know it for sure, but . . . I did." I gave a low, self-deprecating laugh. "Still am. In love with you, I mean. Always will be."

The candles flickered, casting shadows that danced over her face, highlighting the shimmer in her eyes. "Cade . . ." Her voice trembled.

I sat up, unable to hold back any longer, and cupped her face in my hands. "I don't need you to remember who we were," I said, my forehead resting against hers. "I just need you to know who we are right now. That's enough for me. You're enough for me."

She closed her eyes, and when she opened them again, the stars weren't half as bright as she was.

Without thinking, without daring to doubt, I leaned in and kissed her.

Slow. Gentle. Reverent.

She kissed me back with a sweetness that broke me wide open and stitched me back together all at once. When we finally pulled apart, her hands rested against my chest, feeling the way my heart pounded just for her.

"Thank you," she said simply. "For tonight. For everything."

"Always, baby," I murmured against her hair. "I'll spend the rest of my life giving you nights like this if you'll let me." And under that endless sky, with her pressed close and the whole wide world asleep around us, things were finally beginning to feel like they used to, and that was worth everything.

That's when her eyes got a glassy look, and Megan stiffened in my arms.

CHAPTER 27

Megan

I froze, blinking hard. The world around me blurred at the edges, like I was being pulled somewhere else, somewhere deeper. Suddenly, it was another night. Another sky full of stars.

Cade's hand was in mine, the same way it was at that moment—warm and solid, but holding me like I was made of something sacred. I heard my laughter, breathless and free. I was spinning barefoot in the grass, my hair flying around me like a banner. And Cade was chasing me, sporting that same crooked grin he wore when he was happy.

"Gotcha," he'd said, catching my hand and tugging me back into his arms. Then he'd kissed me, right there under the open sky, without hesitation, without fear. Like he knew with absolute certainty that I was his and he was mine.

The memory shimmered, so fragile I was afraid to breathe too hard, in case it disappeared. I sucked in a sharp breath, my hand tightening instinctively around his.

"Meg?" Cade's voice was gentle, his forehead lowering to mine again. "You okay?"

I nodded, but my throat was thick, my heart hammering in my chest. "I-I think I remembered something," I whispered.

His hand stilled over mine, like he didn't dare move, either.

"It wasn't much." I swallowed past the tightness in my throat. "But it felt real. Like a piece of us. Like a piece of me."

I squeezed my eyes shut, trying to hold on to the fleeting image. I tried to recall the way his arms had felt around me, the sound of his laughter in my ear. Not a story someone had told me. Not a photograph. Not a list of facts.

A memory. Mine.

When I opened my eyes, Cade was staring at me like I'd just handed him the stars themselves.

"You're doing it. You're finding your way back."

Tears pricked the corners of my eyes. I nodded, brushing my thumb over his knuckles. "I think I want to keep finding it with you."

The breath he let out was half laugh, half prayer. He kissed the back of my hand, lingering like he was sealing a vow, then rested our joined hands over his heart.

"As long as it takes," he whispered. "As many memories as you want. I'm yours, Megan. Always have been."

I leaned in, pressing my forehead against his chest, letting the steady drum of his heart anchor me. The past was still fuzzy and out of reach in so many ways, but this feeling was real.

For the first time since waking up in that hospital room, I wasn't scared of what I didn't remember. In the glow of candles and starlight, wrapped in Cade's arms, I realized something else.

We weren't just chasing the past. We were writing a whole new story. Together.

Cade eventually shifted and pressed a kiss to the top of my head before pulling back to look at me. "We should probably get this packed up before the critters out here help themselves."

I let out a reluctant sigh but nodded. The night was still

warm. Cicadas hummed softly in the distance, and the candles flickered low, like they, too, didn't want this moment to end.

Together, we moved slowly, almost lazily, gathering up the plates and tossing the leftover food into a cooler. Cade brushed off crumbs and double-checked lids like he wanted an excuse to stay out here a little longer, too. I bent down to blow out one of the candles and felt his eyes on me.

"You know," he drawled, amusement thick in his voice, "I'm pretty sure you're still the prettiest thing out here, even with grass stains on your knees."

I glanced down and laughed. Sure enough, the bottom of my sundress had a faint smear of green. "Well, you're not so bad yourself, ranch man. Especially with all that candlelight helping you out."

He clutched his chest in mock offense. "So you're saying I need all the help I can get?"

I grinned up at him, heart lighter than it had been in months. "Maybe just a little."

He laughed, and that low, rumbling sound wrapped around me like a hug. Then he tugged me gently toward him by the hem of my jacket and pressed a quick kiss to my temple. "Good thing I don't mind working hard for you," he said softly.

The words fluttered against my skin, which caused me to tense in a way I never expected.

We finished packing up as the world was dipped in gold and midnight blue. Cade grabbed the cooler and blanket in one hand, reaching for mine with the other, threading our fingers together like it was the most natural thing in the world.

As we walked back toward the truck, I stole little glances from the corner of my eye. There was a confidence about him. Not loud or flashy, but steady. Like the earth itself trusted him to stay exactly where he was supposed to be.

I wondered, not for the first time, how I'd gotten so lucky to be loved by a man like this. Even when I couldn't remember every moment we'd shared, my heart still knew him.

The sounds of the evening filled the silence until we reached the truck. Cade set everything in the bed, then turned to me, his smile soft.

"Ready to head home, Meg?"

Home. The word caught in my throat for a second, but then I nodded, smiling back at him. *Yeah.* I was ready.

The drive back was quiet, marked by the kind of comfortable silence that didn't need filling. I leaned my head against the window and watched the moon follow us down the winding roads. Every now and then, Cade would glance over at me, his hand resting on the console like he was ready to catch me if I even so much as tilted wrong.

When we pulled up to the house, he parked, turned off the engine, and turned toward me. Neither of us moved. The porch light cast a warm glow over the front door, and moths danced lazily in the beam. But it was like we were still wrapped up in our own little world inside the truck's cab.

Cade reached over and brushed a loose strand of hair behind my ear. "Thank you," he murmured.

"For what?"

"For trusting me. For coming with me tonight. For letting me be part of your story. Again."

Emotion rose thick in my chest, stealing my breath. "I wouldn't want anyone else."

He leaned in slowly, giving me plenty of time to pull away if I needed to. But I didn't. I didn't even hesitate.

Our lips met again for the second time that night. It was soft at first, gentle, and when I leaned into him, he deepened the kiss just slightly, cradling my face in one big, warm hand.

It wasn't desperate.

It wasn't rushed.

It was the kind of kiss that said, *I'm right here. I'm not going anywhere.*

When we finally pulled apart, I rested my forehead against his, breathing him in. The candlelight, the soft music, his hand in mine—it was still wrapped around me like a second skin.

After a few moments, he got out of the truck and came around to open my door, always the gentleman. I smiled at the small gesture, maybe one I'd experienced a hundred times before, and slipped my hand into his as I climbed down.

We walked into the house after he grabbed everything out of the back of the truck, our steps quiet on the porch. The entryway lamp glowed softly, and I took a deep breath as the familiar scent of home washed over me.

Cade set the leftover picnic basket on the kitchen counter and turned to me with that same quiet intensity that had been simmering all evening. I started down the hallway, toward the spare room I'd been staying in, the room that once felt safe, like a place to land when the world had turned unfamiliar.

But that night, it felt different. Like something had shifted.

I paused just outside the door, hand resting lightly on the knob. Then I turned back to him.

His eyes met mine, patient, steady. Always waiting, never pushing.

"Cade?" My voice was soft but sure.

"Yeah, baby?"

I swallowed, nerves and hope tangled together. "Would it be okay if I . . . stayed in our room tonight?"

As he stood and looked at me, all that love and longing written so clearly across his face stole my breath.

Then he nodded once, slow and reverent. "Yeah. I'd love that."

He reached for my hand, and I let him take it. His thumb brushed over my knuckles as we walked down the hall, not to the room that held hesitation and distance, but to the one that held history. Us.

When we reached the doorway, he paused. "You sure?"

I nodded. "I want to start remembering as your wife."

His chest lifted with a deep breath, his eyes shining in the dim light. "Then welcome home, darlin'. Go on in and get yourself settled. I'm just going to use the bathroom."

"Take your time."

I walked into the room that Cade and I shared. A room that I'd had a hand in decorating.

I brushed my fingers over the quilt at the foot of the bed. I could still feel him. Not just his presence, but the warmth of everything we were and everything we could be. He'd looked at me as if I was already his again, the way I wanted to be, completely, fully, and without hesitation.

The evening hadn't just been a date. It hadn't been about retrieving the past.

It was about choosing the future.

I pressed a hand to my chest, feeling the rhythm of something not just returning, but rebuilding. Whatever this was, it was ours. It was worth holding on to. Worth fighting for.

And it was definitely worth remembering.

CHAPTER 28

Megan

I lay there, barely an inch away, watching the way the morning light caught in Cade's dark beard that curved along his jaw. Faint creases lined his eyes, rested now, but shaped by years of smiling. Years of loving, of waiting, of holding the line, even when I couldn't remember how to stand beside him.

God, last night . . .

It played in my mind like a movie reel, from his knock on the door to his hands shaking just enough to give him away to the warm way he looked at me like I was both a memory and a miracle.

And maybe I was.

I didn't know all the pieces of who we used to be, but I knew how he made me feel now. Safe. Wanted. Home.

I rolled onto my side, facing him more fully, propping my head on my arm. He didn't stir, just kept breathing, thick lashes resting against his cheek, his mouth barely parted.

It struck me then how many mornings we might've shared like this before. The comfort of waking in the same bed. The quiet language of love that didn't need words. I didn't remember them.

But I *wanted* to.

I wanted every one of them back.

Still, there was something achingly beautiful about rediscovering it all now, like we were falling in love again in slow motion, every look and every brush of skin carrying twice the weight.

My fingers reached out and lightly traced the edge of the quilt between us. Not touching him, exactly, but close. Close enough. This bed didn't feel foreign anymore. It didn't feel borrowed or distant or like something someone else used to belong to.

It felt like ours.

Even without every memory, I knew the truth of what we had. What we were still building. The little things were adding up. The shared smiles. The way he watched me like I hung the stars. The strength in his silence. The reverence in his voice when he said my name.

He whispered it like a vow, every time.

A soft noise escaped him in his sleep, barely a breath, but I felt it like a tug on my heart.

I should probably get up, I thought, but I didn't move. Instead, I lay there in the hush of morning and let myself have this fragile, glowing moment.

Because something told me life wouldn't slow down for us forever. There would be more hills to climb. More memories to chase down. And sooner or later, this stretch of peace might break.

But for now?

It's perfect.

I didn't need all the answers to know this man was mine.

And I was his.

Still. Again. Always.

His fingers moved first. Just a slow curl, like they were reaching through sleep for something real.

Me.

I stayed still, watching as his brow twitched slightly, lips parting with a breath that sounded heavier than before. I didn't look away, didn't want to miss the moment when he came into the day with me.

His eyes blinked open slowly, warm hazel meeting mine, still hazy with sleep.

"Hey," I said, my voice barely above a breath.

A smile tugged at the corner of his mouth. "Hey," he rasped back.

Then he reached for me. His hand brushed gently over my wrist, fingers trailing up my forearm before settling lightly at the curve of my elbow, anchoring us to the moment.

"You stayed," he said, like he was still trying to believe it.

"I did."

His smile deepened, but it was softer now. More reverent than surprised. The weight of what last night meant was finally starting to settle in. "Wasn't sure if I dreamed it."

"It wasn't a dream. I didn't want it to end."

"Me neither," he said finally, quiet and true.

My hand found its way to the space between us, palm up, open. His fingers slid into mine, warm and familiar, and the way they fit, like they had all along, sent a tremble through my chest. His thumb traced a slow arc over my knuckles.

"You sure?" he asked, voice gentler now. "About last night? About this?"

I knew what he meant. It wasn't just about a bed. It was about stepping into something I didn't fully remember but still *felt*. It was about reclaiming something that had been mine long before the accident stole the memories.

"I'm sure," I said. "I don't remember everything, but I know how I felt with you last night. I know how I feel now."

He let out a breath, almost a laugh, but it was soft relief wrapped in wonder.

"I missed waking up like this," he murmured.

"Yeah?"

"Yeah." He turned onto his side so we were face-to-face. "You used to make this little sound every morning, just before your eyes opened. Like the day had to ask your permission to begin."

I laughed, heat rushing to my cheeks. "I did not."

"You did. Still do," he teased, his grin sleepy but real. "And I always waited for it."

I stared at him for a long moment, heart aching in the best kind of way.

He remembered everything.

And even if I didn't, not yet, I felt it.

All of it.

He leaned in then, slow and careful, his lips brushing my forehead. It was barely a kiss, but it made me feel complete.

When he pulled back, his hand lingered on my cheek. "We've got time. No rush. We'll go slow. Just don't shut me out, all right?"

"I won't." The words came easier than I expected. "I'm not running."

We stayed like that for a long time, wrapped in the kind of quiet you don't want to break. Eventually, the world would start spinning again. Appointments, the nursery, and preparations. Life.

But not yet.

Right then, in that room that used to feel like a story I didn't belong to . . .

I felt at home.

Wrapped in Cade's gaze, his warmth, his patience . . .

I felt like a wife.

Not just someone who'd been his once, but someone who *chose* him now. Over and over again. No matter what storm came next.

CHAPTER 29

*I*t had been a week.

Seven days since she'd chosen *our* room.

Seven mornings waking up to the same soft sound of her breathing beside me, her head tucked beneath my chin.

Seven days of us easing back into a rhythm built on shared smiles, small touches, and conversations that held both memory and discovery.

And that morning, I'd caught her humming.

She was barefoot, standing in the middle of the nursery we'd started painting two days ago, one hand on her hip and the other holding up a swatch of mint green that she said looked "too cucumber and not enough dream." I hadn't known that was a thing, but watching her animated and glowing, I would've agreed to paint the room with moonlight if it made her happy.

She was in one of those oversized sweaters she'd recently found comfort in, sleeves pushed up to her elbows, and a pair of leggings that clung to her legs in a way that made me forget my own name for a second.

"Okay," she said, turning toward me with that little furrow of focus between her brows. "What about this one? Seabreeze Mist?"

I blinked, snapping out of the moment like a man emerging from a fog. "Sure."

She rolled her eyes playfully. "You didn't even look."

"I did." I crossed the room to where she stood. "But to be honest, I was a little distracted."

"By the color?" She gave me that smile, the one that curled slow, like she knew exactly what she was doing to me.

"By you."

Her cheeks flushed, and for a second, she looked down at her toes. A strand of hair fell across her cheek in the same way it always did when she got shy. Even without her memories, that part hadn't changed. She still blushed when I complimented her. Still got bashful when I stared too long.

We stood there for a moment, the morning light pouring in through the window and catching flecks of dust in the air like golden confetti. The baby's crib was still in pieces beside us; we had moved the crib back to the nursery when we had decided to start working on the room.

It felt good. Like building something again. Like *becoming* something again.

She reached up, placing the paint swatch against the wall, but halfway there, she paused. Her fingers faltered.

"Hey," I said softly. "You okay?"

She blinked and shook her head a little, like she'd forgotten where she was. "Yeah, just . . . dizzy for a second."

I moved closer, steadying her with a hand at her elbow. "Let's take a break."

She nodded and let me lead her to the hallway, then to the kitchen, where the air was cooler. She leaned on the counter, one hand splayed over the granite, the other resting lightly over her belly. "I'm fine," she said, as if she were trying to convince herself more than me. "Probably just moved too fast."

"Still." I reached for a bottle of water in the fridge and handed it to her. "You've been on your feet for a while."

"Yeah," she admitted, accepting defeat with a small smile. "Doctor Langston said I could keep moving as long as I listened to my body."

"Then we're listening."

She took a sip of water, then slid onto the kitchen stool. I watched the way her jaw tensed, how her eyes didn't quite meet mine.

Something had shifted. I couldn't explain it. It was subtle—not pain, not panic, just different.

"I was thinking," I said, keeping my voice light as I took the seat across from her. "Once we're done with the paint, maybe we'll hang some of those photos from the ranch. You know, some of the ones you took a few days ago?"

Her lips curved, but it didn't reach her eyes. "Did you print those out?"

"Yeah, when I saw them, I thought they'd be great to hang up somewhere, and why not the nursery? So when the baby looks around, they'll see their mother wherever they look."

She laughed, "That's sweet—" Her breath hitched just slightly, and her hand returned to her stomach.

I stood. "Meg?"

Her gaze flicked to mine. "It's nothing. Just a weird . . . flutter. Not a kick. More like a drop. Or a tug." Her other hand reached across to touch mine, like she could already sense I was spiraling. "I'm probably just tired."

I crouched beside her. "We should call Dr. Langston."

"Cade—"

"Please." My voice cracked a little, barely audible over the hum of the fridge. "Let's not wait. Just to be sure."

She stared at me for a long beat, then nodded.

I reached for my phone and stepped into the hallway, fingers trembling slightly as I dialed.

Whatever this was, it wasn't panic. Not yet. But something in the air had shifted, and I couldn't shake the feeling that we were on the edge of something again.

CHAPTER 30

Megan

I sat at the kitchen counter, my palms flat against the cool surface, willing them to ground me. Cade's footsteps moved through the house like a steady metronome, phone tucked against his shoulder, questions slipping out between clipped nods.

As he spoke with the doctor, something about the sound of Cade's voice made my heart tighten. It wasn't fear, exactly, not yet, but something like it. A pressure beneath the ribs. A quiet echo of the unknown pressing in around the edges.

He was calm, or trying to be, but I'd seen the way his hand hovered over my stomach when I'd said something felt off. And in the silence that followed, the world tilted a little.

He returned a few minutes later, phone call done, keys in hand.

"She can see us now," he said, reaching out gently. "Dr. Langston's already on her way in. They'll do a quick scan. Just to be safe."

I nodded and slid off the stool. "Okay."

The drive was quiet.

Outside, the clouds were tufts of cotton pulled across a sky too heavy with thoughts. The town passed in muted tones as we traveled the now familiar streets and passed sun-bleached signs and a farmer's market banner flapping lazily above the roundabout.

I stared out the window, one hand resting over the curve of my belly. Just crossing over twenty weeks, yet still so early.

Cade reached across the console and threaded his fingers through mine.

I turned to him, giving a small, grateful smile.

It wasn't just his hand that anchored me, but the way he looked at me. Like everything mattered. Like *I* mattered. Not just because I was carrying our baby, but because I was *me*.

"I didn't mean to worry you," I said.

"You didn't. But I'd rather worry for nothing than not act soon enough."

I nodded, letting that truth settle into me.

We turned into the clinic's parking lot. Cade parked close to the front door, then shut off the engine. For a moment, neither of us moved.

I stared at the building's glass doors, watching the reflection's slow dance on the surface. My heart was beating a little too fast, my breath catching somewhere high in my chest.

"Megan."

I turned.

"I know it's probably nothing. But even if it's something . . . we'll handle it."

I swallowed the tightness rising in my throat. "Together?"

He squeezed my hand. "Always."

We walked in, hand in hand. The air was cool, clinical, and the overhead lights emitted a soft hum. The waiting room smelled faintly of lemon polish and time; it was one of those spaces that held one hundred kinds of hope and fear, wearing them into the fabric of the cushions and the faded corners of the magazines no one really read.

I sat beside Cade, close enough that our knees brushed. I secretly wanted Cade to reach over and pull me against him. With so many questions running through my mind, he was the only sure thing I had anymore. I was about to reach for him when the nurse called my name. He stood first, offering his hand before I could even move. Together, we followed the nurse to Dr. Langston's exam room.

My green cotton dress bunched around my legs, so I adjusted the hem, which was wrinkled from clutching it on the ride over. I'd found the dress in the back of the closet, and when I'd put it on, it had felt like a memory I wasn't certain I'd lived.

I just had to hope that it wouldn't become a memory I wanted to forget.

CHAPTER 31

Cade

*M*egan eased onto the exam table. I stayed by her side, my hand never leaving hers. Her grip tightened slightly as the paper crinkled beneath her, the scent of antiseptic mingling with something faintly lavender.

The door opened, and Dr. Langston stepped in. She was calm and grounded in that no-nonsense way that bolstered my trust in her.

"How're we doing, Megan?" she asked.

Megan gave a quiet shrug. "I'm okay. Just . . . off. A little cramping. Not sharp, just there. Last night it felt a little worse."

Dr. Langston nodded, already stepping closer. "How often has it happened?"

"A few times," Megan admitted. "Not every day. But I notice it. Dull pressure, low. Sometimes it wraps around." She gestured toward her abdomen with her hand.

Dr. Langston's brow creased as she palpated Megan's stomach. She was careful. Thorough. But I could feel Megan's breath catch under my palm.

"Externally, everything feels stable," she said at last. "But let's take a peek, just to be sure."

The room went still as she reached for the ultrasound wand.

The gel hit Megan's skin, and she flinched slightly, whether from cold or nerves, I wasn't sure. Her hand tightened in mine, and I leaned in, pressing my forehead to hers.

"I'm right here," I reassured her.

"I know."

And then, there on the screen, like the first time we ever saw it: the flicker. That unmistakable rhythm of life. The baby moved, the faintest wiggle, like it knew we were watching. And then the heartbeat came. A steady, strong thump-thump-thump that settled somewhere deep in my chest.

"There's your little one," Dr. Langston said with a small smile, turning the monitor slightly so Megan could see. "Heartbeat is strong. Measurements are exactly where we want them. That's all reassuring."

Megan let out a soft sigh of relief. Her shoulders relaxed, but she still looked up at the doctor, her voice a little smaller as she spoke. "Then what is it? Why the cramps?"

Dr. Langston hesitated long enough to put a knot in my gut. "I believe you're experiencing early uterine irritability. It's not dangerous on its own, but it can be an early sign of preterm complications. Especially if it starts to intensify or becomes more frequent."

Megan's eyes flicked to mine, then back to Dr. Langston. "So, what does that mean?"

"It means I want you resting. As much as possible. No lifting. No long errands. No driving alone. And I want to start seeing you weekly."

The quiet in the room grew heavier.

Megan was nodding, but I could feel the tension roll off her. Like something was tightening from the inside out. She didn't say anything as we returned to the waiting room and set up her next appointment. Her lips remained sealed until we were almost back to the truck, walking slower than usual beneath the silver sky.

Stopping just before she reached the door, she looked up at me. "I don't want to be useless."

I froze. God, I hated the sound of that word on her lips. "You're not," I said immediately. "Not even close."

"It just feels like . . ." She trailed off, her eyes shining even though she tried to blink the tears away. "Like everything's being taken from me. Like I'm watching our life happen through a window I can't open."

I cupped her cheek and tucked a strand of hair behind her ear. "You're not losing it, Megan. You're in it. Right in the middle of it. Every time you fight through fear, every time you choose to stay hopeful. That's what makes you strong."

Her lip trembled, but she nodded. And I kissed her forehead, because anything more than that might've undone us both.

We climbed into the truck, and the silence was the kind you don't try to fix. The kind that lets you breathe. As I pulled onto the road, I glanced down and saw her hand resting on her belly, light, reverent. It struck me again, just how much she carried.

Not just the baby.

But hope. Fear. The power of a love she was still stitching back together, piece by piece.

This wasn't the easy part.

But it was ours.

And I would hold the whole damn world still if it meant keeping her safe inside it.

CHAPTER 32

Megan

*B*y the time we got home, the clouds had started to roll in. Thin gray streaks tugged slowly across the sky, casting the world in a tired, wintery hue. Cade parked the truck beside the porch and cut the engine, but neither of us moved at first.

I stared out the window, watching a crow hop across the bare patch of grass near the steps, its feathers glossy black against the brown and brittle earth.

The silence in the cab wasn't uncomfortable, but it was the thick kind of quiet you can't push through with words. There was too much emotion, too many things still sinking in.

Early uterine irritability.

Weekly visits. No more driving. No lifting. No long errands.

It felt like every ounce of independence I'd clawed back since waking up in that hospital bed was slowly slipping through my fingers.

"You ready to head in?" Cade asked.

I nodded, but when I tried to open the door, my hand trembled a little. Cade noticed. Of course he did. He was around the truck in seconds, opening the door for me like we'd stepped back in time to a slower, older era.

"I've got it," I murmured.

"I know," he said. But he still offered his hand.

I didn't argue. I let him help me down, and he didn't let go as we made our way inside.

The house smelled like home—warm wood and the faintest trace of the cinnamon candle I'd lit the night before. It felt like a cocoon, even if my chest was tight with all the unknowns. I eased onto the sofa while Cade set down our things, his quiet energy grounding me in a way I hadn't expected to need so badly.

"I'll get you some water." He headed toward the kitchen.

I leaned into the cushions and let out a slow breath. The ache in my lower abdomen was still there, not sharp, just a dull reminder. A warning.

My body was whispering something. I just didn't know what. When Cade returned, I took the glass from him and sipped slowly.

"Thanks."

He sat beside me, his thigh brushing mine. "You okay?"

"I don't know," I answered truthfully. "I feel . . . powerless."

"You're not."

I gave him a small smile. "I know you believe that. But it's hard to feel like anything other than fragile right now. It's like I finally started getting pieces of myself back, and now the rules are changing again."

Cade shifted closer. "You're not fragile, Meg. Not even a little. You're dealing with more than most people could imagine, and you're still standing. That's not weakness. That's grit."

I rested my head on his shoulder, the warmth of his body soothing the edges of my worry. "What if this is just the start? What if something else goes wrong?"

"Then we deal with it together. One step at a time. Just like we're doing with everything else."

His words should have comforted me, and in a way, they did, but the uncertainty of what lay ahead pressed down on me, causing my heart to ramp up its pace inside my chest. I wanted to believe everything would be okay, but belief didn't feel like enough anymore. I needed facts. Reassurance. Guarantees no one could give.

Later that afternoon, Cade went outside to chop some wood. Probably more to burn off nervous energy than to stockpile kindling. I wandered into our shared bedroom that had slowly started to feel like mine again.

I sat on the edge of the bed, running my hand over the quilt that covered it. Tiny, faded flowers had been stitched into the pattern. The frayed corners and threads pulled in places told me it had been used, loved, and washed a hundred times. I wondered if I'd made it. Or if it had been a gift. Another forgotten thread in the tapestry of a life I was still rediscovering.

All my things from the spare room had been moved to our room. I reached for the small journal I'd started keeping after the amnesia, and I flipped through the pages. Most of it was scribbled thoughts, pieced together memories that felt half-real, half-invented. Little notes Cade had given me. Questions I wanted to ask him. The way he looked at me when he thought I wasn't watching. I paused on a page from earlier in the week. A quote I'd written down after overhearing it in a movie:

"Sometimes healing looks a lot like hurting first."

That line had stuck with me. Still did. I rubbed my belly absently. The baby shifted ever so slightly beneath my hand. A flutter. Like a secret shared just between us.

A knock on the bedroom door broke the quiet. "Yeah?" I called.

Cade peeked in, cheeks flushed from his hard work. "You need anything?"

I shook my head. "Just thinking."

He stepped inside and wiped his hands on his jeans, then crossed the room and kneeled in front of me. His hands came to rest on my knees, gentle but firm. "I know this isn't how you pictured things."

"Kind of hard to picture anything when your whole life's a puzzle missing the picture on the box."

That made him smile faintly. "Well, whatever the picture ends up being, I know one thing."

"What?"

"You and me and this little one . . . we're gonna be the heart of it."

Something caught in my throat. Emotion, thick and unspoken.

"I'm scared, Cade."

He nodded, his voice barely a whisper. "Me too. But I'd rather be scared with you than fine without you."

I wrapped my arms around him and buried my face in his neck. We stayed like that for a long time, breathing in sync, the storm inside me slowly quieting under the steady beat of his heart. I wasn't fighting this alone. Things still hid within a fog, but with Cade, I had him fully and completely.

CHAPTER 33

Cade

*T*he wind picked up that night, not wild, not loud, but steady. It made the shutters creak and the trees murmur low against the eaves. I stood at the kitchen sink, rinsing off the last of our dinner dishes, staring out the window as dusk crept in.

The forecast had said nothing about a front rolling through, but you didn't need the news to know when change was coming. You could smell it in the air. Feel it in your bones. And that night, I felt it.

The kind of shift that had nothing to do with weather.

I dried my hands on the towel, tossed it over the back of a chair, and glanced down the hallway. Megan was in bed already. She'd said she was just going to read for a bit, but she'd been quiet all evening, her silences getting longer, heavier. I couldn't blame her. The appointment had knocked the wind out of both of us.

I'd kept it together at the doctor's office, but inside, I was still unraveling. *Irritability.* That word banged around in my head like a warning bell. And when the doctor said *no driving, no stress, feet up, check-ins every week*, it felt like the ground under us wasn't so solid anymore. Especially since she'd been working on regaining her freedom.

I flicked off the kitchen light and walked quietly to the hallway. The house creaked under my steps, same as it always had. These small, familiar noises grounded me. The place was still holding steady, even when my nerves weren't.

I stopped at our room and eased the door open. She was already under the covers, book splayed open on her chest, eyes fluttering shut.

"You sleepin'?" I asked, my voice low.

"No," she murmured, not opening her eyes. "Just trying to get there."

I walked further in and lowered myself to the edge of our bed, which I was so happy to once again share with her. She reached for my hand without looking, and I gave it to her.

"I've been thinking," I said after a minute.

"Uh-oh," she whispered with a faint smile.

"Smartass," I muttered, grinning despite myself. Then I let the smile fall and turned serious. "I think we ought to ask Momma to stay with you when I'm on shift. Maybe even before then. I can't be everywhere, and I don't want you alone if something happens."

She opened her eyes then, blinking up at me. "You think something's going to happen?"

I hesitated. "That's the thing. We don't *know*, and that's what scares me. You're already dealing with so much, Meg. If anything were to happen when I wasn't here . . ."

Her grip tightened slightly. "Okay," she said, quiet but steady. "We can ask her."

It surprised me how easily she agreed. No protest. No pushback. That told me more than anything that she was scared, too. Probably more than she admitted earlier.

"You think I'm breaking?" Megan's voice was smaller than I'd heard in weeks.

"No," I said without missing a beat. "I think you've been holding more weight than anyone should have to. And you're handling it all like a champ."

She gave a soft, tired laugh, then pushed the book aside and scooted over. "Lay down with me?"

I didn't need to be asked twice.

I kicked off my boots, slipped in beside her, and let her curl into me. I felt her exhale into my chest, the weight of her body soft against mine, and I held her close so I could keep the world at bay.

But even wrapped up in her like that, I couldn't ignore the undercurrent in my chest. That tension. That quiet fear. I'd always known pregnancy was unpredictable, but I guess I'd believed—*hoped*—that Megan would be spared the hard parts. That maybe, after everything else, we'd get smooth sailing here.

Now, I wasn't so sure.

And the hardest part of all? I didn't know how to fix it. I didn't know how to protect her from the things we couldn't see coming.

I lay there long after she fell asleep, listening to the wind and the shift of her breath against me. I watched the shadows move across the ceiling and thought of all the things I still wanted to give her. All the pieces we hadn't yet put back together.

I was scared. And I didn't like being scared. But I wasn't backing down, either.

Whatever storm was coming, whatever this pregnancy still had in store, we'd weather it together.

CHAPTER 34

Megan

The ache started in the early hours of the next morning. Weeks had passed since that initial pain, and I thought we'd gotten past it. Not a sharp pain, nothing dramatic or alarming, but a steady, dull pressure low in my back, like something was settling wrong. I shifted under the covers, trying to find a more comfortable position, but it followed me no matter how I turned.

Cade was still beside me, with one arm draped protectively across my waist. His breathing was deep, steady. Peaceful.

I didn't want to wake him.

I moved slowly, sliding out from beneath his arm and sitting up at the edge of the bed. The room was still dark, the outlines of furniture barely visible in the faint blue pre-dawn light leaking through the curtains.

A wave of dizziness washed over me as I stood. I grabbed the bedpost to steady myself, blinking through it. I told myself it was nothing. Probably just normal pregnancy stuff. The doctor had warned me I'd feel more pressure as the baby grew, and considering where I was in this pregnancy, that low ache made sense.

Still, I couldn't shake the tightness building inside me. Not just physical. Emotional. Like my body and mind were conspiring against me again.

I padded down the hallway toward the kitchen. The floor was cold beneath my bare feet. I should've put on socks, but I didn't go back. I needed a minute. Just one minute to breathe.

I leaned on the counter, pressing my palms into the cool granite and letting the pressure ground me. My heart beat faster than it should, but maybe that was just anxiety. The doctor said stress could make things worse. Maybe I was doing this to myself.

Don't spiral, I told myself. *Breathe.*

The truth was, I hadn't wanted to tell Cade about the pressure yesterday. I'd let him think the appointment rattled me more than it did physically, but the truth was, I'd felt off ever since. Not pain, exactly, but discomfort that didn't settle.

I ran my fingers over my stomach. "You okay in there, little one?"

No answer, of course. Just the silence of the room and the faint creak of the house settling around me.

I poured a glass of water and sipped it as I stared out the window. The wind had died down sometime during the night, but the clouds still hung low, the horizon smeared with a dark, threatening gray. The sky looked like it couldn't decide if it wanted to cry or not.

I knew the feeling.

Behind me, the soft scuff of feet on hardwood made me turn. Cade stood in the doorway, shirtless. He rubbed a hand through his messy hair, his eyes still fogged with sleep. The morning light spilled across his bare chest and caught on the ridges of muscle and the faint dusting of hair that led beneath the low waistband of his flannel pajama pants. His skin was golden from days spent working under the sun, but it was the way his body *held* stillness that undid me. That quiet strength just standing there, as if he could shoulder whatever came next.

"You okay?" he asked, voice low and rough with sleep. Concern laced the short phrase.

And I should have answered him. I should have said something about the lingering unease in my chest or the way sleep hadn't come easily after yesterday's appointment.

But I just looked at him.

This man, *my husband*, who looked at me like I was still his world, even when mine felt unsteady. The worry hadn't erased the pull I felt. If anything, it made it sharper. It stirred inside me, even then, tugging low in my belly, fluttering against the ache of everything unknown.

Even half-asleep, with hair sticking up in every direction and sleep lines creasing his cheek, he still made my heart beat in a way that almost felt unfair. Like my body remembered every kiss we'd shared, every whispered promise, even when my mind still played catch-up. He was a breathtaking kind of undone, all tousled warmth and bare skin, a quiet storm of comfort and want. I hadn't just chosen well. I'd chosen the one my soul already knew by heart.

I swallowed as I watched the rise and fall of his chest. "Just couldn't sleep."

He stepped forward without hesitation, the soft floor creaking beneath his weight, and I let him pull me into the circle of his arms. Solid and safe. "Everything all right?"

"Yeah." I nodded too quickly. "Just . . . restless. Back's a little sore."

His eyes narrowed. He didn't believe me. He never said much when I brushed things off, but he never missed a thing, either.

"I'm fine," I added. "I think I just need to take it slow today. Maybe stay on the sofa. Read, rest, binge-watch."

"We'll do whatever you need. I'll move Heaven and Earth to keep you safe. You know that, right?"

I swallowed hard because I did know. And that scared me, too. I didn't want to be the thing he had to protect all the time. I didn't want to be fragile. Or broken. Or a ticking clock of potential complications.

I wanted to be his partner. Instead, I felt like a problem waiting to happen.

I nodded into the silence, hoping he couldn't feel the tears gathering behind my eyes. "I know," I whispered.

He kissed the side of my head and then left me to finish my water, saying something about making breakfast. I stayed there by the window, arms wrapped tight around myself, eyes locked on the gray sky outside.

Something was shifting inside me. And I didn't know if it was just nerves, instinct, or something more.

Regardless, I needed to think about Cade. He was trying to work, manage a home, and hold me together, and that wasn't fair to him. I would need to be careful not to worry him further, even if the worry already filled me up to overflowing. If it meant giving this man a little peace, I'd just learn how to hide it better.

CHAPTER 35

*T*he scent of sizzling butter hit the air before the eggs even cracked. I moved on autopilot: pan hot, bread in the toaster, eggs over-easy, just how she liked them lately. But I wasn't thinking about breakfast.

I was thinking about the look in her eyes when I found her standing at the kitchen window that morning. She'd smiled. Said she was fine. Restless. Just a sore back. But her eyes told a different story, and I read the fear within them.

I knew what it looked like when she was holding something back. I'd known before the accident, and I'd learned it all over again after. Megan had always been strong, but her strength sometimes came with silence. She'd carry everything, good or bad, all alone before ever asking someone else to share it.

Maybe I'd let that go on a little too long.

Even over the sounds of the rhythmic pop of the toaster, I couldn't shake the uneasy knotting in my chest.

What if something's wrong?

That whisper had been following me since Dr. Langston's glance had lingered a little too long on the screen and Megan had grabbed my hand harder than usual.

What if it's more than nerves?

The toast popped. I buttered it with slow, methodical strokes, eyes flicking toward the hallway. I hadn't heard her come out. Maybe she'd gone back to bed. Maybe she was trying to be strong again, alone in our room.

I brought the plates to the table, poured juice into two small glasses, and waited.

Still no Megan.

I glanced at the clock. Nearly half an hour had passed since I'd found her at the window.

Leaving the food, I made my way down the quiet hall. No movement, no sound. Just the stillness of her trying to get through something on her own.

I hated it.

"Meg?"

Silence for a moment. Then, softly, "Yeah?"

"You want breakfast? It's nice and hot."

Another pause. "I'll be there in a minute."

I could hear the effort in her voice. Like she was piecing herself together to face me.

I rested my hand on the doorframe and leaned into it. "You don't have to do that, you know."

"Do what?"

"Pretend it's fine if it's not."

The silence stretched again. "I'm trying, Cade. I don't know what else to do."

I closed my eyes, that ache in my chest blooming again. I wanted to go in, to pull her into my arms, to take some of the stress off of her. But I also knew there were some moments you had to let someone walk through themselves.

"I'm here," I said instead. "No matter what."

"I know."

I stood there a second longer, then returned to the kitchen. She came out not long after, still in her sleep shirt, hair up in a loose knot, face scrubbed clean. No makeup. No performance. Just her.

She slid into the chair opposite me with a small smile. "Smells amazing."

"I used the fancy butter."

That earned me a half-laugh. "You mean the one with the sea-salt flakes?"

"Only the best."

She took a bite and chewed slowly, gaze drifting toward the window. Rain had started to fall in the distance, just enough to soften the sky.

"How's your back?"

Her fork paused. "Still sore. Maybe a little worse than this morning."

"You want to call the doctor?"

She shook her head. "No. Not yet. I'm okay."

But she wasn't eating much.

We fell into a thick silence again.

She's scared.

I'm scared too.

I wanted to tell her I didn't have all the answers, that every time I looked at her, I felt like I was holding my breath, waiting for the next thing to go wrong, but I couldn't. Not yet. Not when she was already trying so hard to stay upright.

"I might swing by the ranch later," I said, changing the subject. "Alden mentioned the south line needs checking. But I'll be close."

She nodded. "Okay."

"You sure you don't want me to stay?"

"No. Go. I'll be fine. I'll probably just rest." But her eyes didn't meet mine.

After breakfast, I lingered in the doorway as she curled up on the sofa, a blanket tucked around her. She had a book open in her lap, but she wasn't reading. I watched her for a second longer than I should have, memorizing the curve of her cheek, the way her fingers absently stroked her belly. Then I turned and left.

But as I stepped into the cool morning air, something in me twisted. Leaving didn't feel right, but she'd told me to go. Ignoring that feeling, I stepped off the porch and headed toward the ranch. If Megan needed some space, I'd give her that, even if it hurt.

CHAPTER 36

Megan

*T*he front door clicked softly behind Cade, and I waited until I couldn't hear the roar of his truck engine before exhaling. I hated this part. The pretending. The small lies wrapped in soft tones like, "I'm fine," and "Just tired."

I pulled the blanket tighter around me, settling deeper into the sofa, the book still lying in my lap, unread. I glanced down, trying to read. The words swam on the page—chapter titles, paragraphs, dialogue—but none of it stuck no matter how much I tried.

My hand found its way to my belly again. It had become a habit, this unconscious tether between me and the little life growing inside of me. I rested my palm there, hoping for some kind of reassurance.

The dull and persistent pain hadn't gone away. I'd felt it on and off for the past few days, but that morning, it lingered. A quiet whisper in the back of my mind.

I should've told Cade more. He'd seen it anyway; I could tell by the way his brow furrowed as he buttered the toast, by the way he hovered in the doorway like he wanted to fix something he couldn't name.

But I couldn't say it out loud.

Because if I said it, then it became real.

And I wasn't ready for that.

I closed the book and laid it on the coffee table. The house felt too still without him in it. Funny how quickly a space could feel warm when someone was near, then hollow as soon as they left.

This place had become familiar again. Home, even. But it still didn't feel like *mine*. Not in the way it probably should have.

And maybe that was part of what made everything harder.

I wanted to remember what it felt like to belong there. I wanted to reach back into the haze of my mind and find solid ground: wedding vows, morning kisses, and late-night talks in bed. I wanted to recall those early flutterings of our baby's kicks, Cade's hand gently finding mine in the dark, his whisper against my hair, and the act of giving life to our baby. Yet all I had were flashes. Half-moments. And this weight in my body that I didn't always know how to carry.

The baby shifted beneath my palm, just a little nudge, but enough to make my breath hitch.

"I'm okay," I whispered, as much to myself as to them. "I'm okay." But I wasn't.

The thought made my throat tighten.

I stood slowly and padded into the bathroom. The light flickered a moment before warming the room, and I leaned over the sink, catching my reflection in the mirror.

My skin looked pale, my eyes shadowed. My hair had been twisted into a messy bun that had slipped sometime during the night.

"You're fine," I said to my reflection. Even my eyes didn't believe me. I stepped back, pressing a hand to the small of my back where the ache had started to spread. Something low and tight. It wasn't constant, but it was there.

Maybe it's normal, I told myself. *Round ligament pain. Growing pains. Nothing to worry about.*

But the truth was, I didn't know. I didn't remember what it was supposed to feel like. I couldn't rely on instincts I didn't trust anymore.

I rinsed my face with cold water, trying to shake the unease. Cade would be back in a couple of hours. I'd rest until then. Try to stay calm. Maybe call the doctor if it got worse.

I decided that it would be best to stretch out, so I climbed into bed in his room. Our room. A place that smelled like cedarwood and laundry detergent. A faint trace of him clung to the pillow beside mine. The covers were still messy from our early morning, his side left untouched.

I curled up on my left side and exhaled slowly, hand finding my belly again. The ache hadn't gone away. I reached for Cade's pillow, brought it closer to me, and cuddled it against my body, breathing in the lingering scent.

It hadn't gotten worse, but beneath it, something else started to rise.

Pressure. Just enough to steal my breath.

I closed my eyes, and I waited.

CHAPTER 37

Cade

By the time I pulled into the driveway, the sky had shifted from soft morning gray to the bleached light of early afternoon. My truck kicked up a puff of dust as I turned into the driveway and caught a corner of dirt and grass in our yard.

The house looked the same as I'd left it, but something in me tightened. A feeling I couldn't shake, like the hum of a storm too far off to hear but close enough to sense in your bones.

I grabbed the bag of groceries off the passenger seat. Megan hadn't asked for anything specific, but something told me she might need the soup, crackers, and ginger ale.

Inside, it was the kind of quiet and still that made the hair on the back of my neck stand up. I set the bag on the counter. I tried not to let my voice sound too eager or too worried. "Megan?"

No answer.

I dropped my keys into the ceramic dish by the fridge and moved toward the hallway, listening. Our bedroom door was closed. I rapped my knuckles softly against the wood. "Hey, sweetheart. I'm back."

There was a pause before I heard the rustle of sheets, and then her voice, low and a little too calm. "Come in."

I opened the door and found her sitting up in bed, back against the headboard, one hand on her belly, the other gripping the blanket like it was holding her together. And there it was, that tightness in my chest, snapping into clarity.

Something wasn't right.

"You okay?" I asked, crossing the room and crouching at her side.

She nodded, but I wasn't convinced. "I-I don't know."

I sat on the edge of the bed and reached for her hand. "Talk to me."

Megan's eyes met mine, and she explained all that she was feeling. She didn't hold back; she went through her list of concerns, and now they weren't only hers. They were mine, too.

I rubbed her hand between mine, trying to stay calm, measured. "Have you called Dr. Langston?"

Her eyes flicked down. "Not yet. I didn't want to make a big deal out of it if it was nothing."

Those words made my stomach twist. "Megan, this isn't nothing. You're halfway through your pregnancy, and you've been having symptoms for days."

"I know," she whispered. "I know I should've told you sooner. I just . . ."

Her voice cracked, and I could see it. Beneath the guilt and the exhaustion, I could see the real fear.

"I don't want anything to be wrong with the baby, Cade."

God, those words caused an ache in my chest. I gathered her into my arms, careful not to jostle her belly, and held her close. She melted into me like she'd been holding herself up all morning and just then gave in.

"We're going to figure it out," I murmured into her hair. "You're not doing this alone."

She nodded against my shoulder, her breath shuddering.

After a moment, she pulled back, and I saw the resolve rising like a tide behind the fear in her eyes.

"I think we should call."

"Yeah," I agreed. "Let's do that."

As she leaned over to grab her phone from the nightstand, her hands trembled slightly. I watched her fingers hover over the screen as she found the number, hit dial, and pressed it to her ear.

I didn't leave her side.

Dr. Langston's nurse picked up first. Megan gave her the rundown as calmly as she could. She handed me the phone when they asked for dates and details that I'd memorized—the week count, our last visit, her blood pressure then.

Eventually, they transferred us to Dr. Langston herself.

"Let's not panic," she said in that voice that always sounded like reassurance wrapped in intelligence. "But I'd like you both to come in now. We'll do a full workup, just to be safe."

We hung up, and Megan looked at me when I got up from the bed.

I wanted to stay strong for her; I didn't want to show how scared I was. I had been so close to losing her in the accident and felt blessed not only to have her but to have the baby, and I didn't want to lose them now. "I'll warm up the truck."

She nodded and brushed a hand through her hair, standing and wincing just a little as she straightened.

I was at her side in an instant. "Easy, baby. Let me help you."

She leaned into me, and I steadied her. I kept one hand on her lower back, even when she said she could do it herself. Sometimes love was quiet. It was a hand that wouldn't let go. A presence that stayed steady when everything else felt shaky.

In the truck, she went quiet again. I glanced over every few seconds, searching her face for clues. Her eyes were fixed on the road ahead, but she wasn't really seeing it. She seemed somewhere in her head, probably a thousand steps ahead of where we actually were.

"You're not alone in this." I felt like I'd said that so many times since she'd come home, but she needed the reminder.

Her eyes flicked to mine. "I know. I'm scared anyway."

I reached over and slid my hand into hers. "Me too."

We didn't talk much after that. The hospital was forty minutes away, and every minute felt like it stretched too long. I kept my eyes on the road, but my mind remained on those tiny kicks I'd felt under my palm those past few nights. The sound of her laugh just days ago when I tried to make her soup and accidentally added cinnamon instead of cumin. The way she looked at me when I said she felt like home.

We'd made it this far. I didn't care if the road ahead was long and uneven. I just needed her and that baby safe. As we pulled into the hospital lot and I parked, she reached for the door handle, then paused.

"Cade?"

"Yeah?"

"If something's wrong ..."

I looked over and met her eyes. "We'll face it together."

She nodded slowly. Then she got out of the truck, and I followed her inside, praying this was just a scare. But somewhere deep in my gut, I felt it. That uneasy tremor.

Like something was shifting under our feet. And we were running out of time.

CHAPTER 38

Megan

*T*he antiseptic scent of the hospital hit me hard. It was the first memory I had after the accident. Cade had been there beside me, just like he was then. His hand never left mine as we walked through the glass doors into the OB wing. The fluorescent lights buzzed overhead, too bright and far too harsh. Everything about the place felt clinical, sharp-edged. It was the kind of environment where news, good or bad, got handed out with plastic smiles and clipped voices. The last time we were there, the news had been good. I just had to hope that this visit would end with more of the same.

Even with a thought of positivity, I didn't want to be there.

Not for this. Not for something that might mean the baby wasn't okay.

Cade helped me into a chair in the waiting room, his hand warm on my lower back. Tension vibrated beneath his calm. I could feel mine, too, unraveling thread by thread with each second that ticked by.

He crouched beside me, close enough that I could see the flecks of green in his brown eyes. "You want some water?" he asked.

I shook my head. "No. Just . . . stay."

His lips twitched into a half-smile, and he nodded. "Always."

I didn't realize how badly I needed that one word until it left his mouth. I leaned back against the chair and closed my eyes, breathing in through my nose and out through my mouth like Dr. Langston had shown me at our last visit. The pressure in my pelvis had eased, but not entirely. It hovered, low and insistent.

I hated how aware I'd become of my body those last few days. Every twinge, every shift in balance. Every time the baby moved—or didn't—I catalogued it like it was a clue to a mystery I wasn't qualified to solve.

I opened my eyes when the nurse finally called my name.

Cade helped me to my feet, and we followed her down a hallway that seemed longer than it should've been. The walls were painted in soft colors, muted sage green and pale blue, as if serenity could be wallpapered on. But I wasn't calm. Not even close.

Once in the exam room, the nurse gave me a gown and asked me to change while she fetched Dr. Langston. Cade turned his back while I undressed. In some ways, I found that silly—he'd seen me naked before—though I appreciated the gesture. He'd been a perfect gentleman.

The gown felt scratchy, impersonal. Like wearing worry. I climbed onto the exam table, the crinkly paper loud beneath me. Cade sat in the chair beside it with his elbows on his knees and his hands clasped between them.

His eyes flicked to mine. "You okay?"

I didn't answer right away. I wanted to choose my words carefully. "I don't want them to tell me something's wrong," I whispered.

"They won't."

"But if they do?"

He stood and leaned in, pressing a soft kiss to my forehead. "Then we handle it. Together."

The word again. *Together.*

A knock on the door came a second later, and then Dr. Langston stepped in, her face composed, her smile gentle but not forced. She was good at the reassuring calm. I wondered if she taught a class on it in med school.

"Hey, Megan. Cade." She came to my side and glanced at the monitor. "Let's see what's going on."

The next few minutes passed in a blur of gel, pressure, and scrolling ultrasound images. Cade held my hand the entire time during the internal exam, and I was glad to feel him there to help through any discomfort. We watched the screen, hearts clenched, until we heard the words that sounded like magic.

"There's the baby," Dr. Langston said. "Heartbeat's strong."

I exhaled hard, my fingers gripping Cade's a little tighter. On the screen, our baby moved just a little, but enough to make something inside me unclench.

"But," she continued, her tone shifting into something more clinical, "your cervix is shorter than we'd like at this stage. Not alarmingly so, but definitely something to keep an eye on."

I blinked. "What does that mean?"

"It means you're at risk of preterm labor. Not immediately, but this kind of shortening can be an early indicator. We're going to monitor you closely from now on. More frequent check-ins, maybe a cerclage if we see more change. For now, I'm putting you on modified bed rest. Nothing strenuous, no lifting, no long walks. We want to keep pressure off that area."

Modified bed rest. The words echoed in my head, louder than they should've.

"How long?" Cade asked.

Dr. Langston smiled kindly. "Ideally? Until thirty-seven weeks."

"That's four months away," I said, the number sinking like a stone in my gut.

"I know." She touched my arm. "But it's for the best. You're doing great, Megan. And so is the baby. This is just a precaution to keep you both that way."

Cade squeezed my hand again. "We'll figure it out."

I finally looked at him then. He didn't flinch. Not once. Not at the timeline. Not at the implication that I'd be grounded for the rest of this pregnancy. His jaw was tight, but his eyes stayed steady. How could he stay so calm? This wasn't the only time he'd received striking news and remained so strong. It was amazing.

He was amazing.

With Dr. Langston's help, we formulated a brief plan of action and left the hospital. I was relieved to learn the baby was still okay, but on the ride home, I struggled to wrap my mind around bed rest and what that would mean for me.

Back at the house, I changed into soft pajamas and curled up on the sofa. Cade put together a tray of food, opting for small portions, just in case my stomach turned again. He moved around the kitchen like it was second nature, present and attentive like he'd always been.

That was the thing about Cade.

He showed up.

Even when everything felt like it might tip off the edge of the world.

When he came back into the room, he handed me a glass of ginger ale and sat down beside me, thigh warm against mine.

"Bed rest," I said, tasting the words again.

He leaned back, arm across the back of the sofa. "Guess that means I'm your chauffeur and butler for the foreseeable future."

I snorted. "That, or I learn to levitate."

He grinned. "Don't push it. I'll duct tape you to that recliner if I have to."

I laughed a little, then turned to him, quieter now. "I feel like my body is betraying me."

"It's not. You're growing a whole human, Meg. That's a miracle, not a failure."

"But I don't even remember how we got here. Our life. This baby. You and me. And now this? I can't even walk around the block without risking something going wrong."

He reached for my hand and pulled it into his lap. "You're remembering a little more every day. And when this baby gets here—"

"When?" I interrupted.

He met my eyes, sure and steady. "*When.*" He overemphasized. "Not if. When."

I nodded, tears pricking the corners of my eyes. I didn't want to cry, but it felt like something had been shaken loose that day. This reminder that even when things looked okay, they could shift beneath me.

Cade had brought in the book I'd left sitting by the nightstand, and I dozed in his arms as he read aloud, his voice slow and deep and full of patience. He wasn't just giving me space to heal. He was *staying* in it with me, and I loved it. I loved Cade Emmett Steele. My mind hadn't caught up with everything yet, but my heart had.

CHAPTER 39

There's something about silence after bad news. It doesn't roar like you'd expect. It settles, slow and dense, like morning fog over the back pasture. That's how it felt in the house the next morning.

The scent of coffee drifted through the kitchen as I stood at the sink, watching the light stretch through the blinds. I hadn't slept much. Neither had she. Megan had curled into my side sometime in the middle of the night, and I'd stayed awake listening to her breathing, trying to memorize the sound of it. It made me feel like things were still okay, like the world hadn't tilted yesterday.

But it had.

Modified bed rest.

Two words I couldn't stop turning over in my mind.

I'd done emergency fire rescues with less adrenaline than I'd felt sitting in that OB room. Every instinct in me had wanted to take control, to fix it, solve it, *do* something, but this wasn't a broken fence or a calf stuck in the creek. This was Megan. This was our baby. And I couldn't cowboy my way through it.

Something shuffled behind me, the sound soft, like slippered feet. I turned in time to see her standing in the hallway, wrapped in that old cardigan she liked and one of my flannel shirts hanging nearly to her knees.

"You should've let me help get you up," I said, setting my mug down and moving toward her.

She shrugged and brushed a few curls out of her eyes. "I needed to move a little. Just to prove I still can."

I didn't argue. I just reached for her hand and led her to the table.

She lowered herself into a chair like she'd aged twenty years overnight. It wasn't the pregnancy slowing her down. It was the uncertainty, and I hated it. Hated seeing her second-guess every step. Hated the way she looked at her body like it was the enemy now.

"I made eggs," I said, sliding a plate in front of her. "Not fancy, but edible."

"Pretty sure anything you cook is edible. You've got that 'man who feeds cattle at sunrise' energy."

"Damn right," I said, and it earned a small laugh.

I sat across from her and watched her pick at her food. She hadn't been eating much lately, which worried me too. But I didn't push. Not yet.

After a few quiet minutes, she looked up. "I feel like I should be doing something. Nesting or prepping. But all I'm allowed to do now is sit."

"You're *growing* a human. That's not nothing."

She looked down at her hands. "It doesn't feel like enough. Not after everything."

I reached across the table and took her fingers in mine. "You don't have to prove anything, Meg. Not to me. Not to this baby. You're doing your best, and that's more than enough."

Her eyes welled with tears she didn't let fall. "It just scares me, Cade. How easily things can go wrong. What if we lose the baby? What if I mess this up?"

"You won't," I said without hesitation. "We won't."

"But we already—"

"No." I squeezed her hand. "We didn't lose anything yet. And we're not going to. We're going to follow every instruction they give us. You're going to rest. I'll handle the house, the errands, everything. And if it gets hard, we talk. If you're scared, you tell me. We'll shoulder it all together, no matter what."

She looked at me for a long time, like she was trying to memorize my face.

"Okay," she whispered. "Together."

The word settled into my chest like an anchor. I stood up, came around the table, and kneeled beside her, pressing my forehead to her belly. "Hey little one," I murmured. "You hang in there for us, all right? Your momma's already doing more than most folks ever could."

Megan threaded her fingers through my hair. Her breath caught, and I thought maybe she'd remembered something. But she didn't say anything, and I didn't ask. Instead, she leaned in and pressed her mouth to mine, soft at first, then deeper, like she'd been waiting for this. Like we both had.

It caught me off guard, the way her lips moved against mine and how her hand tightened in my hair to keep me close. Every ounce of longing I'd been holding back cracked wide open.

It wasn't just a kiss. It was a moment that made my knees go weak, the kind that pulled every memory we'd ever made straight into the center of my chest. I could feel the tremble in her fingers, the quick hitch of her breath. And God, I kissed her back like she was the only thing tethering me to the ground.

When we finally broke apart, we were both breathing hard, foreheads pressed together. I didn't care that my heart was pounding like I'd run ten miles. I'd take this feeling, this tiny, blazing piece of us, over steady ground any day.

I stayed right there with her for a while, her head tucked

under my chin, my thumb tracing slow circles on her back. We didn't say much. We didn't need to.

After a bit, I convinced her that she needed to eat. It wasn't only for her; it was for the baby, and that made a huge difference. She agreed even though she teased me a bit for fussing over her, which I didn't care about as long as she ate.

When the plates were cleared, I settled her on the recliner by the window, tucked a soft blanket around her shoulders, and set her up with a book and a tall glass of lemon water. She gave me that sleepy, grateful smile that always made my chest ache in the best way.

With her settled, I stepped onto the porch to call Jackson.

He picked up on the second ring. "Hey, everything all right?"

"Yeah, we're okay. Just . . . had the follow-up. Doc says she's on modified bed rest now. Cervix is too short."

Jackson whistled low. "That's early." Having had a child himself, he was familiar with all of this, even though this wasn't a situation he'd found himself directly in.

"Yeah. That's what's got me worried."

"You want us to come help around the house? We can get some meals prepped, finish painting the baby room, or anything else you need. With the seven of us working together, plus Momma and Pop in addition, we'd get a whole lot done in a little bit of time."

I smiled despite the knot in my stomach. "That'd be great. Megan's feeling pretty helpless. I think she needs to see things happening around her. Needs to feel supported."

"She's got that with us, her family, and she's got you."

"Yeah." I exhaled. "But I can't fix this with duct tape and hard work. It's just waiting. That's the hardest part."

We talked a little more, mostly logistics, and then I hung up and let the phone drop to my side, my eyes on the quiet stretch of driveway.

I couldn't stop replaying that kiss. The way she'd tugged me down like she couldn't stand another inch of space between us and how her mouth had found mine like it used to. It still buzzed through me, a live wire, sparking hope right through my ribs.

It felt normal. Or close to it. Maybe better than normal, because I knew just how hard we'd fought to get there. And yet . . . beneath that sweetness, a thread of worry tugged at the edges of my chest. The way she'd gone pale that morning. The way her eyes sometimes drifted off like she was searching for a piece of herself she still couldn't find.

I wanted to protect her from every crack in the road ahead, wrap her up in my arms and promise her nothing bad would ever touch her again. But love didn't work like that. It was messier, deeper. It was standing right there, taking every fear on my shoulders if it meant she'd breathe easier.

God, I loved that woman. I loved her enough that some days it scared the hell out of me.

I blew out a breath, scrubbed a hand over my face, and squared my shoulders before stepping back inside. She needed calm, not my restless mind pacing circles around her. And I'd do anything to give her that.

When I stepped back inside, Megan had drifted off, her book folded on her chest, her mouth just slightly parted in sleep. I kneeled beside her and brushed a strand of her beautiful blonde hair from her face.

I'd never let her fall alone again.

This time, I'd catch her.

Every damn time.

CHAPTER 40

Megan

The morning sun filtered through the blinds in soft gold streaks, warming the tops of my bare legs where Cade's oversized flannel shirt didn't quite reach. I lay still, tucked into the recliner like it had been shaped just for me. The soft clink of dishes being put away drifted in from the kitchen, and I imagined Cade moving quietly, trying not to wake me.

But I'd been awake. For a while.

The previous day's appointment had stolen more than peace of mind. It had taken the illusion that I could power through this. That if I just did the right things, ate the right food, thought the right thoughts, this pregnancy would go smoothly.

But it wasn't smooth. I was on modified bed rest. The words had looped endlessly in my head like a skipping record. No stairs. No lifting. No stress.

Right. Because I had so much control over any of that.

I blinked slowly, trying to force away the sting in my eyes. I didn't want Cade to see me cry. Again. I'd already cried the previous night, and it had wrecked him a little. He hid it well, but I could see the tightness in his jaw and the way his hands had trembled when he'd helped me out of the car.

He was trying so hard to carry this for both of us.

Maybe that was the worst part. I didn't want to be carried.

I wanted to carry *myself* and the baby. But instead, I was lying like porcelain on a shelf while he scrambled to hold it all together.

The recliner creaked gently as I shifted and pushed the blanket off my lap. Cade glanced over from the kitchen when he heard me stir.

"You need something?" he asked, wiping his hands on a dish towel.

I shook my head. "Just wanted to stretch. I'm fine."

He didn't buy it. I could tell from the way his brows dipped. But he didn't push.

He came over anyway, kneeling beside the recliner like he had the night before, his eyes searching mine. "I can move the recliner over to the window if you want more sun. Or closer to the TV if you're bored."

"I'm okay," I whispered. "You don't have to fix everything."

He smiled, but it didn't reach his eyes. "It's kind of my thing, though."

"I know."

I reached out and let my fingertips drift along the strong line of his jaw and the soft, scratchy warmth of his beard. God, he felt so solid under my touch, so steady, so heartbreakingly familiar. It was impossible to ignore the way the muscle flexed under my palm, the warmth of his skin, the quiet strength there. This man, my man, strong enough to fix anything, carry anything, but gentle enough to hold me like I was the most precious thing he'd ever touched. Even if I couldn't remember every piece of our life, I knew that much: he was mine. And I was his.

"But this isn't a broken fence or a busted tractor." My voice was softer now. My thumb brushed along the edge of his beard, wanting him to feel just how much I believed that and how much I needed him, just like this.

"No, it's a hell of a lot more important," he said. His hand found mine and held it tight. "I just hate seeing you like this. You're not meant to be still."

"You sound like you've known me forever."

"I have." He smiled in return, and I felt my heart skip a beat.

There it was again—that bittersweet feeling, that echo of something I *almost* remembered. It sat just out of reach, like a word stuck on the tip of my tongue or a dream I lost as soon as I woke up.

"Tell me something," I said softly. "Something about . . . us. Something small."

He hesitated, and then his thumb began to trace slow circles on the back of my hand. "You used to steal my hoodies," he said. "Said they smelled like the ranch and sunshine. You'd wear them with pajama shorts and something from that ridiculous sock collection you have."

I laughed, surprised by the instant joy Cade gave me. "That sounds like something I would do even now."

"You had one pair with tiny cows on them. Moo print. Wore 'em every time you stayed over. Drove me crazy in the best way."

I blinked fast. "Why?"

He leaned in, his smile a little crooked. "Because I'd be trying really hard to be a gentleman, and you'd be curled up on my sofa in those socks and my hoodie, looking like home."

Looking like home. The words echoed in my chest. My throat tightened.

I *wanted* to remember. I wanted it so badly it hurt.

"I'm sorry," I said, voice cracking. "I'm trying so hard. I want to give this baby everything. I want to give *you* everything."

"You are," he said firmly. "You being here, fighting through this. That's everything to me, Megan."

His lips brushed my forehead and lingered there, and I let my eyes close.

LATER THAT AFTERNOON, after he'd settled me in the bedroom with water, my prenatal vitamins, and a fresh set of sheets, I turned onto my side and let my hand settle over my belly.

"You've got a good daddy," I whispered. "The best. And I promise I'm gonna be better for you."

I didn't know what the next few weeks would look like or how many pieces of myself I'd still have to find along the way. But I knew this: I wasn't in it alone. Not for a single breath. Even on the days when my mind felt like a half-finished puzzle, my heart was whole because every kick from this tiny life inside me made my love swell in ways I couldn't put words to. I hadn't met this baby yet, but I loved them fiercely. Unconditionally.

And Cade . . . God, each day with him, each gentle touch, each stolen kiss, was like falling in love for the first time and remembering how to breathe all at once. My love for him was growing louder, stronger, breaking through the fog and stitching the broken pieces back together. Maybe that was the beginning. The start of it all coming back, not because I was forcing it, but because love this deep, this true, doesn't just disappear. Not even when everything else tries to.

CHAPTER 41

Megan

I had reached thirty weeks. The days melted into each other—slow, careful stretches of time filled with modified bed rest, Cade's gentle reminders to take it easy, his brothers dropping off groceries, and his momma fussing over baby blankets. I never thought I'd come to crave the hush of that house, but I did. There was a sweetness to the quiet moments. A stillness I didn't know my heart needed.

I still wasn't wild about being told to stay put, but I was adjusting. The cramping had all but faded, and every soft flutter of the baby's foot against my ribs reminded me that resting was working. I was keeping this tiny piece of us safe.

That morning, Cade sat on the floor near the foot of our bed, sorting a pile of tiny onesies by color. I was propped against a mound of pillows, sipping iced water, my belly rounding out beneath one of his old T-shirts I'd claimed for myself.

"You know," he said, holding up a mint-green sleeper with tiny white horses on it, "I think Jackson got this one just so you'd say yes to horses for the baby someday."

I burst out laughing, the sound bouncing off the walls like a new memory. "It's working. I think that's a keeper."

He grinned and tossed the sleeper onto the Keep pile. Then he looked at me like he was trying to commit me to memory. I wondered if he knew I was doing the same. The way his hair curled at the ends when he skipped his haircut for too long. The faint tan line around his wrist where his watch usually sat. The way his eyes softened every time they drifted down to my belly, like he could see our future taking shape right beneath my ribs.

Maybe looking toward the future was the best call. Despite the time and many reminders, I still hadn't regained most of my memories. I still grieved those lost parts of myself and wondered if they'd ever return.

"You've been quiet," he said, voice low, gentle. "What's spinning in there?"

I toyed with the hem of the shirt. "Just thinking about how different it all feels. A few weeks ago, I felt trapped in this house. Now it feels like . . ." I paused, searching for the words.

He crawled up beside me on the bed and pressed his palm to my bump. His fingers splayed wide, warm, and steady. The baby shifted beneath his touch, almost like it knew him. "This house," he said, "this family . . . we're yours. We always will be. And you don't have to remember every bit of it for it to be true."

I closed my eyes for a moment, letting that sink in.

When I opened them again, I caught him studying me, that same quiet reverence on his face that undid me every time. He brushed his thumb over my knuckles and leaned in to kiss my temple.

"Cade . . ." I started, then paused, my heart beating so hard it almost hurt. "Can I ask you something?"

"Anything."

I shifted, pressing his palm a little firmer against my stomach. I needed his warmth to ground me. "How did we meet? The first time, I mean. Before all of this. Before the wedding, the ranch, the baby. Just . . . us."

His eyes softened, and that half-smile tugged at his lips like the memory lived right at the edge of his heart.

"High school football game," he said. "I was this hotshot wide receiver trying to look tough in front of my buddies. You were out there in that blue-and-gold cheer uniform, hair tied back, shouting chants like your life depended on it. God, Meg . . . I swear, the first time I saw you jumping up and down on that sideline, I thought I'd lost my damn mind."

I let out a small, breathless laugh. "You did?"

He nodded. His hand cupped my jaw, thumb tracing the curve of my cheek. "Yeah. I don't think I even cared about the game after that. Just kept looking over, praying we'd win so you'd be smiling when it was done."

I swallowed the sudden lump in my throat. "And then?"

"A mutual friend dragged me to Fran's diner after the game. You were sitting in a corner booth, eating fries and laughing at something dumb your friend said. I sat down across from you, and you gave me this shy smile like I was someone worth knowing."

I blinked, my vision blurring with tears I didn't try to stop. "You've always seen me that way, haven't you?"

He smiled, his thumb brushing away a tear before it could fall. "Always, darlin'. Even when you couldn't see it for yourself."

Something swelled so big in my chest I didn't have words for it. Just the heat and the ache and the hope that maybe, somehow, we were finding each other again in that quiet room.

He must have felt the same way I did, because his mouth found mine. He kissed me, not rushed or hungry, but patient and full of every unspoken vow we'd laid between those four walls. My hands slid into his hair, and for once, I didn't feel fragile. I felt wanted. Whole.

When we finally broke apart, we were breathing harder than

we had been a moment ago. Cade didn't move far. He stayed so close that his breath fanned warm against my lips, his thumb tracing lazy circles on my jaw like he couldn't stand not touching me.

He grinned and brushed his nose against mine, his voice low and rough with something that curled through my belly. "You keep that up, Mrs. Steele, and this bed rest is gonna be the best thing we've ever survived."

He swallowed my soft, breathless laughter with another kiss. This one was deeper. Unhurried. His hand slid down to rest at the curve of my hip, fingertips pressing just hard enough to remind me that I was his, that I'd always been his, memory or not.

I made a soft sound into his mouth. My fingers fisted his T-shirt as I wished I could pull him closer, all of him, every heartbeat and promise. "Cade . . ." I whispered when he finally dragged his lips to my jaw, planting soft, open-mouthed kisses beneath my ear. My skin tingled under his mouth, every nerve ending coming awake for him.

He laughed, that low, husky sound that always made my heart flutter. "God, baby, you have no idea how much I've missed this." His teeth grazed my earlobe, making me gasp. "Months. You know that? Months of being the good husband. And you here, looking at me like that . . ." His hand slipped under the hem of my shirt, palm hot on my bare skin. "It's gonna kill me."

My breath hitched. I was half laughing, half drowning in the feeling of him. The weight of his hand, the press of his chest against mine. I pulled back just enough to see his dark eyes full of that impossible tenderness that made my heart twist in the best way.

"Good thing you're strong, Mr. Steele," I teased, and brushed my lips across his again. "I need you to hold out a little longer."

He groaned, dropping his forehead to mine, and his thumb

stroked slow circles on the sensitive skin of my belly. "You're cruel," he murmured, but he smiled, his eyes warm with that fierce devotion that felt like home. "But for you, I'd wait forever."

"You won't have to. Because I'm falling in love with you, Cade Steele. All over again."

His chest rumbled with a soft laugh, but his eyes glistened when he whispered back, "Then I'm the luckiest man alive. Twice."

He kissed me again, slowly, reverently, like he was memorizing every breath, every sigh, every heartbeat tangled up between us. His hand drifted back to my belly, cradling the curve of our baby between us like it was the truest thing he'd ever held.

And in that quiet, wrapped up in his warmth, I knew that when the world spun too fast again, I'd look back at those slow, careful days and remember exactly how love made them shine.

CHAPTER 42

*T*stood in the nursery's doorway. My hand braced against the frame like I needed to steady myself before I let her see it. Maybe I did. Hell, maybe this whole thing was as much for me as it was for her.

She'd had a voice in the things she wanted, but between me, Pop, and my brothers, we were her hands, her feet, and the strength that tied together everything she couldn't. Even though Megan had said what she wanted and picked out items from online inventories, she hadn't been able to see it all together in the room in which our child would sleep. I was excited for her to see it.

She shuffled behind me down the hallway, wearing those soft slipper socks that made her steps sound like a secret.

"Cade? What's all this?" Megan's voice floated closer, warm and curious.

I turned in time to see her leaning against the wall, her hair pulled into one of those loose buns she did without thinking. She wore leggings and an oversized sweater. The outfit made her look small but somehow stronger too, like the world couldn't quite touch her when she wrapped herself up like that.

It was one of the outfits she'd recently picked up while "shopping" with her momma. Since she'd been on modified bed rest, we'd found more creative ways to do things. For example, the shopping trip was both of them on the sofa, clicking through options on the computer screen. They might have preferred to go to the store, but we had to do things differently.

I held my hand out to her. "Come here. Close your eyes."

She gave me a look filled with amusement and suspicion. "Why?"

"Trust me."

She rolled her eyes, but her lips curved into that soft smile that still hit me square in the chest every time. She slipped her hand into mine, and I guided her the last few steps. The warmth of her skin, soft against my rough palm, would never be taken for granted again.

"Okay, ready?" I asked, my mouth brushing against her temple.

She nodded, lashes fanning out against her cheeks. "Show me."

I pushed open the door. The daylight rays spilled across the wood floor, catching on the fresh paint and the crib I'd wrestled with putting together. Jackson checked it four times before he declared it safe and ready for the baby to sleep in.

Megan had wanted some history tied into the room, something that was generational, so there came the rocking chair in the corner; we got it from Momma. I was surprised she still had it. It was the same chair she'd sat in and rocked me, Jackson, Spencer, Alden, Graham, Braxton, and Dallas. It probably lasted because Daddy made it, and anything he made would stand the test of time.

Then there were the new frames that lined the far wall—a photo of us the day we signed the papers for this house; a blurry Polaroid of her laughing in the back pasture; an image from our wedding day with our bridal party. Megan told me that since she'd come from the hospital, she'd been unable to tear her eyes away from it. Every time she went into the living room, she would spot it and focus on it. I think it grounded her. She had requested that we put it in the room, and I happily obliged.

"Okay, open."

She blinked her eyes open, and for a second, she just stood there. Silent. Her hand fell away from mine and rose to her mouth. I swear my heart stopped beating as I waited for her to say something.

"Cade . . ." As she walked forward, her fingers brushed the edge of the crib rail. "You did all this?"

I shrugged, rubbing the back of my neck. "Well, I had a lot of help. My whole family stepped in, and they took over when I nearly dropped the dresser on my foot." A small chuckle left my lips. "But, yeah. I wanted you to see it finished. Not just drywall and paint samples anymore. Our baby's room."

She turned to face me then, and there it was, that light in her eyes that told me this wasn't just about paint or furniture. It was about the way she was letting me in again. Letting *us* in.

"It's beautiful," she said, her voice cracking on the last word. "It feels . . . warm. Like it's always been waiting for us."

I swallowed hard, my throat tight with so many things I didn't know how to say. I stepped up behind her and wrapped my arms around her middle, resting my hands on her belly. She leaned back against me, and her warmth settled right into my bones.

"Worth the wait?" I asked quietly, pressing my nose to her hair.

She nodded. "More than worth it. I love it so much."

We stood there like that for a while, just swaying a little, like we were listening for the ghost of a lullaby that hadn't been sung yet. I didn't want to move; my whole world was right there under my hand. I loved how she looked around and took everything in, and she would gasp every so often when she noticed something new. She reveled when she spotted something she'd asked for nestled somewhere inside the space. It made me happy just to listen to her reactions.

"You ever think about finding out?" she asked after a moment.

"What?"

"The baby's gender." She tipped her head back to look up at me, eyes soft but searching. "Do you want to know?"

I let out a small laugh. "Part of me does. But part of me thinks we've waited this long for so much else. Maybe we can wait for this, too."

She made a thoughtful noise. "So . . . no guess?"

I grinned and kissed her temple. "No guesses. I'll be happy with whatever we have. Though, if it's a girl, she'll be as beautiful as her momma. That's all I know. And if it's a boy, I hope he'll know how important it is to protect the ones you love."

She turned in my arms then, her hands curling into the front of my shirt the way they used to when we'd danced in that hallway before we knew how to be grown-ups together. "What about names?"

I swallowed, brushing my thumb across her cheekbone. "Well, we didn't really talk too much about this before the accident, but a few names did cross my mind. I still like Elijah for a boy, or maybe Nathaniel, your grandaddy's name. If it's a girl, you liked Grace or Lila because you thought those names were pretty."

She nodded, mulling it over. "I do like them both. If I had to choose one, I'd go with Lila because it's not as common. There are a million girls in the world with the name Grace, either as a first name or middle."

We laughed together. "Yeah, you're probably right." I tucked a piece of hair behind her ear, memorizing every line of her face like I hadn't done it a thousand times already. "Whatever name we choose, they're gonna know how loved they are. By both of us."

She turned away just enough to look around the room again. Her hand drifted to the wall. Her eyes glazed for half a second, and then she blinked hard.

"What is it?" I asked, worry immediately tightening in my chest.

"I . . . I think I remember this," she said. "Us. Here. You holding a paintbrush, and me laughing because you got white on your nose. It's just a flash, but I see it."

I swear something broke open in my torso, something light and wild. I pulled her close, pressing my forehead to hers. "That's right. Great memory," I murmured. "Best paint job I've ever done. When we moved here, this room was a putrid yellow. Even though we knew we would use it for a child down the line, we didn't want to leave it that way, so we decided to paint it white to go with a clean slate."

She let out a breathy laugh, and her belly moved under my palm—a little kick, like the baby wanted to remind us they were there, too. Ours. Not that we would ever forget, and now with Megan beginning to remember more and more, it was even more exciting to become a family of three. A family of three that could not only pick up where we left off before we diverted down this road, but one that could navigate the potholes and end up right where we needed to be. It might take some time, but we were getting there

CHAPTER 43

Megan

J sat curled up in the old rocking chair, legs tucked under me, Cade's flannel shirt draped over my shoulders like a borrowed piece of him. It still smelled faintly of sawdust and soap—a warm, safe scent that somehow felt older than my missing memories.

Cade crouched near the dresser, fiddling with one of the stubborn drawers that never wanted to slide just right. He'd been at it for twenty minutes, muttering under his breath, pausing now and then to glance over at me, checking, always checking, like he was scared I might vanish if he looked away too long.

Part of me ached for that. Not the fear, but the depth of that care. How could someone love me so thoroughly when I was still half a stranger to myself?

I shifted in the chair and pressed my palm to my belly as our baby kicked gently, then a little stronger. It was a reminder that life kept moving forward, even when my mind wanted to stay stuck in the fog.

"You okay over there?" Cade asked, twisting the screwdriver with a grunt.

I smiled. "Yeah. Just resting."

He shot me a quick, crooked grin. "You sure you don't want to trade places? I could rock in that chair, and you could fight with this drawer."

"No, thank you." I let out a quiet laugh. "You look too handsome in your natural habitat, grumbling at furniture."

He snorted, but his ears went a little pink. I loved that this big, steady man could still blush around me like we were seventeen-year-olds sneaking behind the bleachers.

My eyelids fluttered. The rhythmic squeak of the rocking chair. Cade's low muttering. The warmth of the Texas sunshine on my cheek.

I felt myself drifting.

And then, like someone pulled a sheet off an old picture, it came rushing in.

It wasn't a grand moment. Not a wedding kiss or a baby announcement. It was something simple. Ordinary. So real it made my chest hurt.

I saw myself in a different chair, the one in the corner of our tiny kitchen, the night we moved in. There were boxes everywhere. None of the lights had shades yet, but we didn't care. Cade had plugged in an old boombox on the counter, one I was surprised he still had. He'd turned the dial until the static cleared, and some old country song filled the space.

I was barefoot, standing by the sink. He'd come up behind me, slid his arms around my waist, and spun me around before I could protest. I'd laughed. God, I could almost hear it now, and he'd pressed his forehead to mine, swaying us side to side like we had all the time in the world.

"You know I'm not the best dancer," I'd whispered.

He'd smiled, that crooked grin I loved even before I knew I loved him. "Doesn't matter. You just gotta hold on."

I twitched awake, causing the chair to creak under me as I rubbed my eyes with the back of my hand.

"Meg?" Cade said, closer now. He abandoned the drawer and kneeled in front of me, eyes wide and worried. "Hey, hey. What's wrong? Are you hurting? Is it the baby?"

I shook my head quickly, voice trembling as I said, "No, no. We're fine. I'm fine. It's not that."

I cupped his face in my palms, enjoying the scratch of his beard and the warmth of his skin under my fingertips. I wanted to fall into his arms and stay there forever.

"I remembered something," I whispered.

His brow furrowed, but hope bloomed in his eyes. "Tell me."

"It was the first night here. The old house, before we did anything to it. We had boxes everywhere, and you turned on an old boombox and made me dance with you in the kitchen. I said I wasn't the best dancer, and you told me it didn't matter, that I just had to hold on."

My chest tightened when I saw the way his eyes shone. I'd given him something, a piece of our story that had been lost to both of us for too long.

"Yeah," he murmured, his voice rough with feeling. "Yeah, baby. That happened. You wore a too-cute-for-moving type of outfit, and your feet were freezing 'cause we hadn't figured out the heater yet."

I laughed, swiping at another tear. "Why do I remember that? Of all the things . . ."

"Because it mattered." He rested his forehead against my belly, his hands braced on either side of the chair, grounding both of us. "Because maybe those small moments are the ones that stick when everything else goes dark."

I threaded my fingers through his dark hair, letting my nails graze his scalp the way I knew he liked. "Every day, Cade. It feels like another piece coming back. Like my heart's putting itself back together. For you. For us."

He lifted his head, eyes blazing with a love so big it almost undid me all over again. "I'd wait forever for every piece, Meg. You know that, right?"

I nodded. "What if I never remember it all? I love getting glimpses, and it feels good, but what if that's all that comes back?"

His hands slowly stroked my thighs, directionally going from him to me.

"If the old memories come back, great. But if they don't, this life, right now? It's still ours."

He was such a good man, but I didn't want to settle for only remembering parts. I wanted to remember more of the good life we'd had before everything happened.

He kissed my knee, then stood and leaned over me, pressing his lips to mine. The kiss was slow, unhurried. The kind of kiss that said, *I'm here and I'm yours, no matter how many times we have to find our way back.*

When we parted, I rested my head against the chair as his hand settled over our baby again. The last bit of sunlight slipped through the window, lighting up the frames on the wall. We were messy, imperfect, but holding on.

"I think I'm ready to remember the rest," I whispered. I said that more to myself than to Cade.

Cade just smiled and brushed his thumb along my jaw.

"Then we'll remember it all," he said. "Together."

And in that nursery, wrapped up in the past and the promise of everything ahead, I felt it: I was home.

CHAPTER 44

*I*t'd been just over a week since the nursery reveal. A week of slow mornings, warm meals on trays balanced across Megan's lap, and more than a few restless nights spent watching her breathe, just to make sure she was okay. Modified bed rest wasn't her idea of fun; hell, it wasn't mine either, but we were making it work. Together.

Still, I could tell she was itching to see something besides our bedroom ceiling and the living room walls. So, when Dr. Langston gave her the green light for a short outing, you'd think I'd suggested a cross-country vacation from the way her eyes lit up.

We pulled up the long dirt drive to the ranch in the old pickup she always called a "creaky dinosaur" but loved anyway. The sun was just starting its late summer slide, turning the edges of the fields gold where the grass brushed against the fence line. There was a hint of early fall in the breeze, too, bringing with it that crisp promise of cooler nights and harvest season just around the bend.

I cut the engine and glanced at Megan in the passenger seat. She'd dressed up for this—khaki-colored jeans that hugged her hips, a loose floral top, her hair in that easy braid that made her look about fifteen years younger than the weight she'd been carrying those last few months. Her eyes danced, brighter than I'd seen them in days.

Then she tried to open the door and grunted. "I swear, this truck gets taller every week," she complained, peering down at the ground like it was a mile away.

"I told you I'd get you that little step stool."

"Oh, right, so I can look extra graceful," she teased, but she took my hand anyway. "Help me down?"

I braced her with both hands as she swung her feet out, my palms warm on her hips. I could feel the baby between us, her belly firm and round. She laughed when she hit the ground with a soft thud and her shoes stirred up a little cloud of dust.

"Smooth landing," I teased, brushing my thumb across the sliver of skin just above her waistband.

She swatted at me, but the sparkle in her eyes made my chest ache. That easy, teasing grin that told me she'd forgotten about bed rest and worry and what we'd nearly lost.

I threaded our fingers together, and we made our way around the side of the barn. A few of the cattle stood along the fence line, flicking flies off their hides with lazy tails. The old windmill creaked overhead. The sound was so familiar it felt like its own heartbeat out there. Home.

"God, I've missed this place," Megan murmured, leaning her head on my shoulder as we walked. "It smells the same. Warm hay and . . . horse sweat."

I chuckled. "You know how to flatter a rancher."

She elbowed me lightly, and I swear I felt something settle in my ribs. The universe had given me a few moments where everything was just simple—her, me, this baby, and the land that'd raised me.

I spotted Jackson standing near the chicken coop, arguing with the latch like it had offended him personally. Paige Lieber, his fiancée, stood a few feet away, arms crossed over her chest, her long red hair blowing around her shoulders like wildfire. She caught sight of us first, and her whole face lit up.

"Well, look who's here. It's so good to see you both out!" Paige called, walking over with her easy, sunshine grin.

Megan squeezed my hand, then let go when Paige stepped in and wrapped her up in a hug. I loved watching the two of them together, the way they just *fit*. Paige and Jackson had come by just a few days after Megan moved back home. Ever since the two of them met (both times), they'd gotten along so well. We Steele brothers didn't have any sisters by blood, so anytime a woman entered the fold, whether by birth or by marriage, she earned the title we came up with years ago: *Chosen Sister.* Paige and Megan wore that well.

I watched Megan's shoulders drop a fraction, the tight line of worry easing in a way it didn't always ease with me. Paige had that gift. Maybe it came from wrangling thirty little first-graders every day, making each of them feel safe and special. Or maybe that was just who she was at her core—someone who turned strangers into family without even trying. And for Megan, a woman still stitching herself back into a life she couldn't fully remember, that kind of unconditional welcome meant more than any of us could ever say out loud. It was one of the many reasons I thanked God every day for this family. Seven brothers, a good pair of parents to guide us, and the women we loved, folding right in like they'd always belonged.

"Maybe I should be calling you Mrs. Steele now?" Megan teased when they pulled back.

Paige laughed, waving her hand dismissively. "Not quite yet. For now, I'm saving that title for you and Elizabeth. But give it a few more months. I can't wait." Then she glanced in Jackson's direction.

Jackson joined us, tossing the coop latch one last dirty look as he looped an arm around Paige's waist. "Don't let her fool you. Her clothes have already drifted into my half of the closet and initiated a Striking Steele barn raising. She's basically a Steele."

Paige rolled her eyes, but she was grinning, her cheeks pink. She leaned into Jackson's embrace as she spoke. "We need to do a double date soon. Possibly before that adorable little Steele comes into the world. I know it's been a hard few weeks, but you could use some time away from the house. You can either come to the ranch and we can barbecue and have mocktails, or we can go to a nice little restaurant in town with minimal walking."

Megan's smile was soft, hopeful. "I'd love that."

My heart kicked a little sideways at the ease in her voice. The word *normal* was finding its way back to her tongue.

"Dinner this weekend?" I suggested. "I think a nice little restaurant in town would be just the ticket."

"It'll be nice," Jackson said. "With a few days' notice, I know Momma and Pop wouldn't mind watching Kaleigh."

"It's a date," Paige said, sealing the deal.

We spent the next hour poking around the property. Jackson showed off the new henhouse he'd half-finished. Paige filled Megan in on the latest gossip, from ranch things to our niece Kaleigh and wedding plans. Megan rested her hand on her belly the whole time, eyes bright, cheeks flushed with color that made me believe this was working. This was just what she'd needed.

I couldn't stop watching the way she tilted her face to the breeze and closed her eyes like she was memorizing the shape of the wind. The way she leaned her weight into me without hesitation said everything. And when she reached for Paige's hand as they crossed the barn bridge, it was clear she knew she belonged here, too, with all of us.

We said our goodbyes just before sunset. Megan hugged Paige twice, and Jackson ruffled her hair, earning a playful swat.

He turned to me with that look that said, *You're doing good, bro. Keep her smiling.*

As we drove back down the long dirt road, the truck rattling over the old cattle guard, I glanced at Megan. She was curled up against the door, humming some tune I couldn't quite catch, her eyes half-closed.

"Good day?" I asked softly.

She cracked one eye open and smiled sleepily. "Perfect day. Thank you."

And as the sky turned that dusky pink, the fields rolling by, I felt it settle deep in my bones: this taste of normal, her hand warm in mine, the echo of laughter, the promise of more days just like this was everything I'd ever wanted.

I'd hold on to it. I'd hold on to her, no matter what.

CHAPTER 45

Megan

I'd almost forgotten how good it felt to get ready for something that wasn't a doctor's appointment or a check-in call. It was the weekend now, a few days since Paige had first suggested the double date. Earlier that week, I'd stood in front of my closet and realized I didn't own a single thing that fit this new version of me.

Thirty-one weeks pregnant meant that every old pair of jeans laughed at me from the hanger, and the only dresses I'd kept felt too snug, too short, or just too . . . *before*. Before all of this. Before the blank spaces and the cautious mornings and the slow, careful way my life had been stitching itself back together one heartbeat at a time.

So, Lindsey—bless her relentless, big-sister energy—had dragged me to that little boutique on Main, the one with the hand-painted sign and the salesgirl who called me *honey* like we'd known each other for years. I told my sister I didn't have anything to wear and that I really wanted to look nice, so she took me out after work.

"You deserve to feel pretty," Lindsey had said as she

rummaged through racks of flowy fabrics and stretchy waistbands. "Pregnant or not. This is still *you*, Meg."

I'd stood barefoot on the little pedestal in the fitting room, running my hands down the soft floral dress that skimmed over my belly like it was made just for me and the baby. When I looked in the mirror, I didn't see the girl who'd gotten lost somewhere in her own mind. I saw someone who was trying. Who was still here.

Now, back in the bedroom, I gave the dress one final smoothing over my bump, then added a touch of mascara and the faintest bit of tinted balm to my lips. The ensemble felt simple enough, but when I stepped into the hallway and Cade turned, his eyes widened just a fraction before that slow grin spread across his face. That was the real magic.

He let out a low whistle, the kind that started deep in his chest and made heat bloom up my neck. "Look at you," he murmured, stepping forward, his hands finding my waist like they always did now, protective and sweet. "I'd say you clean up good, Mrs. Steele, but you always do."

I laughed and leaned into his warmth. "You think so?"

He brushed his lips over my forehead, then dipped lower to kiss my nose, my cheek, the corner of my mouth, but never quite close enough until I leaned in to steal the real thing. "I *know* so," he said, voice rough with that familiar reverence. "You look like every good thing I ever wanted."

When we finally pulled apart, we left our room together. Cade grabbed his keys off the hallway table and opened the front door for me like the gentleman he always tried to be. But the real challenge was waiting for me in the driveway.

"Remind me again why we didn't take my car?" I asked, eyeing the passenger side of his truck like it might sprout a staircase if I stared long enough.

Cade chuckled, rounding to open the door for me. "Because

you told me you wanted to feel *normal*, and normal means you riding shotgun while I drive."

"Normal feels an awful lot like an obstacle course tonight," I shot back, bracing one hand on the seat and the other on the grab handle. Cade's warm hands hovered just behind me, ready to catch me if I even wobbled.

"Go on," he coaxed, voice low near my ear. "I got you. Always."

I bit my lip, puffed out a breath, and made a dramatic grunt as I hoisted myself up with Cade's help. Then I settled into the seat with an exhausted laugh.

"You okay?" Cade asked, his grin half smug, half worried.

I shot him a playful glare. "One of these days you *are* going to have to carry me, you know."

His eyes sparked with something that made my cheeks warm. "Baby, you won't hear a single complaint from me."

I rolled my eyes and swatted his shoulder, but my heart was light. *This.* This was exactly what I'd wanted—normal, or at least our version of it.

Cade reached across the console, his fingers brushing my knee. That simple touch was enough to settle the flutter in my chest. "You look beautiful."

I snorted, tipping my head back against the seat. "You're biased."

"Damn right I am."

We pulled away from the house, the last of the sunset painting the sky in soft gold and dusty rose. I rested my palm over my belly. Some days it still didn't feel real. And some days . . . it felt like the only thing that *was.*

"You okay?" Cade asked.

"Yeah," I said, then caught myself. I was still working on not feeling like a burden because of the memory loss, but Cade wanted to know how I felt, even when it wasn't always positive.

"Well, mostly. I feel good tonight. Really good. But I guess . . . I don't know. It's been so long since anything felt normal."

He reached over, and his hand found mine, his thumb tracing lazy circles on my skin. "This is normal. Us. You giving me grief about my truck being too tall. Me wishing I'd bought you a step stool for Valentine's Day." He gave a playful wink.

"You know what I mean. I want to sit across from Paige tonight and not feel like I'm trying to remember the script. I want to *be* your wife, Cade, not just a girl who lives in your house and takes your last name on the forms."

"Hey." He squeezed my hand, waiting until I looked at him. His jaw flexed—that stubborn, tender thing he did when he was trying to figure out how to fix something unfixable. "You are my wife. You're everything to me. This? Dinner, family, laughing at Jackson's jokes? It's all a moment. Every day, we get to choose each other again."

A little swell of warmth pushed against my ribs, bigger than the worry, bigger than the holes in my memory. I turned our joined hands over, running my fingertips along the calluses on his palm. "You always know how to make me feel like I'm not failing at this."

"Because you're not," he said, so certain it almost knocked the air out of me. "You're the bravest woman I've ever met. And you look sexy as hell tonight, so there's that."

I laughed again, covering my face with my free hand. "Oh my God, Cade."

He leaned over at a red light, pressing a quick, sweet kiss to the back of my knuckles. "Just telling the truth."

We fell quiet for a minute, letting the old country song on the radio fill the cab. The baby shifted inside me, a soft roll against my ribs, and I realized how much I wanted nights like this. The small ones. The normal ones.

The twinkle lights strung up along Main Street came into view, followed by the smell of fresh bread and wood smoke already drifting through the open window. I let myself sink into the moment, the hum of the engine, his hand in mine, the tiny flutters inside my belly reminding me that we were building something real. *Again.*

"I'm glad we're doing this," I said, squeezing his fingers once more.

"Me too. Feels like the start of something good."

I tipped my head back and smiled at him, letting the warmth settle into my bones. "It is."

And as we pulled into the lot behind that little Italian place, the one I'd half-remembered from some long-ago date, the one Cade said always made him think of beginnings, I decided that maybe that's what that night was. A new beginning. Ours, for the taking.

Cade helped me out of the truck and led me to the front of the building. The aroma of garlic and warm bread wrapped us in a comforting hug the second he opened the door for me. The hum of soft laughter, silverware clinking against plates, and the low croon of some old love song made everything feel just shy of magical. Or maybe that was just me, feeling more alive than I had in weeks. It felt so good to be out.

Jackson and Paige were already at a corner table near the window, two glasses of wine in front of them. Jackson's grin split wide when he saw us. Paige practically bounced out of her chair to wrap me in a hug before I reached my seat.

"Look at you!" she said, pulling back to hold me at arm's length. "You look radiant."

I laughed. "I feel like a wobbly duck, but thank you."

"Oh, hush." Paige flicked her hand. "You're glowing. And that dress is perfect."

Cade squeezed my shoulder as he stepped past to clap Jackson on the back. "Thanks for getting us a table. Smells good in here."

Jackson winked at me. "Figured we'd get the cozy corner. Keep the crazy to ourselves."

As soon as we settled in, Paige leaned over the table, her elbows propped up like we were two teenagers whispering secrets. "I'm stealing her for a girls' day soon," she told Cade, who just held up his hands in mock surrender. "Shopping, brunch, the works."

"I'm not gonna stop you," he drawled, eyes soft as he looked at me. "Lord knows she deserves it. Though it may have to wait. I don't want anything to happen. She's still on bed rest, and we've stretched the limits enough lately."

We ordered breadsticks, salad, and big steaming plates of pasta that made my mouth water. Cade poured me a glass of sparkling cider from the bottle he and I were sharing, his knee bumping mine under the table in a silent little reminder that he was right there, always.

The conversation meandered, Jackson talking about the latest repairs on the ranch truck, Paige telling me about a new kid in her first-grade class who spent the night with Kaleigh a weekend ago and kept asking her if the principal was Santa Claus in disguise. I laughed so hard I had to wipe under my eyes with my napkin.

These people, this family, they'd wrapped themselves around me like a quilt I didn't know I needed.

Then, it happened again.

Jackson was telling some story about the last time Cade nearly fell off the barn roof while trying to fix a loose shingle. The sound of his voice, that easy, booming laugh, the way he gestured with his wine glass . . . it hit me like a soft punch to the chest.

A memory came to me. In it, Jackson stood in front of a crowd, his tie slightly crooked, his cheeks flushed from champagne.

"*To Megan and Cade,*" he'd said, voice thick but steady. "*May you always remember what brought you together, and may you never forget that even when it's hard, love's the best thing in the world worth fighting for. Here's to the real thing. Messy, honest, and all in."*

I blinked, the memory flickering through me like a film reel catching light for half a second. I didn't say anything. I just reached for my glass, nodding along to the story, my heart doing somersaults in my chest.

Paige caught my eye. She could tell something had shifted, but she didn't comment.

Cade brushed his thumb over my wrist where it rested on my knee, the warmth of his touch anchoring me back to the present. He leaned in, whispering just for me, "You okay?"

I looked at him, at the little smile lines at the corners of his eyes, and I nodded. "Yeah," I whispered back. "I'm . . . good. Really good."

Because I was. I had a new flicker of something, a piece of our puzzle, tucked away safely. Something I'd tell him about later, when it was just us.

Jackson's voice boomed again, pulling us all back in. "All right, who wants dessert? I'm getting the biggest tiramisu on the menu."

Paige leaned over and placed a kiss on his cheek. "We can share. I think if I eat a whole piece myself, it'll be a very uncomfortable night."

Cade's arm draped across the back of my chair, his fingers tracing lazy circles on my shoulder as we enjoyed the remainder of the double date I so needed. This was what getting our forever back looked like. One small, beautiful piece at a time.

IT WAS LATE when I told him. We were curled up on the sofa, the TV was low, and some half-finished movie flickered on the screen. My head was tucked against Cade's chest, and my palm rested over his heart.

"I remembered something," I whispered.

"Yeah?"

I nodded, but I didn't look up. "Jackson and his toast at our wedding. He said, 'May you always remember what brought you together and may you never forget that even when it's hard, love's the best thing in the world worth fighting for.'"

"He was right. His speech was very good, and he kept everyone's attention." I felt his lips place a gentle kiss on my head. It felt so peaceful, so perfect. "You didn't have to tell me. I can understand wanting to keep some memories to yourself."

"I wanted to tell you," I murmured. "It felt like I was holding a piece of us. And now I want you to hold it, too."

What I didn't share were the mild aches on the ride home. Just some discomfort in my back and some tensing in my stomach, much gentler and different from the pains I'd felt before. My body was preparing to do something amazing, and soon enough, we'd be holding a physical piece of us as well.

CHAPTER 46

I stood in the middle of our bedroom nearly four weeks later, looking at the half-zipped hospital bag and the tiny clothes we'd just finished folding. Megan hummed to herself in the next room, her voice drifting through the doorway like it always did when she was calm. Or when she was trying to be.

Thirty-eight weeks. It was strange how a number could feel like a finish line and a starting gun all at once.

I ran my thumb along the little onesie in my hands, the one that said Worth the Wait across the front. And God, wasn't that the truth? We had worked so hard to get to this point: a car accident, amnesia, preterm labor, and bed rest. We'd made it. A part of me wanted to hold it up to the light, memorize every detail, and keep this moment frozen before life shifted again. The other part wanted to grab Megan and our baby, wrap them both up, and never let them go. Because, if I was being honest, I was terrified.

I'd been steady for her. I'd done everything I knew to do. I built the crib, painted the walls, made her breakfast when she couldn't stand for long, kissed every new stretch mark like a prayer. But none of that changed the voice in my head that said, *What if something goes wrong?*

She caught me staring and holding the baby's onesie in my hand like a lifeline. She leaned in the doorway, round belly leading the way, hair all loose around her shoulders. Beautiful. So beautiful.

"Hey," she said, voice gentle. "Earth to Cade."

I let out a shaky breath. "Sorry. Just . . . thinking."

She came to me and slid her arms around my waist. I rested my chin on the top of her head and enjoyed the quiet of her breath, my heart, and the low creak of the floorboards under our feet.

"We're really doing this, huh?" she murmured.

"Yeah." I swallowed, my fingers drifting down to rest over her belly, feeling that tiny kick beneath my palm. "We're really doing this."

She tipped her head back, her eyes catching mine, those same clear blues I fell for at seventeen—and all over again every day after. "Tell me what you're thinking. The real stuff."

I ran my knuckles along her jaw, needing her to feel it too. "I'm scared," I admitted. "Not about you. I mean, not really. You're the strongest person I know. But . . . this baby. Us. Losing any piece of this. I couldn't take it, Meg."

Her thumb brushed my cheekbone. "Then we won't lose it. We've already done the hardest parts, Cade. The rest is the good stuff. The sleepless nights. The giggles. The first steps. Jackson and Paige's wedding next spring and all of us dancing, with the baby half asleep on your shoulder."

I let out a low laugh at that, the fear easing just a fraction. "He's gonna cry the whole ceremony."

"She," Megan corrected, eyes twinkling. "*She* might cry the whole ceremony."

I raised a brow. "Oh, so now you think it's a girl?"

She shrugged, mischief tugging at her mouth. "I don't know. I just like watching you panic."

I shook my head and leaned in to kiss her, slow and warm, like sealing a promise. "I don't care what we have. As long as you're both here. That's all I want."

We tucked the last of the folded clothes into the bag, and Megan shook her head when I double-checked the charger for the camera three times.

"You're gonna be the daddy with ten thousand photos, huh?" she teased.

"Of course! Every first. Every little thing. That's the plan."

As we finished packing our things, the house fell quiet. We brushed our teeth side by side in the bathroom mirror. She wore one of my old shirts, the hem stretched tight over her belly, and I don't think I'd ever loved a sight more.

I drifted off first, half-listening to her flip through a baby name book beside me and muttering names to herself that she liked.

Then, what felt like only a few moments later, I felt her shift, and her palm was flat on my chest, waking me in the dark.

"Cade," she whispered.

I blinked and squinted at the clock. 2:08 a.m. It was definitely more than a few moments. "Hmm?"

Her voice trembled—maybe excited, maybe a little scared, but certain. "My water just broke."

Everything in me went still. Then my firefighter training kicked in. The muscle memory of every drill and real call I'd ever answered.

Stay calm. Assess. Move with purpose, not panic.

It was the same thing they drilled into us at the academy: whether you're stepping into a burning house or pulling someone out of a wreck, you breathe through the adrenaline. One task at a time. Keep your people safe.

Right now, she's *my people. They both are.*

"Okay." I breathed in once, slow and steady, and nodded to her, already swinging my legs over the side of the bed. "Okay. We've got this."

Megan didn't seem as calm; she braced her hands on her belly. "We've got this."

I cupped her face in my hands, kissed her forehead, my girl, my wife, the mother of our child, and for one heartbeat, it all settled. The fear. The hope. The love.

We were ready. We were really, finally ready. We were about to be parents.

CHAPTER 47

Megan

*B*y the time Cade helped me outside, my body felt like a single, sharp heartbeat. A contraction made my breath catch halfway down the porch steps, and I clung to his arm, forehead pressed to his shoulder, eyes squeezed shut until the pain eased enough for me to speak. Cade decided to take my car, and I was grateful. With the pain I felt, I wouldn't have made it into the truck, and I'd have delivered in our driveway.

"I called Dr. Langston," he murmured, his voice steady and sure as he guided me toward the passenger side. "She knows we're coming. She'll meet us at the hospital."

I could only nod. Words felt useless against the rolling tide of pressure and heat inside me. My mind reached for something to anchor me, and it was him. Cade. His thumb brushed gentle circles on the back of my hand as he buckled me in. He paused just long enough to press a kiss to my hair.

"We've got this, baby," he whispered against my temple. "I've got you. Always."

The ride was a blur of streetlights and the hum of tires on pavement. I focused on Cade's voice counting out my breaths, the quiet murmur of reassurance that curled around me like a blanket, even as each contraction built like a wave crashing through my bones.

When we pulled into the hospital parking lot, another contraction hit. I gripped the door handle so tightly my knuckles went white; my eyes locked on his as he leaned over to unbuckle me.

"You're so strong," he said. He said it like a truth he'd stake his whole life on.

Inside, the world morphed into a whirl of warm lights and quiet chaos. The nurses moved quickly. People talked to me from all sides as they pushed me into a squeaky wheelchair. I could feel the eyes on us, the knowing, tender smiles that said they'd seen this thousands of times and yet somehow every single one was new.

They wheeled me into the delivery suite, where pale walls and the soft glow of the monitors greeted me. Cade never let go of my hand. Not once. He stood at my side through the worst of it, whispering the things I needed to hear: how he loved me, how we were almost there, how the baby would be here soon.

My baby.

Our baby.

Cade helped me into a gown, then onto the bed. My world became a flurry of nurses and progress checks and chaos, but through it all, there he stood. Solid. Unwavering.

I tried to hold on to each comforting word he said, but everything blurred around the edges. My mind skittered between the harsh peaks of pain and tiny, unexpected flashes and images that didn't quite make sense until they did. Cade, seventeen, in a jersey under the Friday night lights. The smell of grass and cold bleachers. His grin the first time he asked if he could walk me home.

Another contraction slammed through me, stealing my breath, but underneath it, more memories settled, bright and stubborn. The way he'd brushed his thumb across my knuckles the first time we'd held hands. The first time he'd told me he loved me, my hair wet with rain, and his heartbeat pounding so loud I could feel it through our jackets.

I whimpered, pressing my forehead into his chest as another wave tore through me.

"I'm right here, Meg. Right here. Breathe, baby. Look at me."

I did. And there it was, the way he'd looked at me when he slipped that ring on my finger, hands shaking, eyes shining like I'd just given him the whole world in a single moment.

More images came in fragments, sliding into place like puzzle pieces I hadn't known were missing. Our wedding, candlelight dancing in the old barn rafters, his tie hanging crooked because I'd tugged him close before he could fix it. The way he'd whispered, *You're it for me, Meg. Always.* His laugh when he carried me over the threshold, bumping my shoulder against the doorframe because he was too busy kissing me to watch where we were going.

Quiet nights wrapped up in blankets on the porch, our breath ghosting in the cold air, secrets shared with the stars. The fights, too. The slammed doors, the storm of hurt, the stubborn silences, but always the way we'd find our way back, like our souls were magnets that couldn't stay apart.

And then a flash so sharp it made my breath hitch: the first time we made love. Not just sex, *love*, slow and rough-edged, and so new that it made my whole body feel too small to hold the feeling. I remembered the feel of his hands on my hips, the tremor in his voice when he'd breathed my name like it was both a prayer and a promise. The way he'd kissed every inch of me, unhurried, worshipful. The heat of his skin pressed to mine, the way he'd looked at me when we came undone together, like he'd just glimpsed the rest of his life and found it more beautiful than he'd ever dared to hope.

More flashes, one tumbling after another. The taste of his lips after a long day on the ranch or at the station, sweat and sun and something sweet. The way his strong palms had always made me feel cherished, even when they wandered lower, hungrier. Every stolen moment on the bleachers after the derby had cleared out, the hush of our laughter, the wild thrill of our bodies pressed tight enough to make the whole world vanish.

Every kiss, every touch, every sleepy morning when I'd wake up with my arm draped across his chest, his heartbeat steady under my cheek. It all came roaring back, hot and unyielding and more *real* than the walls of the hospital room.

Through it all, his face held that same patient, stubborn love in his eyes. The boy I'd fallen for, the man who'd waited for me to come home to him, even when I didn't know how, had remained steadfast.

After hours of memory flashes and dizzying effort, a voice cut through the haze. It was Dr. Langston's calm and strong tone, even in a hurried situation. "Megan, it's time. One more push. You can do this."

I locked eyes with Cade, and for a moment, it was like time folded in on itself. Past and present collided. Every version of us that ever was stood right there between our clasped hands.

And then . . . there it was. The cry that split the room open, sharp and new and impossibly alive.

The nurse pressed a tiny, warm weight to my chest, and my whole world cracked open and poured light straight through me. Tiny fingers. The downy swirl of hair at the crown. I couldn't help the tears from falling from my eyes. We were finally holding our child in our arms.

Our son.

Cade's lips brushed against my temple, his shoulders shaking with quiet, joyful sobs. My own tears blurred everything.

I looked up at him, and the pieces clicked into place. They were sharp and sweet.

"I remember," I whispered, the words tearing loose between sobs. "Cade, I remember *everything.*"

His eyes locked on mine, wide and wet. "Everything."

"Everything," I repeated. There were no more flashes of what used to be, no more inconsistencies or a past of darkness. It was all there, fluid and constant.

He kissed me in a breathless, trembling way that tasted like every promise we'd ever made. "Welcome home, baby," he said against my mouth. "Welcome back."

"It's so good to be back." The words slurred as fatigue finally hit me. Whether from giving birth or the mental exertion of the memories flooding back, it really didn't matter; it was the best sort of tired I'd ever felt.

I looked down at our son, at this beautiful, impossible proof that love survived broken memories and bent roads. His tiny hand curled around my finger, warm and strong.

And in that raw, golden moment, I knew I'd never be lost again.

EPILOGUE

Megan

A few weeks had passed since Levi had come barreling into our world, tiny lungs screaming, tiny fists curled tight like he already knew he'd been worth every moment of the wait. We were home, the three of us drifting through sleepless nights and soft dawns and days stitched together with diapers, half-drunk coffee, and the kind of bone-deep love that made every exhaustion feel holy.

I sat on the edge of our bed, folding the last little onesie into Levi's diaper bag for the next day. Jackson and Paige's wedding was in the morning, and I didn't want to be caught without anything for him. I wanted to be prepared.

Cade stood by the dresser, half-dressed himself, barefoot, holding our son against his chest like he was the world's most precious secret. His big hands cupped Levi's tiny back, and he hummed under his breath, not caring if the notes were off-key. He'd gotten so good at being a father.

"Bag's ready for tomorrow," I said softly, trying not to wake the baby.

Cade looked up, eyes bright under the low lamp. "You always did like being prepared."

I smiled. "One of us has to be."

He crossed the room to me, leaned down, brushed my hair off my shoulder, and pressed a kiss to the curve of my neck. "Have I told you today how beautiful you are?"

"Only twice. You're slipping, Steele," I teased, and savored each kiss he placed on my skin.

"You know, I've been thinking," Cade said between kisses.

I arched an eyebrow. "Hmm?"

He shifted Levi so he could cradle our boy in one arm and still take hold of my hand with his free one. "I want to do something for us. For you. For all of this."

I met his eyes. "Cade . . ."

"I want to plan a vow renewal," he said. "Not for anyone else. Just for us. To celebrate every second chance we've been given. To say it all again, with the baby who pulled every piece back together."

My throat tightened. I looked down at Levi. Our Levi Nathaniel Steele. *Levi*. The name that meant *joined*. No more dividing lines between before and after. No more wondering if I'd ever feel whole.

I stretched up to place a gentle kiss on his lips, a calming gesture that always made my insides feel warm. As we separated, a thought came to mind. "Do you know what the best part about all of this is?"

He tilted his head. "What?"

I brought my hand up to cup his jaw, feeling the instant scratch of his beard under my palm. "I didn't just get to fall in love with the love of my life once. I got to do it twice. I have an old memory of what it felt like then, and I have this new memory of what it feels like now. You never left my side. I choose you over and over again. So, I can't think of anything more perfect to commemorate that than a vow renewal."

His eyes glistened, as did mine. Levi let out a soft sigh in his sleep, like he already understood something about this world that I'd fought so hard to remember: love doesn't disappear. It grows. It roots itself deeper.

We moved to the porch to enjoy a little of the warm night air before bedtime. Cade settled into our Adirondack loveseat first, with Levi tucked against his chest. I curled into Cade's side, listening to the steady rhythm of our son's breathing—the softest proof that this life we'd built had found a way to bloom, even through every storm.

I traced my fingers along Cade's wrist, feeling his pulse there, strong and sure under my touch. "You know what this means?" My voice drifted into the warm hush between us.

He turned, brushing his nose against my hair, his lips grazing my temple. "What's that?"

I smiled. "It means the best stories don't really end. They just begin again. And again."

"And I'll be here for every new page." Cade's arms tightened around us both.

I pressed a kiss to the spot over his heart. "So will I."

And there, on that old porch, the first place we ever called home as husband and wife, where we learned how to build a life together, piece by imperfect piece, I knew that this was only the beginning.

Because sometimes life makes you forget what matters most. Sometimes it makes you remember every beautiful piece. And if you're lucky, *truly* lucky, love chooses you all over again.

The End

Steele

BRANSON

ELIZABETH

MOVIE TIME ADVENTURES

ELIZABETH

The summer before ninth grade had a certain magic to it, an energy that seemed to hum in the air, thick with promise and possibilities. The sun hung longer in the sky, casting a golden glow over everything, and every day felt like an adventure waiting to happen. I spent most of those days with my friends, soaking up the freedom that came with knowing it was the last summer before high school changed everything.

That Friday night, we decided to meet at the small local movie theater with the old-fashioned marquee and the sticky floors. It wasn't fancy, but it was our spot, a place where we felt like we belonged. My brother Oliver and I arrived a little early. Since the end of the previous school year, our friend group had somehow merged with his, which meant I got to see more of Branson—an unexpected but welcome benefit.

Oliver leaned against the brick wall, his hands shoved deep into the pockets of his denim jacket. At fifteen, he was tall and lean, with a head of unruly, dark hair that he constantly tried—and failed—to keep in place. His brown eyes were sharp, always seeming to notice things before anyone else, but that night they held a rare softness, a hint of a smile that matched the dimple on his cheek when he looked over at me.

"You're awfully quiet," he remarked, nudging me with his shoulder. "Nervous about something?"

I shrugged and tried to play it cool, but heat crept up my neck. "Maybe. It just feels like . . . I don't know. Tonight's different. Don't you think?"

Oliver grinned, his smile knowing. "You mean because you're going to see Branson?" he teased, his voice light. "I saw you fixing your hair in the mirror for, like, ten minutes before we left the house."

I rolled my eyes, even though I knew he was right. "Shut up, Ollie. I was just making sure I didn't look like a total mess."

"Relax," he chuckled. "You look fine. Better than fine, actually. Branson's going to be over the moon when he sees you."

I nudged him back, but his words brought a smile to my face. "You think so?"

"I know so. He's been looking forward to tonight as much as you have. Trust me, I can tell. The guy barely stops talking about you. It's a little awkward, but oh well."

I laughed softly, feeling a little less nervous, and glanced down the street, scanning for Branson and the others. The anticipation bubbled up inside me again, but it was lighter now, more hopeful than anxious. "Thanks, Ollie. Really."

He nodded, a rare moment of seriousness in his usually playful demeanor. "Anytime. Just remember, I'm still your brother, and I've got to keep an eye on you two."

"Yeah, yeah, I'll keep that in mind."

Bright bulbs lit the marquee, and the smell of popcorn wafted through the air, mingling with the laughter and chatter of people milling around. I spotted my friends down the street, their voices growing louder as they approached. Among them, I saw Branson, his black hair looking almost like midnight blue as it caught the last rays of the setting sun. He was talking to his friend Logan, but when he saw me, his face lit up with a smile that made my heart flutter.

"Hey, Lizzie!" he called out, jogging the last few steps to meet me. He was the only one who called me Lizzie; it was something small that he and I shared. "You've been waiting long?"

"Not really." I returned his smile. "I'm just glad you're here."

We all filed into the theater, the dim lights and the hum of conversation surrounding us. The cool air was a welcome change from the lingering summer heat outside. As we made our way to our seats, I felt a gentle nudge on my arm. It was Branson, his expression a mix of excitement and perhaps a little nervousness.

"Do you want to sit next to me?" His voice was soft enough that only I could hear.

I nodded, feeling a smile spread across my face. "I'd like that."

We settled into our seats in the middle row, surrounded by our friends. The movie started—a lighthearted comedy that had everyone laughing within minutes—but I found it hard to focus. I kept stealing glances at Branson, catching the way he would occasionally glance at me out of the corner of his eye. Every time our gazes met, he'd give me this little smile, like he knew something I didn't.

Halfway through the movie, he leaned over, his breath warm against my ear. "Hey, I've got something for you."

I turned to look at him, curiosity piqued. "What is it?"

"Just wait," he said with a grin. He pulled back his hand and pretended to focus on the screen.

Minutes passed, and my anticipation grew. I tried to pay attention to the movie, but it was impossible with the mystery of Branson's secret hanging in the air. Then, I felt a gentle tap on my arm. I looked down and saw a folded square of paper being slipped into my hand. I unfolded it slowly and used the light filtering from the screen to read the note, my heart pounding in my chest. Inside, written in Branson's neat handwriting, was a note:

Note: *Do you want to be my girlfriend? Check yes or no.*

He had drawn two little boxes beneath the question, one labeled "yes" and the other "no." I couldn't help but smile. It was so simple, so sweet, and yet it felt like the most important question in the world. I glanced over at him, and he was watching me, his expression full of hope and nervousness.

He handed a pen to me. For a moment, I just held it while thinking. Not that there was really a decision to make—I knew my answer—but I wanted to savor this moment, this sweet, perfect moment that felt like something out of a storybook, and he knew how much I *loved* a good story.

With a playful grin, I made a big show of checking the box marked "yes" and then passed the note back to him. He took it, and I watched as he unfolded it, his eyes scanning the paper. When he saw my answer, his face broke into the biggest smile I had ever seen. He looked over at me, and I could see the relief, the joy, the excitement, all shining in his eyes.

He leaned over again, his voice barely above a whisper as he said, "Really?"

"Really," I whispered back, feeling my cheeks warm.

He let out a breath, almost like he'd been holding it this whole time. "I'm glad."

The rest of the movie passed in a blur. It felt like we were the only two people in the theater. We sat closer now, our shoulders brushing, and every time we laughed, it seemed as if our laughter was somehow connected, like we were sharing a secret that only we knew. I couldn't stop smiling, and every time I looked over at him, I saw that he couldn't either.

When the movie ended, the lights slowly came up, and our friends started to shuffle out of their seats. Everyone else needed to get home, but we weren't in any rush, so Branson and

I stayed a bit longer, caught in the warmth of the moment, not quite ready to let it end.

"So," he said, standing up and offering his hand, "since you checked 'yes,' does that mean I get to walk you home?"

I laughed and took his hand, feeling the now-familiar spark at his touch. "I'd like that."

As we walked out of the theater, our hands still clasped, the cool summer night air greeted us. The stars were just beginning to peek out, twinkling in the clear sky. We walked side by side. I glanced over at Branson, feeling the soft squeeze of his hand around mine, and I couldn't help but feel that everything was suddenly brighter.

"I've been wanting to ask you that for a while," he admitted, his voice shy but his smile still confident.

"Why didn't you?" I playfully nudged him.

"I guess I was afraid you'd say no," he replied with a chuckle. "But I'm really glad you didn't."

I stopped and turned to face him, my smile mirroring his. "Me too."

THE FAMILY EMERGENCY

BRANSON

*T*he first few weeks of school had been a whirlwind. High school was everything I thought it would be and more. A mix of new experiences, new faces, and new challenges that left my head spinning by the end of each day. But through it all, there was one thing that kept me grounded, one thing that made it all feel a little less intimidating: Elizabeth . . . my Lizzie.

Being her boyfriend was still something I was getting used to. Every time I saw her in the hallways, my heart would do this weird little flip, like it still couldn't believe this was real. We'd smile at each other, exchange quick notes between classes, and occasionally steal a moment alone in the courtyard. It felt like our own secret world amid the chaos of high school, and I loved every second of it.

Then, one Wednesday afternoon, everything got complicated. I was sitting at the kitchen table, finishing up some homework, when Momma walked in, her face looking unusually tense. My dad followed close behind, a similar worried expression etched across his features.

"Branson," Momma started, folding her arms as she leaned against the counter, "we need to talk to you about something."

I put my pencil down, immediately feeling that familiar twinge of anxiety that always comes with those words. "Okay . . . what's up?"

My dad stepped forward and cleared his throat. "We have to go out of town for a few days. Your Aunt Karen is in the hospital, and we need to be there."

"Oh no." I sat up straighter, immediately worrying about my aunt. "Is she okay?"

"They're still running tests," Momma replied, her voice tight. "But we need to leave tonight, just in case."

I nodded, the news settling in, but then my dad continued. "The thing is, we're not comfortable with you staying here alone while we're gone. It could be a few days, and we don't want you by yourself."

My stomach dropped a little. I knew they were just being protective, but the idea of staying with a relative or one of their friends didn't exactly thrill me. "Can I stay at a friend's house?" I suggested, trying to keep my voice light, hoping it wouldn't sound like too much of a stretch.

My parents exchanged a glance. "Which friend?" Momma asked cautiously.

I hesitated, thinking fast. "Uh . . . Oliver," I blurted. "We've been hanging out a lot lately, and I'm sure his parents wouldn't mind."

My dad raised an eyebrow. "Oliver Myers?"

I nodded, trying to act casual, even though my heart was racing a little. "Yeah, we've been getting close. He's a good guy. And you know his family. They're super nice."

Momma tapped her fingers against her arm and considered this for a moment. "I suppose that could work. If his parents are okay with it. Do you think you could give them a call and check?"

"Of course!" I replied, a little too quickly. "I'll call him right now."

I got up and darted to the living room, where I'd have a bit more privacy, then picked up the phone extension and dialed Oliver's number. He and Lizzie had their own number in the house, so I knew I'd reach either one of them, but I hoped it would be Oliver. I plopped down on the sofa, and my fingers drummed nervously against my leg as I waited for him to pick up.

"Hello!" Oliver's cheerful voice came through the phone.

"Hey, Oliver. It's Branson," I said, relieved he was available. "So, I've got a bit of a situation. My parents have to go out of town for a few days, and they don't want me to stay at home alone. I was thinking . . . maybe I could crash at your place? If it's cool with your folks, I mean."

There was a pause on the other end, and then Oliver's voice came back, sounding amused. "Oh, sure! I mean, I'll have to check with my mom and dad, but I don't see why not. And hey, Elizabeth will be happy to have you around," he added with a laugh.

My cheeks flushed, but I chuckled along. "Yeah, yeah, don't make it weird, dude." I wanted to play it off. If I sounded too excited, then this probably wouldn't work out.

He laughed again. "No worries, man. I'll go ask right now. Hang on."

I waited, listening to the faint sounds of Oliver walking through his house and calling out to his parents. A moment later, I heard his muffled conversation with them. I couldn't make out every word, but I caught enough to know they were considering it. My heart pounded as I waited, hoping this would work out.

Finally, Oliver came back on the line. "Hey, Branson. Good news. They said it's totally fine! You can stay with us as long as you need. My mom just wants to talk to your mom to make sure everything's squared away."

I felt a huge sense of relief. *It worked.* "Awesome! Thanks, Oliver. I'll let her know, and they can figure out the details."

After we hung up, I headed back to the kitchen, trying to keep my expression neutral. "Oliver's parents said it's okay," I told my mom and dad. "They just want to talk to you first."

Momma nodded, already reaching for the phone in the kitchen. "That sounds reasonable. I'll give them a call right now."

I gave her the number, and I listened as Momma and Oliver's mom spoke on the phone. Dad watched nearby with his usual calm demeanor. After a few minutes, Momma hung up, looking relieved. "Okay, that's settled. You can stay at Oliver's while we're gone. We'll leave some emergency money and numbers on the counter before we go. Please be responsible, Branson."

"I will," I promised.

THE VISIT

BRANSON

The ride over to the Meyers' house felt longer than it actually was. My parents were in the front seat, talking quietly about the trip, while I sat in the back, trying to keep my nerves in check. I was excited, sure, but there was also that fluttery feeling in my stomach that wouldn't go away. I glanced out the window as we turned onto their street, spotting the familiar two-story house with dark-blue siding and a white front porch.

As we pulled up to the curb, I saw Mr. Meyers already waiting on the porch, hands in his pockets, smiling in his usual friendly way. Momma parked the car, and Dad turned around to face me. "Remember, Branson," he said, his voice serious but kind, "be respectful, and make sure you help out wherever you can."

"I will, Dad," I replied, and unbuckled my seatbelt. "I promise."

Momma turned off the engine and smiled back at me. "We know you will, sweetheart. Just have a good time, okay? We'll be back before you know it."

I nodded, my heart beating a little faster. The excitement was getting to me; this was going to be great. "Okay, Momma."

We all got out of the car, and I grabbed my bag from the trunk. As we walked up the path, Mr. Meyers stepped forward to greet us. "Evenin', folks! Glad you could make it."

"Thanks for having him, Mark," Momma said with a smile and a shake of Mr. Meyers' hand. "We really appreciate it. With Clay away, we didn't think it would be a good idea to leave him alone, and we didn't want him to miss too much school."

"No trouble at all," Mr. Meyers replied, waving a hand. "We would've made the same choice with ours. We're happy to help. Branson's a good kid."

Mrs. Meyers appeared in the doorway, wiping her hands on a white-and-pink dish towel. Her face lit up when she saw us. "Hello, Branson! Come on in and make yourself at home!"

I turned to my parents, setting my bags down. "Bye, Momma. Bye, Dad."

Momma hugged me tightly. "Take care of yourself, okay? And call us if you need anything."

"Got it," I assured her, hugging back.

Dad gave me a firm pat on the shoulder. "Be good, son. We'll let you know when we get there."

"Great, give Aunt Karen my love," I added.

They waved goodbye as they walked back to the car, and I stood there for a moment, watching them drive away. Once their car turned the corner, I turned back to face the Meyers. Mrs. Meyers smiled at me and gestured for me to come inside.

"Dinner's almost ready, and Oliver's upstairs waiting for you."

"Thanks, Mrs. Meyers," I replied, stepping into the warm, cozy house. The smell of freshly baked bread filled the air, and I could hear the faint hum of music coming from the kitchen.

"Let me take your things," Mr. Meyers offered, reaching out. "You'll be in the guest room, right down the hall."

I handed over my overnight bag, but I kept my bookbag snug against my shoulder as I glanced around the familiar space. Photos and warm colors filled the house with a comforting sort of chaos that felt lived in and welcoming.

I spotted a picture of Elizabeth and Oliver on the wall, probably from a few years prior, and I couldn't help but smile. In it, she was seated beside her brother on a dock as the pair grinned at the cameraman on shore and kicked their feet over the water.

"Oliver, come help Branson with his stuff!" Mrs. Meyers called up the stairs.

A moment later, Oliver came bounding down, grinning. His hair was as messy as ever. "Hey, man!" he said, giving me a high-five. "Glad you made it. Come on, I'll show you to your room." Mr. Meyers gave Oliver my bag.

"I hope you like spaghetti. We're having it for dinner tonight," Mrs. Meyers called up the stairs.

"I love spaghetti," I said before I followed Oliver up the stairs.

"This is you," Oliver said, tossing my bag onto the bed in the upstairs room. "Hope it's okay. At least you're not stuck on the couch."

"It's great, thanks." I glanced around. The space had a kind of old-fashioned charm, with quilted blankets and a framed print of a meadow on the wall.

"No problem. Dinner's in about twenty minutes, and as you heard, we're having spaghetti," he added, before heading out of the room.

I removed my bookbag and focused on making myself comfortable. I could hear voices from the kitchen, the clatter of dishes, and the soft murmur of Elizabeth's laughter. My chest tightened a little at the sound. She was just down the hall, and I couldn't wait to see her.

DINNER WAS LIVELY, just like I expected it to be. The Meyers were a close-knit family, and it showed in the way they talked and laughed with each other. The table was set with big bowls of spaghetti, garlic bread, and a tossed salad. I sat between Oliver and Mr. Meyers, with Elizabeth directly across from me.

Elizabeth glanced at me with a small smile, her eyes flickering with a secret glint that only I could understand. My heart raced a little at the way her foot brushed mine under the table. That tiny, hidden touch sent a spark of excitement through me.

"So, Branson," Mrs. Meyers asked as she passed the breadbasket to me, "how's school treating you? Are you adjusting to high-school life?"

"Yeah, it's been pretty good so far," I said, taking a piece of garlic bread. "A little overwhelming at first, but I'm getting the hang of it."

"Glad to hear it." Mr. Meyers nodded approvingly. "And you've got Oliver to show you the ropes. You two seem to be getting along well."

"Yeah, Oliver's been great," I agreed, giving Oliver a friendly nudge.

Elizabeth stifled a laugh, quickly turning it into a cough, and I bit back a grin. We'd only been in the same room for a few minutes, and already it felt like a game of how much we could get away with.

After dinner, we moved to the living room. The Meyers insisted on playing a game—a family tradition of theirs—and I found myself teaming up with Oliver against Elizabeth and her Momma. I couldn't help but steal glances at Elizabeth every chance I got—her smile, the way she brushed her auburn hair back from her face, and the way her eyes sparkled when she laughed.

We were deep into a game of Pictionary when Oliver called out, "Hey, no cheating!"

Elizabeth giggled and shot back, "I'm not cheating. You're just terrible at guessing."

"I think you're just too good, Elizabeth," I teased, my eyes meeting hers. I couldn't resist jumping in.

She gave me a small, secret smile, one that made my stomach flutter. "Maybe," she said, drawing another card, "but I'll never tell."

LATER, when everyone finally called it a night, I headed up to the guest room to change for bed. I was about to close the door when I saw Elizabeth standing in the hallway, a shy smile on her face.

"Hey," she whispered, glancing over her shoulder to make sure no one was around. "Can I come in for a second?"

"Of course," I whispered back, then stepped aside to let her in. "It is your house after all."

She slipped into the room, and I closed the door quietly behind her. She looked around the small space, then back at me, her expression soft. "I just . . . wanted to say goodnight," she murmured.

I felt my heart swell. "Goodnight, Lizzie," I said, stepping closer.

She reached out and took my hand, her fingers warm against mine. For a moment, we just stood there, letting the silence speak for us.

"I wish we didn't have to sneak around like this," I said quietly.

She bit her lip and brushed her thumb over my knuckles. "I know. I've been trying to tell them. I swear I have. But something always gets in the way."

I raised an eyebrow, fighting a smile. "Like what?"

She gave me a playful shove with her shoulder. "Like Mom bringing home that new puppy last week? Or Dad deciding to fix the fence and needing me to hold boards for three hours straight?"

I laughed under my breath. "I guess I can't compete with a puppy."

She leaned her head against my chest, and my heart tripped over itself. "It's not that, Bran. I was going to tell them the other day, but then your mom called and asked if you could stay over. And I didn't want it to mess anything up, you know? I wanted them to say yes."

I tilted her chin so I could see her eyes. "I get it. Really. We don't have to rush it."

She smiled, a little relieved. "You're not mad?"

"How could I be mad when you look at me like that?" I teased, brushing my thumb across her cheek.

She giggled, cheeks turning pink. "Promise you won't get tired of waiting?"

I leaned in, so close I could feel her breath on my lips. "Not a chance."

This time when I kissed her, it wasn't so quick, just long enough for my whole body to feel it, soft and sweet and full of all the things we hadn't said yet. When I pulled back, her eyes were bright, her smile so warm it made my chest ache.

"I missed you," she whispered.

"I missed you, too." I tangled my fingers with hers, giving her hand a gentle squeeze.

She glanced back at the door, reluctant. "I should go before they notice I'm gone."

I nodded, though I didn't want to let her go. "Okay, but just know I'm right down the hall if you need me."

She laughed softly, the sweetest sound I'd ever heard. "Good to know. Sweet dreams, Branson."

"Sweet dreams, Lizzie."

She slipped out the door, but her warmth stayed with me long after.

THANK YOU FOR READING

Thank you for joining me on this journey. I hope this story brought you laughter, swoons, and a few unforgettable moments with the Steeles.

If you enjoyed the book, the best way to support an author is by sharing the love:

- Tell a friend
- Leave a review
- Spread the word on social media

Your voice helps stories find new readers, and it means more than you know.

Want bonus content, sneak peeks, and early updates on the next book in *The Striking Steele Saga*?

➡ Join my newsletter or my Patreon for your next Decadent Dose of romance!

Thank you for reading, supporting, and believing in these stories.

More cowboys, more warm moments, and more heart are on the way.

ABOUT THE AUTHOR

Dawnlyn Holman writes the kind of stories she wanted to read growing up. She remembers writing stories and screenplays as a child and spent her whole life honing this skill; finally ready to share her work with the world, she's a driven, up-and-coming author. Her fantasy worlds are nothing short of exciting, and she hopes to give people a thrilling place to escape the day-to-day boring bits of life.

As a high school English teacher, she hopes to instill a love of reading in that age group. When she's not working at her day job or writing, she can be found planning her next travel destination, watching movies, playing board games, and spending time with friends and family. She's a 2021 National Novel Writing Month and Camp July 2021 winner and hopes to make writing a more serious endeavor. Dawnlyn lives in Pennsylvania with her family and two dogs and is happily plucking away at the keyboard, telling the next story.

Playlist

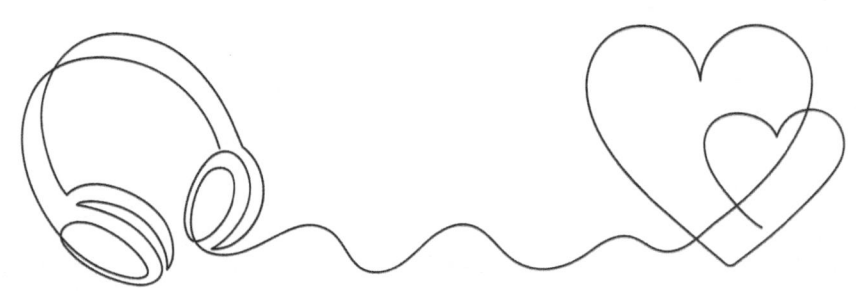

SCAN ME

01:02   02:00

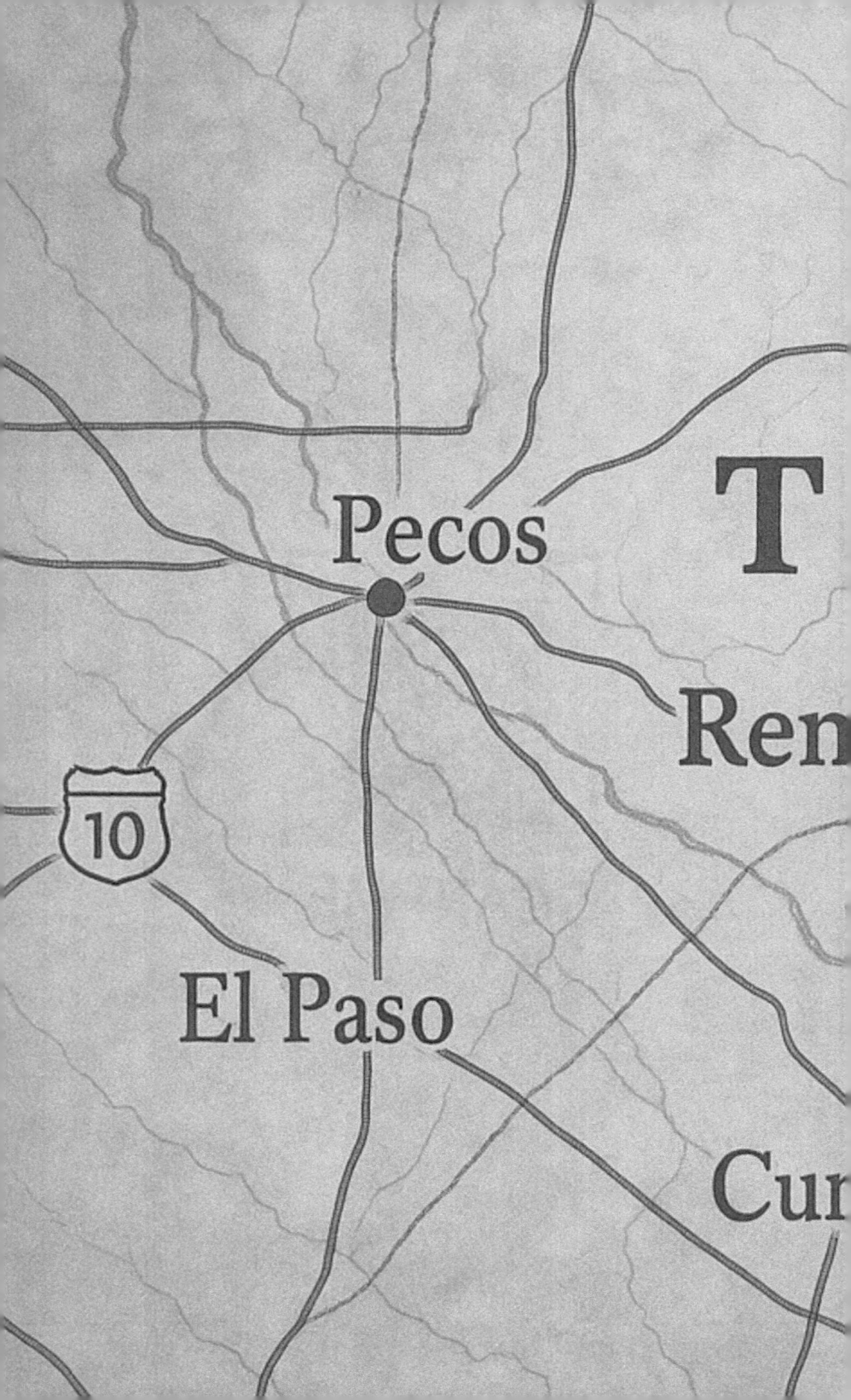

Odessa

EXAS

ngton

Odessa

Pecos River

erland

ALL ABOUT REMINGTON

Remington, Texas, is a vibrant and bustling city located in the heart of the Lone Star State. As the 10th largest city in Texas, Remington boasts a population of approximately 200,000 residents and spans an area of approximately 75 square miles, offering a perfect blend of urban amenities and small-town charm. It's located between El Paso and Odessa and just south of Pecos.

The city's history dates back to the late 1800s, when it was founded by settlers attracted to the fertile lands and the promise of prosperity. Originally a stop along a key cattle trail, Remington quickly evolved into a bustling hub for ranchers and farmers. The town's name honors the pioneering Remington family, who played a crucial role in establishing the community.

In its early years, Remington flourished as an agricultural center, with vast fields of cotton and corn dominating the landscape. The arrival of the railroad in the early 1900s further boosted the city's economy, facilitating the transport of goods and attracting new businesses. The historic downtown area, with its preserved 19th-century architecture, serves as a testament to this bygone era, featuring charming storefronts, a classic general store, and a vintage post office.

Today, Remington seamlessly blends its agricultural roots with modern developments. One of the city's main attractions is The Plaza, a lively and popular hangout spot for both adults and teens. The Plaza features a variety of shops, restaurants, and entertainment venues, including a state-of-the-art movie theater, an expansive arcade, and a rooftop café offering stunning views of the city skyline. Whether it's enjoying a night out with friends, catching the latest blockbuster, or simply strolling through the bustling marketplace, The Plaza is the heart of social life in Remington.

The annual derby at the Steele ranch, a beloved tradition, draws visitors from neighboring towns and showcases the community's rich heritage. Residents of Remington take pride in their city's rich history and work together to preserve its unique character while fostering a welcoming environment for newcomers. With its friendly faces, picturesque landscapes, and strong sense of community, Remington, Texas, is a place where the past and present harmoniously coexist, making it a great place to live, work, and play.

ACKNOWLEDGMENTS

Every new book is proof that stories don't grow alone; they grow because of the people who keep believing alongside the writer.

First, I thank God. His hand has guided every chapter, every idea, every step of this journey. When doors opened, when creativity sparked, when I found strength on the hard days, He was there. May this story touch hearts in the ways only He can design.

To Mom, your support doesn't just lift me; it anchors me. You celebrate every milestone, big or small, and remind me that talent is nothing without perseverance. Life got really hard while working on this novel, but together, we made it through. Thank you for the prayers, the pep talks, and the unwavering belief that I could do this.

To Aunt Lora and Auntie M, your constant encouragement and faith in my dreams have never gone unnoticed. From the beginning of this series until now, you've been two of my greatest cheerleaders, and I am blessed beyond measure to have you.

To my brothers, Marc and Chris, thank you for answering my strange questions, brainstorming solutions, and helping make sure my characters don't do anything that would embarrass them too much in the real world (embarrassing moments are fun to write about). Your humor and advice still shape these stories in ways readers might never know, but I always will.

To my editor, Brooke, you've now survived five books with me (and a short story), which surely deserves its own award. Thank you for challenging me, sharpening my words, and helping me grow stronger with every draft. You make me a better writer, and this book is better because of you.

To my cover designers, once again, your creativity gave this story a visual heartbeat. Seeing the characters come to life on the cover is one of the greatest joys of the process. Thank you for bringing your artistry into this world with such care and vision.

And to my friends, near and far—thank you for cheering, sharing, messaging, reading, and believing. You celebrate every win like it's your own, and you never let me forget why I started this journey.

This book is for all of you—for the love you've given, the faith you've shown, and the ways you've helped me keep going.

With all my heart, thank you.